A Scone
of
Contention

A Scone

of

Contention

A KEY WEST FOOD CRITIC MYSTERY

Lucy Burdette

CROOKED
LANE

NEW YORK

Published in the United States by Crooked Lane Books, an imprint of The Quick Brown Fox & Company LLC.

Crooked Lane Books and its logo are trademarks of The Quick Brown Fox & Company LLC.

Library of Congress Catalog-in-Publication data available upon request.

ISBN (hardcover): 978-1-64385-624-7
ISBN (ePub): 978-1-64385-625-4

Cover illustration by Griesbach/Martucci

Printed in the United States.

www.crookedlanebooks.com

Crooked Lane Books
34 West 27th St., 10th Floor
New York, NY 10001

First Edition: August 2021

10 9 8 7 6 5 4 3 2 1

For the gang who shared the magical Scotland adventure: Sue, Jeff, John, Steve, Yvonne, Susan, David, Robin, and Jack— and Wendy, who was there in spirit

Chapter One

Whoever said cooking should be entered into with abandon or not at all had it wrong. Going into it when you have no hope is sometimes just what you need to get to a better place. Long before there were antidepressants, there was stew.
—Regina Schrambling, "When the Path to Serenity Wends Past the Stove," *The New York Times*, September 19, 2001

The phone rang, and I felt a shiver of worry as my guy's name flashed on the screen: *Nathan Bransford.* A ghost walking on your grave—that's how my grandmother would have described the shiver. I tried to shrug that off as an old wives' tale, but . . . My new husband, Nathan, was a detective with the Key West Police Department and utterly serious about fending off disruptions to his work. Texts were tolerated. Calls not so much. And that meant he never called without an utterly serious reason.

"Hi, sweetheart," I said. "What's up?" I couldn't help worrying about him, always. Considering that we had reservations to fly to Scotland tomorrow, where we'd be staying with his sister and her husband, now I was also concerned about a police emergency interfering with our long-delayed honeymoon trip. But I was learning the rules of married life, one of them being don't instantly show him that you're worried because that makes him feel weak or something even worse. And definitely don't show that *you're* worried that *he's* worried.

He cleared his throat and his voice came over the line a little more rumbly than usual. "I heard from my brother-in-law today while at work. Honestly, my sister sounds a bit"—there was a pause—"unhinged, is the only way to describe it." He was again quiet for a minute, and I could hear him cracking his knuckles, echoing Evinrude the cat, who was crunching on the dog's kibbles. "To make things worse, he insists that I play golf. In fact, he's already made three reservations. At one of the fanciest courses in the world, where duffers and hackers like me don't belong. I'll be in the deep end, way over my head. Plus, a round of golf lasts a lifetime, and that will cut into my time with you."

Nathan had grown up in a family where golf was a given. As part of his teenage rebellion, he'd dropped it cold as soon as he left home for college. "It'll come back to you, like falling off a horse. Oops, sorry—mixing my metaphors. Don't worry about me—I know I'll love your sister. How bad could she be if her husband's planning all that golf? And besides, Miss Gloria makes everything a party." I paused. "Sounds like you're getting cold feet about the trip," I said, keeping my voice light.

"No cold feet, but this sure isn't turning into much of a honeymoon."

I snickered. "We gave that up when we asked Miss Gloria to join us. And she's going to make the trip so much richer. She's so excited—she's researching her family tree on Ancestry and she's made a little map marking where all her relatives might be buried."

We were all headed to Scotland, a delayed honeymoon for Nathan and me, and the first trip abroad since her husband's death for Miss Gloria. Nathan had offered to take me anywhere I wanted to go. I chose Scotland because of *Outlander* and *Shetland,* natch, and because I wanted to meet his mysterious sister, whom I'd only recently learned about. When I'd broken the news to Miss Gloria, my fellow fanatic *Outlander* watcher, she'd said mournfully, "Scotland was the next trip Frank and I were going to take. And then—poof— he was gone. Dead of a heart attack and not traveling anywhere but to the morgue. I'm so happy for you, Hayley," she added. She really meant that, but she had a shimmer of tears in her eyes.

Later that night, Nathan suggested that we should invite her along. I was shocked. "It's our honeymoon," I reminded him. I would have loved to have her travel with us, but I was afraid my new husband would regret it once we were on the road. Traveling with an old lady might be a challenge. Not that anyone who knew her would describe Miss Gloria as old. Some days she showed more zip than me—and I was fifty-something years younger. And if she did happen to droop, the tiniest catnap brought her roaring back to life.

"We're already spending most of the week with my sister," he said. "Miss G would only be an improvement."

On the phone, Nathan heaved a big sigh. "Now the plot's gotten thicker. My mother's coming."

I almost choked on the swallow of water I'd just taken. I'd gotten to know Nathan's mom right before New Year's. We'd survived a harrowing situation that left us filled with respect for one another. However, she was tall, formal, and super-accomplished, and she still scared the pants off me.

"She's worried about my sister too," Nathan continued, "but she hasn't seen her in a couple of years, so she figured our visit would be an easy way to work herself into the mix. I assured her that you wouldn't mind." I could hear him taking a big breath. "I'm sorry."

"We'll figure it out," I said briskly. "I'm sure it will be fine. I've got to run. I've got scones in the oven and only the barest bones of an article on the computer screen."

I'd wheedled a week of vacation out of my bosses at *Key Zest* magazine but then felt guilty about dropping the ball and offered to write a special section on Scottish food and music for the next issue—*Hayley Snow, traveling correspondent*. In addition to the article I was committed to send by tomorrow—a roundup of restaurateurs' opinions about the Mall on Duval Street, I'd promised a couple of scone recipes. I've always been and probably always will be an overachiever, once I get my compass aimed at the right point. And my bosses weren't going to turn me down, even if it was my so-called honeymoon.

The Mall on Duval had been a brainstorm from our new-ish mayor. It involved closing several blocks of the busiest strip in Key West to car and truck traffic on weekend evenings, in order to increase foot traffic and attract locals as well as visitors. The jury was definitely out on whether it was a raging success or the worst mistake since the harbor dredging that opened the gates to the influx of giant cruise ships.

I got up from my lounge chair on the teak deck and walked into our new houseboat, our home. Nathan and I had been living here two weeks and I still had to pinch myself to believe it was real. Though we'd spent months pouring over plans and many more months waiting for workers and materials to show up, the outcome was, in a word, stunning—without a whiff of flashy.

Our builder, Chris, had managed to secure Dade county pine lumber from a demolition project that now found a new life as my kitchen counters and drawers. He'd also managed to find Dave Combs, an amazing contractor and woodworker, who helped to execute our dream to polished reality. At the deep end of the counter, he had built shelves where I lined up my pottery containers holding baking supplies; and above that, vertical slats for my prettiest plates; and a little higher, a glass-fronted cabinet for the flowered blue china mugs and teapot that had been handed down from my grandmother's kitchen. There was a separate shelf for my cookbooks, and a gas stove on which every burner worked without coaxing or danger of explosion, and even a special cabinet that exactly fit the mammoth food processor that my mother-in-law had given us as a wedding present. From a wrought iron rack on the wall and ceiling over the stove hung an assortment of pots and pans, whisks, cheese grater boxes, and the other tools of my trade.

Though I wrote food criticism for a living, I lived for feeding my family and friends. The new kitchen made that activity almost purely pleasurable. There were, of course, trade-offs that came automatically with living on a houseboat—neighbors were close by, and the water all around us amplified every sound. That meant we shared our neighbors' music, no matter the genre. And we heard every woof and meow from every furry resident. And space was at a premium. That meant that our bed, three steps up from the double oven at the end of the kitchen, was built into the wall of the bedroom, with reasonable walk-in space only on his side, and a smaller mattress than a well-muscled man might prefer. As newlyweds, we did not find this close proximity to be a drawback. And we loved waking up in the morning and looking out on our aqua-blue watery world. On nice days, we opened the sliding doors so the whole world became part of our bedroom.

We had no room for houseguests aside from a berth on the living room couch, but since the people I loved most also lived on this island, I could easily survive with that restriction. I had a small built-in desk in the living area, and pale green walls that set off the rich woodwork and matched the color of the sea on a stormy day, and a special slot for Evinrude's litter box, and room for a bed for Nathan's dog, Ziggy, too. I couldn't believe that I lived here, married to a sweet and sexy hunk of a guy, with Miss Gloria, one of my best friends, next door, and my old college roommate and dear friend, Connie, right up the dock.

I heard the sound of a cowbell ringing, the system we had set up to alert me that Miss Gloria was out on her deck and available for conversation. She insisted I should feel free to ignore the call, but so far I had not failed to respond. It wasn't an easy transition for either of us, my moving out along with two members of our furry menagerie. Easy access with the toll of a bell made the change go more smoothly and feel less draconian.

I poked my head out the door and called over.

"Are you ready for a tea and scone break? I have some banana date scones coming out of the oven in five minutes."

"Are you kidding?" she asked. "I'll set the table. Bring the guys with you."

She didn't need to mention that, as both—Evinrude, my cat, and Ziggy the dog—had already gotten acclimated to the sound of the bell. Bell equals treats plus fun with old friends.

I pulled the fragrant scones out of the oven, the air now scented with the aromas of pastries browned just right plus the richness of bananas and a pile of butter. I transferred three of them to a yellow gingham plate, another wedding present, this time from Connie. I added the butter dish and a little bowl of freshly whipped cream and another of raspberry jam to the tray. Then I poured hot water into the blue flowered teapot and covered it with a tea cozy in the shape of a sheep that had been a gift from Nathan's sister. Following my gray tiger and Nathan's exuberant min pin, I started over to Miss Gloria's place, navigating the gap between the deck and the sloshing bight with care. Next time I should remember to heat the water in her kitchen.

Miss Gloria's two cats, handsome black Sparky, and adorable and mischievous orange tiger T-Bone, were waiting on her deck. She snatched the orange kitten up so he wouldn't wind between my legs and trip me.

"Are you working?" she asked. "I hate to bother you when you have so much—"

"You never bother me," I said patiently. "Remember what we agreed on after Nathan bought the boat?" I settled the tray on the table in between the two lounge chairs and gestured to the place next door.

"Friends and family first," she said, her eyes twinkling. "Your mother and I taught you well, didn't we?"

I'd spent a good part of the last few years here on this deck, talking with my friend and absorbing the life rhythms of Houseboat Row. "The recipe called for banana nut, but I changed out the nuts for dates," I said. "There's a ton of Irish butter already in the mixture, but I thought we might need a little melted butter on top too." I split open one of the scones, watching the steam drift up, and slathered it with Kerrygold butter. We each grabbed a half, doused it in whipped cream and jam, and tucked in.

"Heavenly. Maple syrup?" she asked, quirking her white eyebrows into peaks.

"Your palate is getting so sophisticated," I said with a big smile. "What else is up this morning?" I removed the sheep cozy, poured tea into each cup, and stirred in a tablespoon of honey. This was mango honey, with a hint of ripe fruit, that I doubted you could get anywhere outside of the Florida Keys. And it was the second week of June, ushering in the hot and sticky summer season, not hot tea weather at all. But both of us had gotten so excited about the impending trip that we couldn't let a day go by without practicing taking a proper Scottish tea.

"Two things," she said. "I want to go over my packing one more time. And I need you to remind me how to get into my Ancestry account. I fell asleep last night while I was looking at my family tree, and Sparky walked on the keyboard, and now I can't remember how to get back there."

"Easy yes on both," I said, popping the last of the sweet and buttery scone into my mouth. I cut the third confection in half and buttered that too. As we ate, I described the phone call with Nathan. "He's worried that his sister is flipping out," I said.

"What are the symptoms?" she asked, stroking Evinrude, who had pushed onto her lap and was eying the bowl of whipped cream.

I reviewed the conversation in my head, coming up with not much detail. "I didn't even ask. He was so busy telling me that his mother's joining the trip, that question never even came to my mind. I'll find out more tonight."

"Helen is coming too? This doesn't sound like much of a honeymoon. I could bail out—maybe your mother should be going instead of me, since Nathan's mother will be there."

I cut her off before she could work herself into a lather. "Don't be silly—she's too busy to go on a trip right now. And we love that you're coming. We wouldn't have it any other way."

Forty-five minutes later, we'd polished off every crumb of our tea and gone through everything in Miss Gloria's suitcase, which she had laid out on the bed in my former bedroom. I wondered how it was possible to feel so thrilled with my new home and new husband and yet sad about leaving this cozy little space. Evinrude, who had followed us in, circled around several times on the pillow, appearing puzzled, then curled up for a snooze while we inspected the suitcase.

I advised Miss Gloria to remove the shorts and bathing suit and add another sweater and a raincoat. Early June in Scotland was rumored to be both chilly and wet. And being petite and thin, she tended to feel cold in even the warmest weather. And as she hadn't gone swimming in Key West for the past decade—too nippy for her tastes—I doubted she'd be paddling about in the cold lochs of Scotland.

"Besides, they do have clothing stores in Scotland, I am told," I said with a wink. "We can buy anything we've forgotten." Then we went to her computer, where I restored her access to her family tree with a few quick strokes of the keyboard and watched two videos of Scottish bagpipers, admiring their music and their swinging kilts and well-muscled calves.

"Thanks so much," she said, hugging me warmly. "Are you going downtown this afternoon?"

"Yes, I need to spend at least an hour wandering Duval Street and interviewing a few of the restaurant owners and diners. Somehow I have to get this article finished before we leave."

"Would you mind running me over to Sunset? I feel like I need to touch base with Lorenzo before we go to your mother's for supper."

Lorenzo was our Tarot card-reading friend who set up every night at Mallory Square to advise visiting tourists about their lives. Some people dismissed him as a fruitcake, but I knew better. He had a deep spiritual connection with the universe around him. And he understood the unconscious motivations of the world and the people he met better than anyone I'd ever known, with my psychologist friend Eric Altman running a close second.

We agreed that Miss Gloria could spend the time while I was interviewing people having a little tipple of wine at happy hour, and then we would both buzz over on my scooter to talk with Lorenzo. And after that, run to my mother and Sam's place for a pre-trip going away dinner.

We clipped on our helmets, Miss Gloria grabbed my waist, and I fired up my scooter and pulled out onto Palm Avenue. The traffic was light, a welcome change from the hordes that flooded Key West in the high season from December through March. I enjoyed all the seasons of our island but a break from the partying crowds was welcome. I took White Street to Southard, and parked my bike in the assigned area at the corner of this one-way road, which would leave us very near to the blocks designated as a pedestrian mall.

Each week, in the local papers, I'd read articles assessing the effects of this pedestrian mall project. The restaurants along these blocks were thrilled with the opportunity to expand their space to outdoor seating right on the street. Others, retail places without that same option, insisted that their sales were dropping. And restaurants outside the three-block mall often complained that they weren't allowed the same outdoor open seating, and suggested that their sales were being siphoned off by the lucky few. The dispute appeared to be coming to a head soon.

I settled Miss Gloria on the couch outside the art gallery Duval Destiny and brought her a tiny glass of complimentary chardonnay. She had not an inch of room for new art on her walls, and these psychedelic roosters and orgasmic naked women certainly wouldn't be her style even if she did, but the owners didn't seem to mind her occasional appearance. To my mind, she was an asset, as she never let a tourist pass by without chitchatting with them about supporting local businesses and artists.

As I walked closer to the Italian restaurant where I planned to start my research by questioning my waiter acquaintance Cheech (so nicknamed for his spacy appearance), I heard a loud noise—the crack of a gun?—and then a panicked voice yelled, "He's got a gun! Help! A gun!" Then all around me people began shouting and crying and running and pushing—both ways, toward the noise and away from it.

I froze for a moment, with my heart pounding. The spate of mass shootings in the news had us all in terror that we would experience this kind of event firsthand. No matter where you were headed or what the event might be, the bad guys could find you. Churches, movie theaters, schools, shopping centers—nothing was sacred. Nothing was safe. Which definitely put a damper on the Key West party mood.

Nathan had insisted on drilling the entire family on how to behave in the case of an active shooter: First, you should look for the exits when you arrive at any destination.

Second, if you are caught in an incident, evacuate and run if at all possible. If escape is not possible, drop, roll, hide, and call it in. In that order. And silence devices so beeps and messages won't give you away to a killer intent on hunting victims.

If there is no other option, fight.

It must have killed him to tell us all of that, especially the fighting.

I sorted quickly through the possibilities. If I headed to the teeming sidewalk, I was afraid I'd be crushed by the panicked crowd. Running down the less-crowded middle of the street was out too. If there really was a crazy person shooting, I'd become the perfect target. As Nathan advised, I dropped to my knees on the pavement and rolled into the gutter. Too late, I froze, wondering whether I'd gotten the rolling bit mixed up with a fire emergency.

Chapter Two

Everything depends on the moment the spice hits a hot pan: whether it sizzles with a mouthwatering fragrance or turns to ash.

—Sasha Martin, *Life from Scratch*

My face ended up smooshed near the white-stenciled words on the curb above the drain, warning potential litterers, "Anything discarded here will wash into the ocean." The gutter smelled of stale beer and cigarette butts and pizza, but strongest of all was the stink of my own fear. I curled into the smallest human ball possible, knowing that I could still be an open target for a crazed shooter. Should I get up and run to help Miss Gloria? Nathan had drilled the same safety information into her head as he had mine, with great patience. I had to think she'd be hunkered down behind the art gallery furniture. Or maybe she'd been smart and quick enough to run inside.

Hearing more muffled shouts but no gunshots, I crab-walked toward better cover—a nearby trash can. I peered around the edge to see what was going on. I heard the sound of footsteps pounding and two different voices yelling, "Drop the gun! Hands above your head! Police!"

Then I heard the clatter of metal on pavement and saw two hands stretched high above the heads of the crowd. Tourists and bystanders had begun to push toward the scene while two fierce police yelled at them to move back. More officers came running down the street, some with guns drawn and some with police dogs loping beside them.

"Stand back," a tall officer shouted to the crowd. "You need to clear the area."

Miss Gloria came up behind me and tapped my shoulder. "I think you're okay to come out from behind the trashcan now. The only bad guy they seem to have trapped is Ray."

"Ray?" I stood up and brushed the grit off my knees, realizing I had scraped them raw in the flurry of activity. Ray was my dear friend Connie's husband, father of the adorable baby Claire, and a very talented and peace-loving artist. I could not imagine him getting into an altercation with the cops, especially over a gun.

She took my elbow and we moved to the sidewalk, close enough that we could hear the men talking. Shouting was more like it.

"I panicked," Ray was explaining. "I heard gunshots and got spooked. I would never shoot anyone, I swear. My gallery manager was there—she saw everything—"

"You'll need to come to the station," said the biggest cop, the same man who had stopped me for running through a stop sign on my scooter after Christmas. He was intimidating because of his size and his bald head, but he seemed like a nice enough man. If you liked tough police personas. Which, being married to one, I suppose I did. Before migrating to Key West, I didn't know one single policeman. I'd never imagined I'd end up with so many police officers in my life.

"You can't brandish a weapon in a public space. It's a crime," the cop said.

"But it was self-defense," Ray told him. "Or it would have been." His voice trailed off weakly, as though he recognized he was in deep trouble. The crowd around him had gotten louder, offering their own opinions and observations.

I caught Ray's eye and shouted above the din. "Do you need anything? Do you want us to come with you? Call Nathan?"

He shook his head, the expression on his face bleak, then marched down the street with a cop at each elbow. Should I text Connie? Or butt out and assume Ray would call her? I decided to text Nathan instead and ask him to check up on Ray. Better not to terrify my friend until we had some facts. I also needed to let Nathan know that although we had been on the scene, we'd suffered nothing more than a few scary moments.

The tourists who had gathered around to see the cause of the commotion were encouraged by the police to move on with their evening activities while the authorities continued to investigate the incident. I felt a little shaky and not at all interested in writing this "woman on the street" article that I had promised my bosses. As usual, I had loaded too much onto my plate. But this time I wasn't going to try to choke it all down. Interviews about the Duval Mall experiment were not going to be possible under these circumstances anyway. Everything would still be here when we got home from our trip. I sent a quick text off to my two bosses, explaining that Duval Street was a disaster following a possible shooter incident and that I'd do the Mall article on my return. Which was all true. But most of all right now, I needed to see Lorenzo and then share a meal with my mother and Sam, and then, finally, check in with Connie and Ray.

* * *

Ten minutes later, we parked the scooter in the lot off Mallory Square. With sunset not due until after eight, the crowds were light on the plaza. The sun was still blazing high in the sky over the horizon, and the air felt hot and still and smelled of yesterday's popcorn. Even the seagulls were quiet, perched on the edge of the pier, facing in toward the square, on the lookout for a breeze or a handout. We found Lorenzo free at his booth near the edge of the water.

"What happened?" he asked, getting up to greet us. You both look upset."

Miss Gloria explained the incident on Duval Street. "It was enough to rattle the sturdiest of souls. All those people running and shrieking, and us with no idea what was really going on."

"The world's gone mad," he said in a somber voice. "We're all at sixes and sevens." He gave us each a hug and then sat back down and reached for his deck of cards.

We perched on the two folding chairs across from him, our hands clenched on the blue tablecloth. "You know what isn't helping?" I added. "I think we're both nervous about traveling." I glanced at my friend, and she nodded her agreement.

"We want to go, we're so excited. But at the same time, it's a little scary too," said Miss Gloria. "I haven't been out of the country in many years, and Hayley's never been abroad. And Key West is comfortable. It's home."

"And we like being able to check in with you when we feel like the world's rocked off its rails," I said. "You're our security blanket."

A wide smile lit up his face, and he pulled the deck of colored Tarot cards out of our reach. "I don't need to read any cards to tell you that this will be the trip of a lifetime. Everybody feels a little anxious going somewhere new. You can let that stop you, or you can acknowledge the feeling and then go anyway. It's so wonderful that you're sharing this trip together. And if you need to talk with me while you're away, your mother can come over with her phone and we'll FaceTime." He reached across the table to gather a hand from each of us, and then squeezed. I felt his warmth spread through my fingers, and that made me feel the tiniest bit teary.

"Should we bring you back a redheaded man in a kilt?" asked Miss Gloria, once he'd let go of our hands. Lorenzo had had a longtime partner in his life, but no new fellow recently. And he loved the Jamie character from *Outlander* as much as we did.

"Perfect!" said Lorenzo, and we moved aside for his next customer, a large woman in a bright purple shirt, who was pacing behind us.

"I read about you in a mystery book," I heard her say. "I still can't believe you're here and you're real."

He chuckled. "Very real."

Then we motored over to my mother's home, located on a street a block from the waterfront in the Truman Annex. We could smell something delicious before we even got inside the house.

Mom met us at the door. "I wasn't sure what kind of cuisine you'd have in Scotland," she said on the way to the kitchen. "But we made a shepherd's pie and a nice, light lime sponge cake for dessert. There was no point in trying to replicate fried fish and mushy peas—we can't compete with what they do with a deep fryer!" She gestured at the big center island, where they'd set up bottles of wine, one red and one rosé, beaded with cool droplets. "Pour yourself a glass of wine and then we'll eat."

"I was so excited at the thought of making Scottish rumbledethumps," said Sam as he pulled a bubbling casserole from the oven. "That would have involved leftovers and no meat—not proper for a send-off meal. But I still love the name."

"This dinner sounds amazing," I said. "And we could use some comfort food about now."

While Miss Gloria explained the gun incident at Ray's gallery, I went to the sink to blot the blood oozing from my knees and wash the scrapes off. No telling what organisms might lurk on the Duval Street pavement.

"Poor Ray was having an absolute fit," I said. "I couldn't even believe he had a gun with him. But I'm sure I'll hear the full story once we get home to Houseboat Row tonight."

We took our seats out on the porch and inhaled every bite of Sam's ground beef and veggie casserole, which swam in a thick gravy and was topped with mashed potatoes and turnips. "The Scottish people are going to beg for this recipe," said Miss Gloria to Sam. "Do you mind writing it down so Hayley can make it?"

Sam began to scroll through his notes, to send the recipe to Miss Gloria's phone. I got up from the table to help my mother clear the plates.

"Nothing from Connie or Ray?" she asked, as we loaded dishes in the dishwasher.

"Not a peep." I brought out my phone and navigated to the Key West police Twitter account. "Let's see what the authorities are saying."

I read the most recent tweet aloud. "'No active shooter was discovered on the Duval Street mall. One individual has been taken in for questioning. Police searched the area and found no credible threat. Visitors are advised to take caution and report suspicious activity.'"

The tweet further down their page from earlier in the afternoon reported a possible shooting, with police on the scene. "Anybody in the area should shelter in place and evacuate when cleared."

It seemed pretty clear that they had determined there had been no gunshot before Ray's panicked reaction, and that perhaps visitors to the area had also panicked, including Miss Gloria and me. This was the good news and the bad news about social media. Important information could be spread quickly, but often it was inaccurate and sometimes inflammatory. I reported this latest news to my family while Sam cut us wedges of a light and lovely lime sponge cake.

"I've read about other incidents like this," Sam said, passing the plates around. "Even in Times Square, people heard what they thought were gunshots, and the noise turned out to be the backfiring of a dirt bike. And in Boca Raton, a panic was started by popping balloons."

"I hate that the world has come to this," said my mother, looking sad. "I'm glad you'll be getting away for a bit. Is it true that they don't allow guns in Scotland?" She gulped and threw a worried look at me. "Do you think Nathan is planning to bring his handgun? I wonder if that would be permitted?"

Chapter Three

*He knew it was crazy, but then he could feel his mind
being eaten away at the edges. It was like mice nibbling
at a piece of rotting carpet, leaving his thoughts ragged
and frayed.*

—Ann Cleeves, *Harbour Street*

Upon our return to Houseboat Row, I took Ziggy for a quick walk along the edge of the parking lot, noticing that Connie and Ray's lights were on at their place farther down the dock. No sign yet of Nathan.

"I'll be back shortly," I told the animals once I'd returned the dog to our place. "I'm going to run down to Connie's boat to get the facts. We aren't leaving until tomorrow." They both stared at me, Evinrude, impassive, from his perch on the plaid dog bed; and Ziggy, worried. I knelt down and kissed him on his shiny head. "We have so many pet sitters lined up that you will be begging for some alone time." This might be true of Evinrude—he was a cat after all—but it was hard for Ziggy to get his fill of human attention. Passing the Renharts' boat,

I could hear their TV cranked up to full volume—sounded like a rerun of *Everybody Loves Raymond*. Further up the dock, strains of classical music wafted out over the water from Mrs. Dubisson's boat. This was something else I appreciated about our pier in paradise—we weren't homogeneous, and yet we didn't judge one another.

I hopped from the wooden walk to Connie's front porch and tapped on my friend's door. A few minutes later, I heard the clack as her peephole opened. Then the door swung open and Connie invited me in. "I was hoping you might stop by," she said. "Ray is beside himself. He's having a beer up on the deck. Do you have time to join us?"

"Nathan's not home yet, so I have some time. Just a finger." She poured me half a glass of pinot grigio, and I followed her up the steps. "Has the baby gone to bed?"

"Yes, thank goodness. Tonight was an easy night. If anything can be labeled 'easy' with a toddler." She laughed but she sounded tired. And worried. I couldn't remember the last time she'd checked on a visitor through her peephole.

We emerged onto the roof deck, where Ray was splayed out on one of their lounge chairs, with a beer in hand. A CD of the *Soul of Key West* played at a low volume. The night sky was unusually clear, allowing a swath of stars to shimmer in the distance over Garrison Bight and the Navy base. A night made for chilling out with your wife. Ray, however, looked anything but relaxed: I could see the lines of worry on his face, etched in the unflattering glow of the streetlight from the walk below.

"Goodness," I said, wondering how to approach him and deciding on direct. "That was so scary tonight on

Duval Street. I'm glad you're home. What in the world happened?"

"It's a long story," he said—and then clamped his lips together as though that was the end of it. "Not a big deal really."

Standing at the head of his chair behind him, Connie rolled her eyes. "I'd say getting hauled off to the police station for drawing a gun on Duval Street is a pretty big deal. Maybe Hayley can help, if you let her."

"I got spooked and I panicked," said Ray. "Turns out some kid popped a bunch of balloons, and I thought it was a shooter. That's it, end of story."

And I could see that tonight, for him, that was the end of the story. But Connie's anxious face told me there was a lot more to it. She circled her hand as if to ask me to try again.

"Everybody gets spooked these days," I said. "How can we help it? Every time you turn on the news, there's a report of another mass shooting. I don't blame you a bit."

He jutted his chin out, drank more beer, and said nothing.

"Nathan's got us all jacked up too," I continued, "about how to react in a crisis." I perched on the chair next to Ray and showed them my skinned knees. "I dropped and rolled, exactly as he prescribed. Only he didn't predict that I'd end up in the nastiest gutter in town. And I think you're supposed to roll if you're on fire, not if you're getting shot at." I laughed a little, trying to lighten the mood. It wasn't working.

"How is it going with your show?" I asked.

Ray had been a painter as long as I'd known him, and lately it seemed as though he might be on the cusp of breaking out. His artistic style had evolved over the last couple of years. Now he worked mostly in watercolors, which I knew were difficult. I'd taken a one-day class at the Studios of Key West, thinking I could learn a few tips and capture the Key West scenery. Instead, I'd ended up with a brown muddy mess on my canvas. Even the teacher, who, I was certain, hoped that her sweet support would garner good reviews from her students, was speechless in the face of my final product. I had not signed up for another class.

For a wedding gift, Ray had painted a scene of our dock for me and Nathan. It encompassed all three of the homes I had lived in and treasured since landing in Key West—Connie's place, Miss Gloria's, and now ours. And the kindness and thoughtfulness of this gift brought me to tears.

The artist's life could be heartbreaking—no artist or writer I knew felt they were being paid or appreciated for what they were worth. But very few of them were willing to give up chasing that dream. I knew it broke Ray's heart to see his wife trudge off every morning to work alongside her employees in her cleaning business. He would have much preferred being able to support her and their baby without her income. Even if she did insist she loved her customers and her job.

He shrugged and let a sigh escape. "I've had a lot of people looking at the paintings, but no buyers yet. The prices are high—but I had to do that because the gallery's commission is high too. And it's the shoulder season. And they only hung my stuff last week. And I'm sharing the showing with Jag."

"His friend from art school," Connie explained.

He cast a worried look at Connie, and she responded with a reassuring smile. "They wouldn't have asked you to show there if they didn't think you'd sell. We knew this would be hard going in. But you're going to make it big, I'm sure of it." She paused. "What had you so jumpy? Why did you pull the gun?"

She had to be working hard to keep her voice even, not accusatory, as I would have been. Ray didn't answer, and I could feel the tension between them ratchet up a few notches.

A flash of light caught my eye, and I glanced toward my houseboat and saw the headlights of Nathan's SUV as he pulled into the parking lot. "Look, you guys take care, and let us know if you need anything. I better go check in with my husband."

Connie stood up to walk me out. "Have a wonderful time in Scotland," she said. "We will keep an eye on the boats. Luckily, the weather report for next week appears completely benign. And I'm sure Nathan will have half the Key West Police Department doing drive-bys."

I kissed Ray on the top of the head and followed Connie down the stairs.

"I didn't even know he had a gun," she hissed in a low voice when we reached the front door. "He's worried about something, and he won't say any more about it. He thinks he's protecting us, but all it does is make me more anxious. And the timing could not be worse—with this big show on Duval Street. He could be on the edge of real artistic success, and instead, he's breaking down and pulling guns, and that could ruin everything. Who wants to buy art from a gun-toting nutjob?"

I hardly knew what to say, so I kept any advice to myself and gave her a big hug. "Listen, don't hesitate to call me anytime. If I'm sleeping, I'll turn the ringer off. Don't think twice about it, okay?" I put my hands on her shoulders. "If you have any worries or questions, call the police department and ask for Steve Torrence. And I'll find out right now whether Nathan's heard anything, and I'll text you instantly." I squeezed her shoulders and then drew her into a hug. "Everything will be okay. Love you guys to death."

I trotted back up the finger to greet my husband.

"I wondered where you got off to," Nathan said when I walked in. "I knew you couldn't be far because the scones were here. But the furry gentlemen wouldn't tell me anything."

I threw my arms around his neck and gave him a big kiss. "The truth is, this vacation can't come soon enough. I don't care how many kooky relatives are cramming themselves into our honeymoon or how bad the weather is or how much golf you have to play. I need a change of scenery. And some time with my new husband."

A smile lit up his face. "Same back at you. Now what in the devil was going on this afternoon with your friend and his gun?" He tipped his chin in the direction of Connie and Ray's home.

"I was going to ask you that. He wouldn't tell me anything. Why is it," I wondered, "that a person in trouble with the law won't explain why they did what they did?" I was remembering incidents with both my friend Lorenzo and my psychologist friend Eric, when their insistence on keeping secrets private made them look guilty as hell.

"Usually," said Nathan, "they are covering up some kind of secret that feels worse than what is known. The problem here is that he brandished a gun in a public place. And balloons or no balloons, that's a serious charge with serious consequences." He frowned. "I don't know Ray that well—"

"But I do," I broke in. "He's the sweetest, kindest guy, with not a violent bone in his body. He had to have been feeling threatened. Although why in the world he was carrying a gun . . ."

"You'd be surprised to know," said Nathan, "that not everyone shares your views."

He wasn't really smiling, and we were both exhausted and edgy about the trip, so I made the smart decision to head this conversation off before we got into a fight. I wasn't even going to ask whether he planned to bring his gun to Scotland. Not tonight anyway. I nudged the conversation in a different direction.

"Speaking of secrets, I didn't get a chance to ask you what is really going on with your sister. Why does everyone think she's losing it?

"She's jumpy," Nathan said. "That's the biggest symptom. She keeps trying to tell her husband that someone's trying to sabotage her project. And he keeps thinking she's having PTSD. Which would be understandable considering what she went through as a teenager. It's been almost fifteen years."

I had recently learned that Vera had been abducted by a killer many years ago, but managed to escape. Another girl had not been so lucky. Surely that was enough to make a person jumpy, especially, as Eric liked to point out, at a time like an anniversary of the original horrific event.

Chapter Four

Tasting a sauce, the master dipped first and second fin-
ger, tasted his forefinger and held the second finger to be
licked by Apollo. Thus the chef knew the cat's taste and
moreover had great respect for its judgment.
                    —John Steinbeck, *The Amiable Fleas*

I woke early the next morning to finish packing, water the
plants, and give Ziggy a decent walk. Walking would help
me as well, burning off some of my travel anxiety. The plane
from Miami to Edinburgh didn't leave until seven o'clock this
evening, but because any small accident could shut down the
mostly two-lane road that traversed the Florida Keys, travelers
were always advised to build in extra time. Lots of it.

As it turned out, we had an easy enough time getting to
the airport—getting through security, not so much. Nathan
had suggested I go through the line first, Miss Gloria next,
and him at the end to help with any stray luggage or other
issues. I sailed through, collected my shoes and suitcase and
laptop and liquids in their clear bag, and waited for my friend.

"Whose bag is this?" a stern TSA agent asked, holding up Miss G's pink backpack.

"That's mine," she said, waggling her hand in the air and grinning. "Is there a problem, Officer?"

But he only grunted and motioned her to the stand at the end of the rolling belt. "Do you have anything sharp inside?" he asked.

She looked thoughtful and then guilty. "The penknife my husband gave me before he died. It's tiny though. It would not work for a hijacking."

I groaned and clapped a hand over my eyes. We should have gone through her carry-on bag as well as the suitcase.

As the agent began pulling things out of the pack, I saw a look of dismay cross her face. She had added a bottle of her special anti-wrinkle cream, definitely larger than the 3.4 ounces allowed. She patted her face with one hand. "Oh, my goodness, that's too big, isn't it? Look what happens when I do use this—I'd hate for you to be responsible for how I look when I don't."

The man finally cracked a smile. He ran his wand over the top of the bottle, then opened it, sniffed, and replaced it in her bag.

She flashed a big grin and leaned closer to him to whisper. "I won't tell if you don't."

A few hours later, we took off without incident and were served a plate of rubbery chicken and a tipple of wine. Once the dinner trays had been removed, Miss Gloria tilted her seat back and went to sleep in an instant. Her ear rested on my shoulder, and I could feel my shirt getting damp from sleep drool. On the other side of me, Nathan had dozed off, too, and was snoring, though he looked miserable, his arms crossed and long legs cramped by the seat in front of him.

I was too wound up to sleep, worried about Connie and Ray and the gun incident, also concerned about our animals and whether they'd mope about being left alone. And I didn't like leaving my mother and Sam behind when I was certain they too would have enjoyed the trip. And finally, I tried not to think about how we were in a metal tube hurtling over the Atlantic Ocean with not a shred of control over our destiny. Even with all those thoughts clogging my emotional channels, I must have dozed off during the night, as I was woken by the pilot's announcement to return seats and tray tables to their upright and locked position. I could smell coffee, but I'd slept right through breakfast.

As we circled the city and approached the airport, Miss Gloria sprang to life, chattering about her two other trips to Europe and how much she was looking forward to Scotland. My brain felt slow and mushy, like something Evinrude might have dragged in from the parking lot and left as a gift on the deck. I ran my fingers through my curls and hoped I rallied in time to make a decent first impression with my new in-laws.

The head flight attendant came down the aisle and asked Nathan in a hushed voice whether his grandmother needed a wheelchair. Miss Gloria leaned across me to look the woman in the eye.

"My hearing is crackerjack—probably better than yours, young lady. And I am not his grandmother, he is my boy toy. And no, thank you, I don't need a wheelchair," she announced. "Unless you need a ride somewhere—then I'll be happy to push you."

The flight attendant turned a bright pink, and we all burst out laughing. I squeezed my friend's hand, grateful again that we'd stumbled into such a wonderful friendship.

We landed smoothly, filed out of the plane, and set out toward the baggage claim. I recognized Nathan's sister, Vera, without introduction. She looked like a younger version of her mother—tall, slender, and lovely, only with a curtain of wavy brown hair and green eyes like Nathan's. I felt suddenly tongue-tied. She rushed up to give Nathan a hug, and he introduced her and her husband, William, to Miss Gloria and me.

"I am so pleased to meet you finally," she said, holding me by the shoulders after a brief hug. "I can't believe Nathan didn't tell me he was getting married until after it had already happened. We probably couldn't have made it to the wedding, as we're both in the last throes of big projects. But isn't that just like a brother not to say a word? And as you probably heard already—or maybe not, as Nathan's not the greatest communicator—my mother and I have not been in the closest touch lately, so she didn't mention it either."

I hardly knew what to say to that, but luckily the men returned with the luggage, so I was spared the possibility of saying the wrong thing. Miss Gloria and I nodded off in the backseat, the lull of conversation between Nathan, Vera, and William a comforting backdrop.

I woke again as the car tires bumped over what felt like cobblestones. Then we turned into a lane lined with stone houses, the stones a pale yellow that made the homes glow when the sun hit them, and a small driveway leading to a sweet detached garage. We trundled into the backyard, which was surrounded by orderly stone walls and lined with flower gardens.

"This is beautiful!" exclaimed Miss Gloria. "It's like something from a fancy house and garden magazine."

"It's a little early for the best display of flowers," Vera said apologetically. "We really hit our stride in July."

The home was constructed of stone as well, with a chunky red tile roof and a bright red painted door. We followed our hosts into a cozy kitchen. The back wall behind the six-burner gas stove was brick, weathered to a soft pink as if it had been there for years. There were tall ceilings and exposed dark beams and beautiful views out the front windows of more gardens and more stone homes.

"I'll light a fire in the living room," said William in a charming brogue, "while you show our guests to their rooms. And then Nathan and I have to look over the golf club situation. If he doesn't like what I have in the garage, I'll have to make some calls."

"I thought I was staying in a motel with Helen?" asked Miss Gloria.

"We have two extra bedrooms, and it seemed silly not to use them," said Vera, waving us toward the back hall. She turned to look at me. "William and I were thinking we would move out of our master suite upstairs, and then you could have your private bathroom," she said to me. "The honeymoon suite. Nathan never did like to share with girls. Growing up, he complained bitterly about how much space my beauty potions took up." She smirked and patted her cheeks.

Miss Gloria and I laughed. "He's over that. If you could only see the space where we lived with Nathan when we first got married. We have sharing a bathroom down to a science," I said. "Please, we'd feel more comfortable without bumping you out of your room."

"This room is for Gloria," said Vera, leading us into a small bedroom with a blue-flowered quilt on the four-poster bed. At the end of the bed, two glossy gray tiger cats were sleeping on a pale blue afghan, making me feel instantly homesick for Evinrude. One of them opened his green eyes and blinked, then bolted off the bed and disappeared down the hallway.

"That was Archie," Vera said with a fond smile. "He loves me and only me, I'm afraid." The second cat jumped off the bed and began to wind around Miss Gloria's legs, talking loudly in secret cat chirps.

"This is Louise," said Vera. "She's highly opinionated, so my advice is do what she says."

Miss Gloria scooped up the big cat and rubbed her cheek on the distinctive black M on her forehead. "I don't know if you believe in signs from the universe," she said to Vera. "But I sure do. And cats on the bed are speaking to me. You take the first shower," she told me. "I'll stretch out with this lovely Scottish kitty for a few minutes." With Louise draped over her shoulder, she headed for the bed.

"She's darling," said Vera as we started down the hall to the second bedroom. "I'm really so pleased to meet you both."

"Same here. I'm sorry we didn't ask you to the wedding," I said. "I didn't even know for the longest time that you existed. Nathan finally told me why you'd moved to Scotland, but I had to squeeze it out of him."

She gave a little laugh, though the situation wasn't all that funny. "I don't know what is wrong with my family. Somewhere back in our history, our ancestors decided they were safer keeping their own counsel. And now we seem to be doomed by our ridiculous inability to talk about anything important."

As she passed by a brass sconce on the wall, I noticed that she looked tired, with gray circles under her eyes, as though she, too, had flown on a red-eye. We turned into the second bedroom, which had its own fireplace, and robin's egg–blue walls and a four-poster bed covered with a fluffy white duvet.

She crossed the room and flipped a switch on the wall. "This fireplace is gas," she said, "so we don't have to keep up with stoking two fires."

"I may never leave this room," I said. "It's so lovely. Your home is incredible and so cozy."

Her smile lit up her face. "Come out to the kitchen when you're ready, and I'll make you a cup of tea and we can have a proper chat." She disappeared into the hall.

It felt glorious to wash off the grit of traveling. I washed and dried my hair and dressed in clean clothes slightly more stylish than the yoga pants I'd worn on the plane. Then I headed down the hall toward that beautiful kitchen, feeling a bit more normal and definitely hungry. I stopped outside the kitchen door when I heard raised voices. Were Vera and William arguing?

"I can't believe you're going off for three days and leaving me to entertain—you know how stressed I am about—"

I tried to back away, but it was too late. They'd heard me. Vera whirled around to face me with a frozen smile of welcome on her face.

"We'll have an early dinner, something light, if that's all right," she said after a beat of silence. "I figure it's always best to get on the time zone of wherever you are and not stress the digestion. I made cream of vegetable soup and some cheese scones. I feel a bit badly that I didn't make a roast or something fancier, but usually when I get off a plane, I'm not in the mood for a big meal or a big hunk of meat."

"That sounds perfect," I said. "Do you mind if I take photos of your food? I promised my bosses that I would document everything I ate. I'm the only food critic at our little magazine, and people notice and gripe if there's an issue without food and eating." I was blathering now, wishing Nathan was here to back me up, carry the conversation in some other direction. Did his one and only sister wish we hadn't come?

The rest of the day passed in a blur of exhaustion—a walk around the neighborhood, the dinner of creamy vegetable soup and two servings of cheese scones slathered with butter, and finally a nip of Scotch whiskey in front of the fire. I tried to stay awake to be polite but ended up excusing myself to go to bed at the same time as Miss Gloria, a few minutes after eight.

"I'll see you shortly," Nathan said, getting up to kiss me. "Don't wait up."

"Not a chance." I grinned.

Chapter Five

*But the truth was that as much as she loved Arbutus and
held a cautious regard for Gladys, sometimes Madeline
felt like she would scream if she spent one more hour at
the kitchen table with yet another cup of coffee.*
—Ellen Airgood, *South of Superior*

The next morning, I woke and rolled over to feel the
space beside me in the bed. Empty. And I could hear
Miss Gloria exclaiming over the flowers outside the window
and sweet-talking the cat. Apparently, I was the last one up.
I dressed quickly and hurried to the kitchen. Nathan and his
brother-in-law were out in the backyard, looking at several
bags of golf clubs leaning against the garage.

On the kitchen table was an empty plate with only crumbs
remaining and half a cup of tea. There was a list in Miss
Gloria's handwriting that I recognized as places she hoped
to visit, many related to her favorite episodes of *Outlander*. A
second note from Vera invited me to make myself at home—
she had gone to Edinburgh to pick up her mother. I put the

kettle on and fished in the fridge for milk and butter, yearning for the sharp jolt of caffeine that I'd find in a café con leche from the Cuban Coffee Queen back home.

I sat at the table, drinking tea and enjoying the most wonderful banana date scone, even better than the one I had made for Miss Gloria before we left. I felt sluggish with jet lag and generally discombobulated about landing in this place so far in miles and spirit from Key West. The kitchen door opened, and Miss Gloria and Helen clattered in from the garden.

I stood to greet my mother-in-law and gave her a warm hug and a kiss on the cheek. "How wonderful that you could be here the same time we are," I said, mostly meaning it. We'd come to like and respect each other on her December visit to Key West, though she still scared me a little. She was so reserved and talented and opinionated—and tall.

"You won't believe how cute this town is," Miss Gloria said. "We walked around a little bit, but I didn't want to see everything before you got up. Bring your breakfast out to the back patio—they have the cutest garden. And Vera says it's not very often this sunny in June, so we should take advantage of it."

I popped the end of the scone into my mouth and carried the mug of tea to the backyard as Miss Gloria had suggested. Vera was kneeling on a blue pad, weeding her flowers. The rest of us took seats at a wrought iron table, to visit with her as she worked. Nathan and William emerged from the garage.

"Probably now that everyone's together, we should talk about our plans this week," said Vera, sneaking a quick look at her brother and not looking at her mother at all. "This is not ideal when you've only just landed yesterday, but we've accepted an invitation for cocktails and dinner tonight. Luckily, it's within walking distance, so when dinner is over, our travelers can be excused and get to bed at a reasonable hour."

Nathan swallowed, his Adam's apple sinking and rising. "A cocktail party?"

"I'm truly sorry," Vera said, perched on her haunches with a handful of dead-headed flowers, and now looking at me. "Some of the people are my business associates, and others are William's golf buddies. I hope you don't mind, but I've arranged for a little tour of some of the most beautiful places in the country." She started talking faster, as if to leave no room for dissent. "Nathan and William will meet us on the Isle of Mull, and they will also see Iona—both of them are too lovely to miss. But unfortunately, golf is my husband's primary passion. And once he heard Nathan was coming, he signed them up to play in a tournament this week, and there's no money back. And it would kill him to miss a round of golf with Nathan anyway." She looked apologetic. "This isn't much of a honeymoon, is it?"

"So everyone says." I tried to smile graciously, but all these plans made me feel a little grumpy.

"I'm sure it will be fine. Just give us tea and scones along the way," said Miss Gloria. "And maybe a wee dram of whiskey at night."

"The point is tomorrow and the next two days, unfortunately, William has commandeered your husband for this golf tournament. It will take up their evenings too." She stood up and brushed the mulch off her knees.

Nathan looked a little queasy and glared at his brother-in-law. "You did not say anything about a tournament. My game is not tournament quality."

"Not a care about that," said William, adding a hearty laugh. "The main thing is you'll be playing the Old Course which you've probably seen many times watching the British Open on the telly. Better still, we'll get to play several of the other courses, which may actually be even nicer, and meet some local Scottish laddies and drink Scottish whiskey. I believe they have bagpipes lined up to serenade us on the final hole. And I made my best guess of your waist size, so you'll be able to wear my family's Campbell plaid kilt for the final evening. And for tonight as well."

Now Nathan's face reflected sheer horror.

"I can't wait to watch all this," I said, trying to act effusive since he obviously couldn't muster a whit of enthusiasm. I knew coming in that this wasn't going to be a traditional honeymoon, but it was turning out even worse than I'd expected.

"Do tell us more about what's on the docket for the rest of us," said Nathan's mom. "What's this about a tour?"

His sister sighed. "I think I told you about my big publishing project."

From the expression on Mrs. Bransford's—Helen's—face, I wondered if she had been told anything about this. I certainly hadn't heard any details other than that Vera seemed to be losing it in some subtle way. Helen raised her eyebrows, which might have meant "no" or maybe "tell me again." Or something else in the Bransford dialect that I had yet to decipher. There was a coolness between them that left me feeling sad and uncomfortable.

William answered. "Vera landed a huge contract for a book about traveling to and absorbing Scotland's thin places. She's working with several old friends, and that makes it even more special."

I snuck a look at Nathan's sister. She was smiling, but it was not the kind of smile that looked like it came from the joy in one's heart. This smile was pasted on to cover something—I wasn't sure what.

"Tell us about thin places," her mother said. "I've heard the term used, but I don't quite know what it means." Her voice was flat, devoid of judgment. But I wasn't convinced that it didn't lurk beneath the surface.

"Thin places are places where the earth and heaven are close, where the distance between them has shrunk," Vera explained. "Sometimes people say the veil between heaven and earth has lifted in such locations. Islands are often thin places—they are cut off from undesirable physical and psychic influences."

Nathan's brows drew together, his expression perplexed. Under his tough cop exterior, though I'd found him to be more emotional than I'd first imagined, he was not a deeply spiritual man. Expressions such as "lifting the veil between heaven and earth" would not be in his wheelhouse.

"Like Key West," explained Miss Gloria. "Lorenzo talks about the same thing. He says there's a current running around our island that protects us. And that people who are drawn to visit don't realize it's the spiritual nature of the island

41

pulling them. They misinterpret that invitation to mean getting drunk on Duval Street." She chortled, making everyone smile.

"Now that's a big jump," said William, "from spirit to spirits."

"Lorenzo says that Key West is a Capricorn, more concerned about money than anything else—where that money's coming from and in whose pockets it will land," I added. "It sounds odd, I know, but cities have astrological signs exactly like people."

Helen nodded politely. "Fascinating words from a fascinating man." She had met Lorenzo briefly during her visit last winter, and they had discovered more in common than I would have imagined. She turned her attention back to her daughter. "So, thin places?"

Vera continued, "I proposed the project as a recasting of some of the history behind Scottish tourist sites. Many tour groups pitching *Outlander* and *Game of Thrones* sites as a way to understand Scottish history and religion have grown hokey and money-hungry—they skim along the surface and pitch the kind of tourism that appeals to the lowest common denominator. It's not all about guessing what's under the kilts of our men."

I didn't dare look at Miss Gloria's face for fear that we'd both break into hysterical laughter, which would have seemed so rude.

"I'm hoping this project can counteract some of that and help teach people how to cultivate their spirituality in our precious thin places," Vera continued. Her expression was very serious, and I had the bad feeling she knew we were on the verge of laughing, though that had mostly to do with feeling giddy with jet lag and very little to do with her project.

"I'm very proud of her," William said, putting a defensive arm around his wife's shoulders as if to block any disagreement from the rest of us. "Not only has she landed a huge advance for this book, but her book will return dignity and truth to our history."

Vera flashed a lopsided grin at her husband. "Not everyone is as excited as you are, darling." She turned back to us. "There have been problems with people who believe I'm pretending to be an expert when I am actually nothing but an outsider. Not even born in Scotland."

I understood this perfectly, as the same dynamic occurred on our Key West island. There was a constant turnover of artistic and foodie and literary types, and the new arrivals seemed to believe they understood the culture better than anyone who had come before. My good friend and police officer Steve Torrence always said that the folks who made the biggest splash coming in were the first to bail out with any signs of trouble.

"I can imagine how that would be controversial," I said. "Natives to our island are called conchs. But you can't be one unless you were actually born there. When I write for our magazine, I try to be super clear that these are my opinions, that I'm not trying to speak for the world. I'm not trying to pretend to be anyone but myself."

"And you're almost perfect," said Nathan with a big grin.

"Almost?" I punched his arm and turned back to Vera. "You're working with several people on this book? I bet that can be tricky."

Vera sighed, her shoulders tightening visibly. "Yes. And we are arguing a bit about which of the places we've researched have to be cut. Our draft has run long, and the publisher isn't budging. Especially because of the photographs, it's an expensive project. All that to say again that we're so sorry about the party that we must attend tonight. I'm afraid nothing about this visit is going the way we would have hoped or planned. Since we're crashing toward the deadline, I wasn't able to put any of this off," she said and then shrugged.

Which caused me to wonder what else wasn't right. Whatever I'd overheard them arguing about last night was probably in the mix.

"Turns out the summer solstice can be the best time to photograph special places," Vera said. "I promise the scenery will be stunning. Meanwhile, since the golf doesn't start until tomorrow, I thought we could all walk around town, see some of the sights, grab a bite of lunch?"

"I was going to take Nathan to the driving range," William said, frowning a little. "According to his fatuous claim, he's very rusty."

"It's not a fatuous claim—it's a fact. I haven't touched a club since I was twenty," Nathan said, turning to me. "Is that okay with you if we don't join you?"

"Sure," I said, assuming that was what he wanted. "We'll have an all girls' lunch instead."

A Scone of Contention

After an hour of spinning through the ruins of St. Andrews Castle and Cathedral and admiring the glorious juxtaposition of blue sea of the Firth of Forth against weathered stone and green grass, Miss Gloria and I were beginning to droop. The cobblestone walkways and streets, though beautiful, had begun to pound my ankles, spreading an ache up through my calves to my knees.

Vera noticed. "You two need a spot of tea," she said. "Before we adjourn inside to lunch, I want you to see one more thing. It's not a thin place, but I think you'll enjoy it." We walked back across town and stopped in front of a coffee shop called the Northpoint Café. A plain brown bench sat below the picture window.

"People say this is where Kate met Wills," said Vera. "At the very least they either had coffee here or flirted on the bench outside the picture window."

"Kate Middleton? Oh, I love Kate," said Miss Gloria. "That wedding! And remember how she came out of the hospital carrying her firstborn baby? She was stunning! Even though she must have had a staff to buff and puff her so she looked like a million dollars." She perched on the bench and pretended to flip her hair back like a princess. "I didn't think that was quite fair to the rest of us women—it warped our husbands' expectations about what a new mother should look like. And our own. But I don't suppose she chose it. She does what the royal family requires of her, and she does it with grace and beauty." She held one hand up to simulate a royal wave, and we all three snickered.

Vera beckoned us inside the busy café. As we were seated, my phone buzzed, and Connie's face came up in a FaceTime call. She looked distraught.

"Excuse me, I need to take this," I told the ladies. "Order me something light, okay? Soup and half a sandwich or a scone maybe?"

"Hello?" I answered once I was seated outside on Will and Kate's bench. "Is everything okay?" I could see that she was pacing on Miss Gloria's deck. T-bone, Sparky, and Evinrude were in a furry, purring pile on my former lounge chair, with Ziggy beside them, but six inches away. None of them looked injured, nor did they appear to be pining for us. The houseboat looked homey and peaceful, and I was surprised by the zing of homesickness that pierced my gut.

"All is well, I just wanted to check in. How's Scotland?" she asked.

I held the phone up so she could see the cobblestone street and stone buildings. "Beautiful. Nathan's sister looks exactly like his mom, and they live in the most adorable house. Though the family dynamics are complicated, as you can imagine." I could have gone on and on, but I was certain she hadn't called to hear about my trip. "What's up?"

"I hate to bother you, but I'm in knots," she said. "I can't get Ray to tell me why he pulled the gun out or even why he had a damn gun in the first place." She started to cry. "We've had to put all our savings toward hiring a lawyer who *may* be able to get the charges reduced *if* they can find bystanders to confirm that either he himself was threatened or he didn't flash his weapon in a threatening way. His weapon. Since when has my sweet Ray felt like he needed a weapon? And now his lawyer wants him to have a psychological evaluation, but so far Ray's refusing."

I didn't want to say this to her, but having been right there on the scene and scared to death by the crowd's panic, I could understand why brandishing a gun was a big deal. "Do you think he would talk to Eric?" I asked. Eric was a dear friend in Key West, a psychologist who had been through a difficult time when he'd been accused of a crime he didn't commit. "He has such a gentle way about him. And besides, he knows exactly what it feels like to be on the wrong side of the law."

"I can ask," Connie said, sinking down on the chaise lounge beside the cats. "But I'll bet he'll refuse. It's like he's withdrawing into himself. He's spending all of his time at his studio on Stock Island and refuses to say what happened or why." Evinrude stalked over and rubbed his jowls on her iPhone so the whole screen was filled with gray fur. I liked to think he recognized my voice.

"I miss you, kitty," I said, clucking at him. "Mommy will be home soon. If it was me," I said to Connie, "and I'm not saying this is the right thing for everyone, I would go down to the gallery and ask some questions. Talk to the owner. Who was there when he pulled the gun out? Were there any conflicts between the staff and Ray? Did he say anything to you that morning that now seems out of character? Was he antsy or depressed? More wound up than usual? Has he been angry with anyone? Scared? You could ask my mother to go with you," I added. "She's pretty good about nosing into things. I come by it honestly." We both chuckled and she swiped at her tear-streaked face with the back of her hand. "Wasn't this his big breakout moment? Is he having mixed feelings about that?"

"Yes, it was supposed to be," said Connie in a voice as soft as a whisper. She reached to stroke the nearest cat, Evinrude, again. "I have no idea why he'd want to sabotage himself. And his family's future."

"Hayley?" Miss Gloria stuck her head out of the café, bringing me back to the present moment. "Your soup is here already." She looked and sounded exhausted. I needed to get off the phone, eat lunch, and get my friend back to the house for a nap.

"Text me tomorrow, okay? Let me know what you find out."

Returning to the table, I felt torn, not quite settled in Scotland and yet so far from home. I felt it again, the shiver on the grave. *You're tired,* I told myself. Everything will be fine.

It was after two by the time we got back to Vera's home, though lord only knew what time it really was in my body. Nathan had warned me to try to think only of local time in order to dispense with jet lag and get settled more quickly. Easier said than done. I washed my face and put on a pair of yoga pants and a T-shirt, and prepared to attack a power nap. I heard a soft tap on the door.

"Come in."

The door cracked open and Miss Gloria's elfin face appeared.

"Everything okay?" I asked. "Come on in."

"It's beautiful here, isn't it? I can't wait to see more of the countryside." She paused, plucked at a few wayward peaks of white hair. "But I am a little worried."

I patted the bed beside me. "About what?"

She crossed the room and perched on Nathan's side of the bed. "It might sound silly. But I didn't realize that Vera's husband is a Campbell. I never asked you their family name."

"And that's a problem because . . .?"

"Because my mother's people were MacDonalds."

She stopped speaking, as though that was all I needed to know. But it explained nothing to me.

"Say a little more about that?" I suggested.

She heaved a troubled sigh. "My ancestors lived in the Highlands, in Glencoe, where we will be going with Vera, I'm sure. It's well known for being a thin place. And many of those same people were massacred by the Campbells. William's people."

She looked so distressed that I needed to understand. Clearly, I should have been reading more Scottish history. "And how long ago did all this happen?" I asked.

"In the 1600s. But they wiped out most of the clan. And we have long memories. I still sense that loss right here." She pressed her hand to her chest, and I could almost see her heart pounding like a little bird.

"I can imagine how distressing that bit of history would feel," I said—though, in truth, I couldn't quite imagine getting that upset about something so long ago. On the other hand, I didn't know the details of the massacre, and I was a lot younger than Miss Gloria and more concerned with the here and now than my ancestors' lives. And this was likely a failing of my own. All that aside, I knew that Miss Gloria had a special connection with spirits from the past. I'd seen this in action watching her take visitors on guided tours of the Key West Cemetery. I didn't understand it, but I believed that her experience was unusual and true. And a little exhausting.

"Let's get a little rest. We're both tired. And then we can figure out what to do when we're fresh." I reached over to give her a hug.

Though, honestly, what was there to do? Demand reparations from our host, Nathan's brother-in-law? I sighed. Old hurts and the damage they'd done were hard to heal and impossible to undo.

Chapter Six

She'd fermented cabbage with radishes, and cauliflower with haricots vert and carrots. The spice mixtures were not as hot as the traditional kimchee—a concession to the bland English palate—but still had a good bit of pop. The spicy, crunchy veg made a perfect counterpoint to the soft creaminess of the smoked lamb and beans.
—Deborah Crombie, *A Bitter Feast*

By five o'clock, we were refreshed as much as we could be for Vera's friends' party. I had scrounged the only skirt from the bottom of my suitcase and attempted to steam out the wrinkles, while Miss Gloria decked herself out in a sweat suit beaded with sequins. Vera's husband had harangued Nathan until he folded and agreed to wear a borrowed kilt sewn from the official Campbell tartan, finished off with a waistcoat and a traditional sporran hanging from his waist.

"Doesn't he look amazing?" William asked, once they'd marched into the living room where we waited. The fabric of their kilts consisted of rows and columns of green and blue separated by black lines.

"He's got the legs for it, that's for sure," said Miss Gloria, grinning. "Look at the muscles in his calves! He could give Jamie in Outlander a run for his money. Did you know," she added, ignoring the fierce blush that had spread over Nathan's cheeks, "that men used to carry cooked oatmeal in those pouches? That sounds a little disgusting, doesn't it? It would make an awful mess."

"It must have been some kind of dried grain," I suggested, only glad she was focused on the contents of the sporran rather than questioning him about what he was wearing under the kilt. Or even worse, launching into a discussion of the Campbell–MacDonald conflict. We'd have time over the week to explore that quietly.

We strolled through the streets of St. Andrews, passing clusters of young people, some wearing flapping black or red graduation gowns.

"The gowns were traditionally worn at all Scottish universities," said William, scowling. "Now they mostly trot them out for special occasions, which I find appalling. Where is their sense of history and tradition?"

"Keep in mind that he's the man who convinced your husband to wear a kilt," Vera said with a laugh. "And he's a full professor at the University." Then she began to describe the cast of characters that we would encounter at the party. "Ainsley and Dougal are the hosts tonight. You are not likely to see a penthouse this grand again except perhaps in your dreams or an Architectural Digest. It overlooks the 16th hole of the Old Course, so they are besieged by celebrity guests when the British Open takes place in this town."

"I'm getting the idea that should mean something very important," Miss Gloria whispered, catching my elbow and pulling me toward her. "I'm not sure this will be our crowd."

I laughed. "But Nathan will love talking about the golf course with the others. Even if he claims to hate golf, I can see that it's in his blood. And if they're friends of his sister's, I'm sure we'll enjoy them."

An elevator whisked us up to the penultimate floor of a stunning red sandstone building. Inside, a hallway that looked like the entrance to a museum gallery led to a living room where a set of stairs swept up to another floor, resembling something out of Downton Abbey. I felt stunned by the glamour, and I could see that Miss Gloria's mind was just as boggled.

"I promise we won't stay late but I wanted you to see the house and meet a few friends," said Vera. She dropped her voice to a whisper. "It's astonishing, isn't it?"

She introduced us to her book team, including Glenda Findlay, a slender blonde woman with dark brown eyes; her husband, Gavin, somewhat corpulent with watery blue eyes and a reddened nose; and Ainsley, the hostess, her beautiful auburn hair swept into a stylish knot. She had a spray of freckles across her cheeks that I imagined she'd hated as a teenager, though they looked adorable now. She was standing next to a tall man with pronounced laugh lines and a red kilt.

"Welcome to our home!" Ainsley said. "This is my husband, Dougal. We're so excited to meet Vera's family. Come get a drink and meet some friends."

We were plied with flutes of champagne and introduced to a series of people with thick brogues. "I'd love to show them around," Ainsley said to Vera. "You've seen it all, and you probably have to chat with the golfing set."

Vera laughed. "Unfortunately, I do. That would be wonderful—your home is a dream."

Then Ainsley whisked us through a tour of the downstairs rooms: a dark wood paneled bar with striped club chairs and floor-to-ceiling drapes and chandeliers and Doric columns; a separate den with pink plush tufted chairs and a gilt fireplace (for the lady of the house?); and, at my request, a peek into her glorious kitchen.

"Wow," I said, stepping out of the way of a waiter carrying a tray of what looked and smelled like sausage rolls encased in puff pastry.

Miss Gloria snagged one as the waiter floated by. She blew on the end to cool it off, then took a healthy bite and nodded her approval. "Hayley can't help it. Even though she has a brand-new kitchen, she contracts a bad case of appliance envy each time she sees someone else's." She waved the end of the sausage in the air. "These are marvelous by the way. The truth is Hayley can cook anywhere. She made amazing dishes when she lived in my floating tub, and that was by no means a show kitchen."

"You cook?" Ainsley asked me, looking a bit surprised. "We'd heard that Americans eat all their meals out."

"She's an amazing cook," Miss Gloria said. "And she's also a restaurant critic."

"I write about food for a magazine in Key West, the town on an island at the very bottom of Florida. I'm on the hunt for the best scones in Scotland," I said with a grin. "Or die trying."

"We can help with that," said Ainsley with a warm return smile. "My personal favorite is a hint of citrus or cinnamon when serving at tea, but you might prefer cheese, which the chef is serving with dinner tonight."

She then introduced me to the cook standing at the stove—Grace, a sturdy young woman who wore chef's whites and brown hair pulled back to the base of her neck with a yellow ribbon. I studied her as she pulled a heavy tray of pastries out of the oven. She had a square face, a cleft in her chin, and powerful forearms. She slid the tray onto the counter, wiped her hands on her white apron, and turned to greet us. "Pleasure to meet you."

"You may find the very best scones right here in Grace's kitchen. You'll see." Ainsley grinned, then explained to Grace, "Hayley is a food specialist."

"Not really a specialist, but I do love to eat. And those are gorgeous," I told Grace, pointing to the fragrant baked goods, which were striped with cheese and smelled like heaven, if heaven was butter and cheese, which sounded about right to me.

She cut into one of the golden scones and offered pieces to each of us. "Hot!" she warned, as if we were food toddlers.

I nibbled and closed my eyes to savor the perfect flavor and buttery crumb, which left me almost speechless. "These are absolutely divine. Maybe you'll share the recipe?"

"I will," she said. "And I would love to show you around the kitchen properly tomorrow when things aren't so hectic, if Miss Ainsley doesn't object?"

"Of course not," said Ainsley. "And maybe you could take her to the market when you go in the morning, if that suits her schedule? Vendors come from all around the countryside, with farmhouse cheese and heritage pork, Scottish game, organic vegetables and fruits, honey," she explained to me. "Grace does most of our shopping from these local folks."

"I would love that so much," I said, glancing at the young chef, who nodded shyly. I arranged to meet her here at the house at eight AM.

Then Miss Gloria and I followed Ainsley up the elegant sweep of stairs and down a hall to more steps leading to the roof terrace that they shared with other tenants in the building.

"This view is sensational," I exclaimed, looking over the wide, flat West Sands Beach on one side and out to sea, and the kelly-green golf course on the other. "Aren't you lucky to live here!"

She nodded. "The weather can be iffy, but it's Scotland and we're Scottish, so we expect that."

"How did you meet Vera?" I asked.

"We all went to University here in St. Andrews," she explained. "Glenda, Vera, and I were inseparable pals that first year. We had big plans to become artists and writers and share a garret in Paris while we waited for our talents to be discovered. We certainly never intended to remain in this town."

She laughed. "But life has a way of finding its own path, and we found soon enough that getting married shackled our ankles a bit and curbed our plans to travel as free birds. I've never really gotten back to my art, though I can't complain about my life." She shrugged, gave a wry little laugh. "Vera has been discovered because of her brilliant writing, but the rest of us are still waiting."

"What kind of art were you studying?" I asked. "I'm guessing because of your home that you're a designer."

Again, her laugh was light, but I sensed a hint of regret underneath. "Most of the paintings on the walls are mine. And I planned the decorating, but as far as professional design, life has gotten in the way. I suppose that should have been obvious going in, that marriage and the trappings of adulthood become a wee cage of sorts. But it never occurred to me. With this project, I'm hoping to make up for lost time."

"I never found being married to my Frank to cramp my style," said Miss Gloria, turning away from the view to look at our hostess. "We wanted a lot of the same things in our lives, and we both liked some of our own space, and had separate friends and hobbies. And that meant I was almost always happy to see him at the end of a day."

"I wish I'd met him," I said, squeezing her hand.

She smiled back at me. "And Hayley here is a newlywed so hopefully she hasn't experienced that trapped feeling—and won't. In any case, if you've ended up in a cage, it's definitely gilded," said Miss Gloria to Ainsley, adding a warm laugh that took some of the sting out of the comment.

"But Vera mentioned too that you are all working on a joint project," I said. "Will you tell us more about that? You must be involved with design."

Her face brightened. "You guessed correctly. Design, and also organization. I have a knack, it turns out, for herding cats. But the subject is a passion of mine too. All of us except for Vera are Scottish nationals," said Ainsley. "And over many conversations, we came to realize that we were appalled by the influx of tourism."

She sighed. "It's not that we object to people learning about our country, but we do object to tourism based on inaccurate portrayals of our country and its history. And we object to sacred sites trampled by careless guests. Our project is designed to counterbalance that. We plan to tell an accurate story of our history and display photographs of the most gorgeous sites in our country, but also raise questions about the way tourism may be threatening those exact qualities. And we hope that our book will offer a template for how best to absorb these sacred places."

She patted her elegant twist of red hair and continued. "I'm certain it's not only Scotland that is suffering. My husband and I took one of the ferries from Stranraer on the west coast over to Northern Ireland last fall. We wanted to see the Giants Causeway and hear some Irish music. Do you know that site? It consists of enormous columns of basalt rock along the coast, formed by a flow of lava, and it has many myths associated with it."

Miss Gloria and I both shook our heads.

"It wasn't exactly a beautiful day, rainy and cool. Even so, the place was overrun with tourists. Busloads of visitors posed in front of the rock formations with their umbrellas, and kids tore around as if it was one big playground. Of course, the Giant's Causeway has been designated a World Heritage Site and everyone should be entitled to enjoy it. But we felt disoriented and overwhelmed, rather like a panicked herd of sheep being driven to the marketplace, I imagine. It was impossible to truly experience and absorb the magic of the setting."

"This happens in Key West too," said Miss Gloria sadly. "The more people crowd in, the more the beauty is obscured. Lorenzo—that's our tarot card–reading friend—likes to say that money rules Key West. And money and magic don't fit together that well."

"I think Iceland has suffered in a similar fashion, mostly because *Game of Thrones* was filmed there," I said. "Too many tourists watched that show and then rushed across the ocean to cram themselves into the famous spaces."

"And the Justin Bieber YouTube video was part of Iceland's appeal too," Miss Gloria added. "The one with him walking on that narrow ledge of rock? I must have watched it a hundred times, and I wasn't the only senior on that soul train." She winked at me. "Iceland's on my bucket list now, and I don't even like heights."

"It's really a problem without a good solution," Ainsley said, "because on the one hand, we want our beautiful country to be seen and enjoyed. And maybe it's not fair to put a value judgment on tourism. And who should be the arbiter of taste? And who will be assigned to man the gate?"

A gong rang in a distant room. "Dinner is served," said Ainsley. "Just in time before we all sink into a great quagmire of depression."

Chapter Seven

There he got out the luncheon-basket and packed a simple meal, in which, remembering the stranger's origin and preferences, he took care to include a yard of long French bread, a sausage out of which the garlic sang, some cheese which lay down and cried, and a long-necked straw-covered flask wherein lay bottled sunshine shed and garnered on far Southern slopes.

—Kenneth Grahame, *The Wind in the Willows*

She ushered us back down the hallway and into a cavernous dining room. I was seated next to one of Vera's cowriters, Gavin Findlay, and across the table from another man wearing a kilt, with Nathan's mother cattycorner and Nathan and Miss Gloria at the far end.

Ainsley leaned between me and Gavin to introduce us. "Gavin, this is Hayley, Vera's new sister-in-law. We are so happy to have her visiting. Hayley, Gavin is my old friend Gloria's husband and simply a brilliant photographer." She patted us on our shoulders and smiled, though her left eye seemed to be twitching as if she was sending me a message. He slung an arm around my shoulders and squeezed. I could smell the scotch on his breath, and a whiff of cigar.

"Always glad to make the acquaintance of another beautiful woman," he said.

"Lovely to meet you," I said, trying to ease out of his grip. "I'm struggling to keep everyone straight, so remind me which beautiful lady is your better half?"

He looked confused for a minute.

"Your wife, I mean," I added.

"Glenda's down there." He gestured at the slim blonde at the end of the table, who wore a purple gown with a deep slash of cleavage. She was glaring at us, or me anyway. I flashed her a big smile and shrugged her husband's hand off my back.

"So then, Vera has a sister. She never said anything about that." Gavin tucked a white napkin into his neckline and drained the glass of Scotch he'd brought to the table.

I opened my mouth to correct his assessment of our relationship, but Gavin had already begun to explain that he was the photographer for the book, but also what he referred to as the "concept man." Across the table, Helen Bransford widened her eyes and mouthed "Good luck" in my direction.

Two waiters and Grace the cook began circulating around the big table, serving wine and appetizers to each of us. Grace whispered about the dishes she was serving as she reached me.

"Bubble and squeak patties," she said, "otherwise known as cabbage and potatoes. And these are Scottish eggs wrapped in sausage."

I smiled my thanks and snapped a few photos before I bit into them. Absolutely divine, crunchy outside and soft and savory inside.

"What is the concept of this book?" I asked Gavin. "Ainsley was mentioning the push–pull of tourism versus ecology and beauty of the spaces. And Vera writes about sacred places, I think." By now I was somewhat confused about how all these people were working together and what the end product would be. "How will your project be different from other tour books of Scotland?"

His lips curved into a disdainful frown. "Just like Vera not to bother to explain how very different this will be."

I felt my mental hackles rise on my sister-in-law's behalf. "We rolled in from the US yesterday and are a bit staggered by jet lag. In other words, we haven't delved into every conceivable angle of your project—we're doing our best to get acclimated." This was a dinner party and I needed to try to smooth over my testiness, so I added, "Though I'd love to hear about it."

"My concept is called interactive tourism," he said, folding his hands over his stomach in a satisfied way.

"I'm not familiar with that term," I said.

But before Gavin could explain it to me, if in fact he had had any intention of doing so, the man next to him began quizzing him about the book.

"My female coauthors—" Gavin slapped his hand on the table—"are interested in reality. Which I find insufferably dull. We've seen that in a thousand history books and guidebooks to Scotland. I am interested in sharing historical virtual reality with visitors. And that means there will be a live link for each of the sites in the book connected to a virtual experience of Scottish history, as well as a downloadable app. But most exciting to me is, once you've purchased the Oculite headset, the experience goes from dull to immersive and astonishing!"

"So, give us an example of what might we see," his dinner companion urged, before I could get my question out: What in the world was an Oculite headset?

"So, for example, if you were visiting the Great Wall of China," said Gavin, "you would no longer be looking at the remnants of an old stone wall. After downloading my new app and purchasing the headset, you would literally experience the attacks of the Huns—the clashing swords, the thwack of mace or javelin, the screaming horses. The only thing missing would be the smell of burning flesh—and you better believe I'm working on how to simulate odors as well. After that might come scenes of slaves building the wall, which was designed to repel further attacks. You wouldn't forget *those* historical events."

This was sounding like a book experience that I would never, not in a million years, purchase or read. And it also did not sound like the same book that Vera was writing. It didn't actually sound like a book at all; it sounded like an expensive video game.

Gavin continued to hold forth on his version of the project. "Similarly, many tourists visit Glencoe in the Highlands. You can drive through the mountains on those narrow roads, with buses hurtling toward you, and then pile into the visitor center with hundreds of other tourists, and then walk through a basically boring landscape and see nothing. Or you can Velcro on the eyepiece for my virtual reality experience and see a reenactment of the massacre of Glencoe. The triumph of the Campbells." He honked a loud laugh and signaled for the waiter to refill his glass with red wine.

I dearly hoped that Miss Gloria was too far away to hear this man crow about experiencing the massacre of her clan. Trying to focus on the plate of cock-a-leekie soup that had been served, I blew on a spoonful of hot broth, then tasted leeks and a rich chicken stock, lots of black pepper, and a hint of thyme. And sunk at the bottom of the bowl were pieces of prune, which lent a sweet finish to the savory dish. As we finished the soup course and dove into the shepherd's pie, followed by a roast lamb with baby red potatoes, I chatted with the man on my other side, who was a golfer like Nathan and William. As dull as it might have seemed, hearing about putts and sand bunkers and the history of the Old Course was suddenly preferable to the alternative conversation.

"I have a theory about the third stage of life," Gavin was saying in a voice that had grown louder and louder over the course of the meal and could no longer be tuned out. "First there is childhood, then adulthood, and then what—old age? I and a handful of French philosophers prefer to call this third stage the *troisième age*." He glanced around to see who was listening. "I believe this stage of life is based on curiosity."

Which struck me as almost hysterical as he had not shown a shred of curiosity toward anyone else in the room. He had not asked one question of his tablemates, even those of us who were obviously not local. And all that aside, his French accent was atrocious. I tried to ignore him and make mental notes about Grace's recipes.

After the dinner plates had been cleared, Grace served small green salads—"to clear your palates," she told us. I snapped a quick photo, focusing on the nasturtium garnish, thinking that some of the greens that made up the salad were unfamiliar. I'd have to remember to ask what was used. Next Grace circled around with a bottle of whiskey and poured each of us a finger of alcohol over ice. "Edradour single malt cream whiskey with hints of butterscotch, chocolate, and hazelnut," she told us.

I took one sip of the whiskey—only to be polite, as I had never been a fan of sweet after-dinner drinks—and found it delicious. It was not at all sweet; it tasted creamy and smooth. I nibbled on shortbread and a few pieces of gorgeous cheese that were being passed by uniformed waiters, hoping they might absorb some of the alcohol. The new people I'd met began to swim together in a boozy blur. Miss Gloria looked knackered too, like a cut flower that had fallen out of its vase and was lying limply on the table.

As I was thinking about how to signal to Nathan that it was time to clear out, at the far end of the table, Gavin's wife, Glenda, suddenly doubled over, moaning in pain.

"Oh my goodness," said Ainsley, leaping out of her chair and rushing to her side. "What's wrong? How can we help?"

The guest who'd been seated next to her sprang up. "Should we call emergency?"

"Do you feel nauseous?" another voice asked.

The other guests chimed in with more questions.

"Is her abdomen tender?"

"Has this happened before?"

"Does she have a history of drug use?"

"Is her stomach swollen?"

"Do you suppose it's a case of appendicitis or diverticulitis or some other infected internal organ?"

None of that would be helpful to hear if a person was feeling ill.

"Call poison control," a voice boomed out.

That last comment came from Gavin, who had arrived at her side. I was hoping his wife was too distracted by her pain to absorb it.

Vera's face had gone ashen white, and she stood over her friend, wringing her hands helplessly. Ainsley bustled around giving orders and gently pushing people away from Glenda. "Friends, please stand back and let her breathe. Is she taking any new medication?" she asked Gavin.

But he only shrugged. "No idea."

"How much did she have to drink?" she asked the people who had been seated on either side of her, including Miss Gloria.

But my friend looked woozy, exhausted from the jet lag, I suspected. And she too would've been a fan of the cream whiskey and probably tippled more than one glass.

"I'm sorry," she murmured. "I said yes to everything that was offered and I wasn't watching."

"Maybe some of us should clear out of the way," said Helen Bransford. "It won't help her to have fifteen tipsy guests sucking up her air."

I could have kissed her.

"I'm going to stay behind, make sure she's okay," said Vera. "Do you mind staying with me?" she asked Nathan. "In case . . ." Her words trailed off, but her eyes were pleading. "And maybe William could escort the rest of you home."

I had to admit it was a relief to get out of the stone mansion, away from too much to drink and too much heavy food, and far away from my bombastic dinner companion. Of course, I was worried about Glenda, but I had nothing to offer that might help her. And I couldn't wait to breathe in some cool sea-scented air and return to the comfort of our own temporary beds.

As we walked, Helen chatted with her son-in-law and I quietly quizzed Miss Gloria. "Did you notice anything wrong with Glenda over the course of the night?"

"Honestly not," said Miss Gloria. "But I was feeling a little droopy myself, trying to make sure I didn't slide under the table. Too much excitement and sausage and cheese and whiskey." She glanced at me. "That sounded terrible, as though I don't care a fig about her. I feel awful that it ended that way, but on the other hand, I'm so glad to leave the party and hit the hay. I guess I'm still jet-lagged."

"Me too, on all of the above," I admitted. "Let's hope she recovers quickly and it blows over tonight."

William deposited us back at home and then left to drive my mother-in-law to her hotel. Miss Gloria and I headed directly to our rooms. I washed my face and brushed my teeth and collapsed under the covers. I woke when Nathan climbed into bed sometime later.

"Is she all right?" I mumbled.

"At first she refused medical assistance."

"Why refuse help if she was feeling that sick?" I wondered.

Nathan sighed and spooned his chest against my back. "Don't ask me. Then not ten minutes after, she insisted that she had probably eaten something that didn't agree with her. Perhaps the sausage wasn't fresh or the lamb or the chicken soup had sat out on the counter too long. As I was about to leave, she took a turn for the worse, and Gavin got a bit hysterical, saying he was certain she must have been poisoned. At this point, she was rolling around on the carpet, clutching her stomach. And then Gavin announced that the authorities needed to be called."

The word stabbed through my foggy, sleep-craving brain like a knife. "Poisoned? Really? By whom? I heard him say to call poison control before we left, but I assumed he meant food poisoning—or maybe he'd gotten upset watching her discomfort. Did he mean someone at the party tried to do her in?"

"Damn good questions. I told them that since they worried that something was amiss and she was obviously in distress, we should call an ambulance along with the authorities. Glenda agreed—she looked a little scared by that point."

"At least they had one calm head on the scene."

"At least this time it's not my job to sort it out. Isn't this supposed to be a honeymoon?" He sighed. "Finally, the ambulance came and carried her off. I hate that my sister is a wreck over it. And so of course is her friend Ainsley because it was her house and her dinner party. And her chef and her food." He burrowed down beneath the comforter and pulled me closer. "And apparently Mr. Gavin has a direct line to the chief inspector who promised to send someone over instantly. At that point, Vera and I were dismissed. We may all be questioned again tomorrow if it turns out that they suspect foul play.

"Let's not talk about it anymore tonight, okay? I can't believe I'm playing in a golf tournament in the morning." He groaned. "Whose idea was it to come to Scotland anyway?"

Within seconds, his breathing grew slow and easy as he dropped off to sleep. I lay awake for much longer, puzzling over the possible poisoning incident. Had I seen anything that was off-kilter in the kitchen? I had been so distracted by Gavin's buffoonery that I'd noticed nothing out of order at Glenda's end of the table. I also thought about Nathan's sister. True, she seemed very much wound up about her project. I liked her very much, but I hadn't spent enough time with her yet to get a sense of whether she was really anxious about something she interpreted as threatening, or whether the men around her simply couldn't handle her being emotional and having strong opinions.

Either was possible.

Chapter Eight

"I rather like you," she said. "You're growing on me like the mold of well-aged Roquefort cheese, but I like you."
—Samantha Verant, *The Secret French Recipes of Sophie Valroux*

Although part of me—the part that would have loved to sleep in—regretted agreeing to an early rendezvous with chef Grace to visit the market, I was glad once I got up and moving. I knew I would enjoy touring Ainsley's professional kitchen with all its fancy European equipment, and I really looked forward to an insider's tour of the local farmers market, too—grist for the mill for a future article in *Key Zest*. And besides, this outing would give me a chance to question Grace, not only about food and cooking in Scotland but also about the disastrous way the party had ended last night. I dressed quickly and trotted across town to Ainsley and Dougal's home. The sky was a brilliant blue, but the wind appeared to be blowing from the ocean and whipped across the open square, knifing through my clothing. I was glad I'd grabbed one of Vera's fleece vests from a peg in her hallway, along with my pink Key West Police Department ball cap.

Grace was waiting for me outside the lobby door, pacing along the edge of the flower garden that stretched the length of the building. Some of these flowers had already begun to bloom purple and pink, and I suspected that their placement in the direct morning sun against the stone building meant they'd gotten an earlier start than the plants in Vera's garden.

"Oh, I'm so glad you came," she said. "I was terribly afraid you wouldn't. Do you mind if I take you inside to the kitchen first, before we visit the market?"

"Of course not," I said, thinking she didn't look like a happy chef about to show off her fabulous kitchen equipment. She looked as though she had a lot of worry on her mind. And why in the world would she imagine that I wouldn't show up?

We took the elevator upstairs, and she ushered me down the hall to the kitchen. The space was quiet and clean— nothing in the process of being chopped or peeled on cutting boards, no pastry rolled out on the marble counters, nothing simmering on the stainless eight-burner stove. As far as I could tell, not a single dish was cooking—or even in the early stages of being prepared.

She closed the swinging door behind us and turned to face me, her expression haunted. "I suppose you heard about Glenda last night?"

"I saw that she took ill, but we left right after," I said. "My husband mentioned when he came in a little later that she was a bit hysterical and that an ambulance was called. And the police." She looked so distressed that I reached out to put a comforting hand on her back. "Why, is there more news?"

"Of a kind." She shuddered as though she was controlling her tears. She began to speak in a rush, so quickly that I had to struggle to understand the torrent of accented words.

"She seemed to be feeling a little better, but then she got sicker and her husband announced to everyone that she believed she had been poisoned. He would not rest until the local police were called."

So far, her chronology matched what Nathan had reported the night before.

"Several officers came in last night, and after some discussion, they were told to clear every bit of food out of the fridge. The chief constable even had one of the policemen dig through the garbage where I'd scraped the dinner plates. And they hauled those scraps off, and every plate on the counters too." She flung open the refrigerator and then the trash cabinet to show me how empty they were.

"Oh dear," I said, "that sounds so distressing. Were there new developments this morning?"

"She's alive, thank God, and they sent her home from emergency after pumping her stomach. I can only assume they'll be testing the contents."

The way her lips quivered, I was afraid she would start bawling at any moment.

"I know how hard you worked on that meal, and every bite of it was amazing. What a terrible end to the glorious night." But in my head, I was also thinking that they must have had a good reason to suspect foul play to take the situation that far. Sweeping in to clear every edible morsel out of the kitchen made it appear as though they expected to find something wrong with the food.

"It's not only that the meal was ruined," she said, "it's that they might think I actually tried to kill her. I would never— why in the world—I can't tell you . . . I hardly know her!" She looked like she was trying hard not to burst into tears, but barely hanging on to her composure. I patted her back and steered her toward the door.

"Let's take a walk over to the market, and you can tell me about it. I was so looking forward to getting your insider's view on shopping."

As we walked over the cobblestone streets toward the market, I quizzed Grace further about the events of the night before. Unfortunately, I'd seen more than my share of poisoning events over the past few years, so the questions came easily. "While you were getting ready for the dinner, did you notice anything unusual at all?"

Her expression looked simultaneously puzzled and hopeless.

"I know that's a very broad question, but what I'm trying to get at is, did anybody leave anything unusual in your kitchen? An ingredient you hadn't ordered, for example? Or did someone you didn't expect perhaps visit the kitchen? Did your hostess hire any extra help that night?"

She shuddered with emotion and fell quiet for a few minutes, then shook her head. "I can't think of anything out of the ordinary. I did all the cooking. We got deliveries as usual— smoked fish and sausage and greens and vegetables and cheese.

I accepted most of them myself, though it's possible . . ." She paused. "I had the lamb marinating ahead, so that was already set. But nothing out of place. Not that I noticed. And Miss Ainsley hired the same two waiters she always uses to help me serve. There's nothing dodgy about either one."

So far, her memory was producing zippo, zero, zilch. "It might come to you when you're not trying so hard. Memories are like that." I smiled reassuringly. "Did Ainsley seem upset or tense about anything to do with the dinner?"

"She seemed happy," Grace said quickly. "She loves to entertain. And we'd talked for ages about the menu, and it was all coming together so beautifully. And she loved having guests from America." She managed a small smile. "We had such fun thinking about what you might enjoy and how to showcase Scottish food."

I smiled back. "And we loved every bite. I have to say you ended on such a high note with the cream whiskey and those heavenly cheeses. And butter cookies too." I nibbled on my lip, trying to think about how to unravel what had really happened. "Did you happen to notice anything odd when Glenda and her husband arrived? What I'm getting at is, was there any tension between them and the other guests or our hosts?"

Her eyes grew wider and, in what felt like slow motion, filled with tears.

I slung my arm around her shoulders and gave a comforting squeeze. I wasn't sure why that particular question would cause her to fall apart, but clearly I was pushing too hard, too fast. "That's too many questions at once, isn't it? Let's go back to things in your kitchen. Tell me about the process of planning and preparing the meal."

She nodded and swiped at her wet cheeks. "Of course, we started preparing for the dinner days ago. I made some of the hors d'oeuvres ahead of time so I could pop them in the oven right before the guests arrived and serve them hot. The sausage rolls freeze up perfectly, for example. And for the cock-a-leekie soup, naturally the broth has to be prepared ahead. If it has a few days to settle, the flavor is so much better. And it's easy to skim the fat."

I nodded. Soup always tasted richer if you could hold off eating it for a day or two to allow the ingredients to meld.

"And as I mentioned, I set the lamb to marinate the day before with garlic and rosemary and olive oil. Is this what you mean? Am I telling you too much?"

"It's exactly right," I said. "The thing is, you don't always know what you're looking for, what will help solve the mystery of what happened to her. For that reason, I like to hear everything." I chuckled. "You can probably tell that I love hearing about food anyway."

The streets had gotten busier as we approached the Fife Farmers Market, and up ahead I could see the colorful tents of the vendors and begin to hear cheerful conversation between them and the shoppers. Dogs were barking and a rooster crowed, and the scent of the most wonderful grilled sausage wafted by on a wind gust, beckoning us closer. Grace led me down each of the aisles, urging me to taste samples from the vendors of local cheeses, handcrafted oatcakes, pickles and mustards, sausages, and cottage pies made of wild venison and game birds. There were also booths stocked with luxury candles, bouquets of colorful flowers, and knitted hats and tartan scarves. I reminded myself to come back around, after circling the market with Grace, and choose souvenirs to take home for my friends and family.

The shoppers, too, were picturesque, people wearing shawls and scarves against the chill, carrying baskets, negotiating prices in thick Scottish burrs. The vendors greeted Grace warmly; some wanted to know how her dinner party had turned out, and what she was shopping for today, and others had obviously heard rumors about Glenda's unfortunate illness. The cheese maker next to the flower vendor seemed to have heard all about the party's disastrous ending. He came out from behind his booth, smoothing his hands over a pristine white butcher's apron. He had rusty curls, thick eyebrows, and warm brown eyes.

"Is the woman all right?" he asked in a low voice. "Did they determine what caused her illness? I am hoping it wasn't cheese . . ." He had a smile on his face, but at the same time he looked absolutely serious—and worried.

Grace glanced at me and then explained: "This is Blair, whose family makes goat and sheep's milk cheese from the animals on their farm not too far from here. That's why it's called farmhouse cheese. You tasted two of them last night."

"Your cheese was amazing," I said, reaching over to shake Blair's hand, which was strong and calloused, as though he was a man familiar with hard work.

He gestured at the refrigerated case with a stunning array of cheese on three shelves. "These aren't all mine, but I belong to a cheese makers' coop, and we take turns manning this booth." His gaze flitted from mine to hers. "Tell me what happened?"

Grace took a step closer and lowered her voice. "They're testing the contents of her stomach. Unfortunately, the incident occurred at the end of the evening"—she glanced at me for confirmation, and I nodded—"right after I served the cheese. That's why I'm not buying anything for the house today—don't worry, they weren't concerned about the cheese specifically. But Glenda seems to think someone tried to poison her, and isn't the cook the obvious suspect? Ainsley agreed that I should skip preparing anything at all, at least until we have the facts."

He frowned, the lines on his face deepening. "You know Glenda's a hammy queen. Always looking for the spotlight. Has to be, with a husband like the one she's got. She probably felt overlooked at the dinner table and figured this would draw all eyes to her." He rubbed a hand over his forehead and grimaced.

Grace did not look convinced, and neither was I. Who ever heard of pretending to be poisoned in order to get more attention and move the spotlight in her direction? And another thing—hadn't Grace just told me that she barely knew Glenda? Blair made it sound as if they both knew her perfectly well.

"You've known Glenda a while it seems," I said to Blair.

He snuck a furtive glance at Grace. "St. Andrews is a small town. I worked for her some years ago until I recognized that cheese was my true calling. She's a very rivalrous woman, and

I got the sense that she believed that her good fortune could be taken away from her at any moment. I was quite relieved to be away from her, truth be known."

Grace was looking more and more glum as he talked, and he seemed to realize he wasn't helping. Could he mean that she believed her good fortune was Gavin? He had not seemed like such a prize to me.

"Was there anyone you didn't know at the party? Did Ainsley hire people to help you out in the kitchen?" he asked. The same questions I'd wondered about.

Grace shook her head. "All the regulars attended, mostly her friends who are working on that Scotland book and a few golfers. And Hayley and her family, of course. We'd never met, but then they didn't know Glenda either and would hardly have a reason to want to do her in."

"If we wanted to end the evening, we could have pled jet lag. We'd have no reason to poison one of the other guests," I tried to joke. "Her husband, maybe. He's a bit of a blowhard," I added.

Blair got a funny look on his face, and I realized I'd probably said too much. I was scrambling to think how I could fix that faux pas and coax him to say more about Glenda and Gavin, but several new customers approached the cheese stand. Grace tugged on my elbow, and we backed away to allow him to attend to them.

"He seems like an awfully nice fellow," I said.

She gave me a quick smile and nodded.

"You mentioned you didn't know Glenda terribly well," I said to Grace. "But Blair called her a hammy queen. Which is kind of a perfect description. Are you certain you haven't had any run-ins with her in the past? Something that would give you the idea she was out to harm you in particular?"

Grace blanched. "I can't think why she'd be unhappy with me. The women had a number of meetings about the book project here at the house," she said, "and Ainsley asked me to provide the cream tea, which of course I did."

"What does your cream tea menu consist of?" I asked. Not that I thought this would provide any kind of clue to possible psychological discomfort between the women, but more because the very words "cream tea" had me salivating, drawn like a moth to candle. After last night's delicious spread, I suspected that her tea would be spectacular too. Thinking about her baked goods, I was having trouble concentrating. I wanted to hear her menu and hoped she might share her recipes. And besides, some people got great ideas by clearing their minds of everything—mine came when I was focused on food.

"Often I'd make a standard scone and serve it with clotted cream and a wee bit of raspberry jam. And sometimes Scottish cheddar shortbread cookies, although if I remember correctly, Glenda did not care for those. *A cookie should taste sweet, not lie in wait like an unpleasant brackish ambush,*' she'd say."

I visualized those cookies from the cheese course after dinner. They were sharp with cayenne and good cheddar and just the right amount of salty. To me, one of those wafers would never come as an unwelcome surprise. "Is there a certain kind of butter that works best for you in the scones? At home I started experimenting with Irish Kerrygold, and it seems softer, which changes the texture a bit, right?"

She was looking at me so oddly that I finally realized how far I'd veered off track. I pushed my mind back to the problem at hand. "While they were having these meetings to plan the project, was there any particular problem or tension between the women? Can you put your finger on anything out of the ordinary in their relationship or their work together before the party?"

She glanced over at me again, and from the worried look on her face, I thought she was probably doubting whether she ought to be talking behind her boss's back. "I wouldn't even ask you this kind of thing," I added, "if it wasn't for the poisoning accusation."

"They knew each other forever, since college," she said. "I imagine there was the usual amount of bickering. But no one thing stands out." She glanced at her watch and turned around.

"I need to get back to the house," Grace said. "Do you want to walk with me?"

"I'll stay a bit longer," I said. "I want to look at all these wonderful booths again. If either of us hears something new, we'll be in touch?" I exchanged cell phone numbers with her, then bid her goodbye and returned to the florist to choose a bunch of cut flowers as a small gift for Vera.

All this food gave me a powerful urge to cook, or at the very least, eat. I restrained myself from buying dinner ingredients as I didn't know what our host's plans were for the next few days. But houseguests are always hungry, and Vera might be too distraught to plan meals. And wasn't cheese always welcome? Besides, I had the impression that Blair had something more to say about last night's disaster than what he'd already told us. Returning to his counter, I bought several pieces of his family's cheese and then chose a glorious hunk of Dunsyre Blue, strong and peppery and streaked with blue. I took a picture of the label that described how the cheese was aged in an old stone farm building.

"What makes blue cheese appear blue?" I asked Blair.

He grimaced. "It won't sound right, but we add mold cultures before the cheese is ready to be aged, and then the cheese is salted and spiked with stainless steel rods to allow the mold to grow into those lovely blue streaks." He grinned and I did too. Unless you stuck to raw vegetables—which were safe but kind of boring and plain, a lot of food went through an ugly phase on the way to becoming delicious.

"What else should I choose for a hostess gift?" I asked. "For snacking. Something I could compare to the Dunsyre?"

In addition to a wedge of his sheep's milk feta that I'd overlooked, he steered me toward a lump of Strathdon Blue, made further north in Scotland in the Highlands. I could picture a whole feature on cheese in my *Key Zest* piece.

I accepted the package from Blair. "I hope you don't mind me saying that it appeared you knew more than you said earlier about the people involved in the incident at Ainsley's home last night." Then I waited. No telling how willing he'd be to share facts, or even gossip, but worth a try.

He leaned across the counter to whisper. "Glenda's husband is an awful pig. He made a pass at Grace not long ago at another of Ainsley's gatherings. Pushed her into the pantry, pawed her private places, and slobbered all over her."

"That's disgusting," I said, remembering the unwelcome feeling of his arm draped across my back and his wife's angry glare.

"She was horrified," he said, nodding grimly. "And terribly afraid she'd lose her job if she said anything to Ainsley. And for certain she wouldn't mention it to Glenda. I wanted to go pummel that arsehat, but had to agree that the best course for her sake would be keeping her silence and her distance. She hoped he was drunk and would forget all about it." He brushed a few crumbs off his cheese cutting board and straightened his knives, the frown still on his face.

"Anything else?" I asked. "Maybe the incident had nothing at all to do with Grace, but is it possible that someone on the outside had it in for Ainsley? Maybe someone who makes her deliveries?"

"I deliver the bigger cheese orders if it's too much for Grace to carry, and the butcher does his meat, and so on." He crossed his muscular arms and squinted. "But for the sake of argument, how would this work? Say a person wanted to poison a certain guest in the party. They would have to target the exact hunk of cheese that guest would be consuming, not poison everything. And if they wished to target one particular plate, Grace would have had to be involved in order to know which food to serve to the victim."

His face got red. "I'm blathering on, but you see it makes no sense. Grace would never hurt anyone. And besides, it wouldn't work. You could end up poisoning the wrong party or, for that matter, the whole party."

"I do see. It would be very difficult to pull off and lots could go wrong. But thanks for talking to me. And for the cheese lesson." I smiled and took the package that he'd set on the counter. "I know we'll enjoy every bite."

Once I'd finished my perusal of the shops, I paused on the cobblestone lane that led back to the center of town. The sun had risen just enough to take a bit of the chill out of the air. I was glad that Nathan would be having a glorious day on the golf course, but to be honest, I missed him a little, and he hadn't even left yet.

I started back to my sister-in-law's house, mulling over the strange conversations I'd had at the market. One thing I needed to know for sure: aside from her husband assaulting Grace in the closet, did Glenda and Grace have an unpleasant history? And what about Blair and Grace? She hadn't said anything about a relationship between them, but he was awfully protective of her.

And who might want to ruin Ainsley by poisoning her guests?

Chapter Nine

He was about to sip the tea cooling in the mug on the table in front of him, but then the thought of the rat poison in the unfortunate woman's coffee made him stop.
—Ragnar Jonasson, *Rupture*

My phone rang as I reached Vera's home; it was a FaceTime call from Connie. I quickly stashed my cheese in the fridge and rested the flowers in the sink, and then accepted the call and sat at the kitchen table. As the screen came into focus, I could see that Lorenzo, Connie, and my mother were all on Miss Gloria's deck, sipping cups of something steaming. The cats were there too; T-Bone, Miss G's orange kitten, had splayed across Lorenzo's lap, and the other two snuggled against his legs.

"Hi everyone," I said, realizing there was only the barest hint of light in the sky beyond our boat and that I couldn't see their faces clearly. "Isn't it the middle of the night in Key West?"

Ziggy woofed as soon as he heard my voice, looking around frantically for the person that went with the words.

Mom scooped him up and stroked him, trying to calm him down.

"It's early, but we all miss you so much that we decided to meet for a breakfast call," Connie said, gesturing at the others. "I hope you don't mind that we helped ourselves to tea and some scones I found in the freezer. We wish we were there with you. We figured that eating scones in Key West might help us pretend to be in Scotland."

"I don't mind a bit, and I'm sure Miss Gloria won't either. We are eating our body weight in scones here anyway."

"How are you enjoying Scotland?" my mother asked. "I can't wait to hear all about it."

"It's lovely, beautiful. This morning I went to the farmers market with the chef of one of Vera's friends. I tasted the most amazing cheeses. And sausages, oh my gosh. Sam would be in heaven. In a little while, Nathan and William tee off in their tournament, and the rest of us are going to visit some kind of local site. We're still a little bit off-kilter because of the time change."

"Of course," said my mother, "don't they say it takes a day to adjust to each hour of change?"

"I hope not," I said. "That would mean we won't feel right until the day we're coming home." Then I noticed Connie's face, which looked pinched and gloomy. "How are things there? Did anything get resolved with Ray?"

She shook her head sadly. "I did talk with him, just as you suggested. I pleaded with him to tell me what's going on. And then I told him about Eric and how people think they have to protect secrets and that often makes things worse."

"So true," said Lorenzo, "people are funny that way. I offered to read some cards for him."

"But Ray being Ray, he of course wants nothing to do with that," said Connie.

"Mercury is in retrograde," Lorenzo said, shaking his head. "Not always the best time to have relationship-altering discussions. And it's a full moon. We're going to get a whopper King tide here in town, and that makes everyone even more crazy than they already are. Not only because of the moon, but because people panic when they see the water on the streets. As well they should." He frowned and patted Connie's arm. "That's not to say your husband is crazy—more that people in general are crazy. Because the world we know has gone mad."

"So true, dat," said Miss Gloria, who had come up behind me and put her hands on my shoulders. "I am so happy to see your familiar faces. Though I admit it makes me a little bit homesick to see you all sitting on my deck," she added, her voice wistful. "Even though it's beautiful here and we have some wonderful things planned. Did you tell them about the dinner party last night?" she asked me.

"Not yet," I said. "We were talking Ray and scones."

Vera came into the kitchen, her face looking grim. She pasted on a smile. "I guess I should always look for you two in the kitchen."

I introduced her to my mother and my friends on the screen. "Can you imagine, this is Nathan's sister?"

"I could pick her out of a lineup in a New York minute," said my mother. "Except, don't tell Nathan I said this, but you're much prettier." We all laughed. "What happened at dinner?"

"Someone from the party last night got sick—she had terrible stomach cramps, and I gather she's trying to pin this on the chef," said Miss Gloria. "The cops came around this morning, asking questions. Nathan pressed them until they admitted they'd discovered traces of digitalis in her stomach contents."

"Digitalis? Does she have a heart arrhythmia?" I asked, looking at Vera.

At the same time my mother said, "Isn't that used for congestive heart failure? Does your friend have a heart problem?"

Vera shook her head no, then turned to me. "I came to let you know the men are leaving, and we should be in the car shortly after so we don't keep the others waiting." Miss Gloria saluted, and Vera smiled and left the room.

My mother whispered, "She seems wound up."

I nodded glumly. "A lot of pressure on her project. Before we go, tell me quickly about Ray," I said.

Connie sighed. "In a nutshell, Ray won't tell me anything about what's bothering him. I did exactly what you suggested and went down to Duval Street to the gallery to talk with the owner and Ray's friend Jag. Jag is an artist too, and he's known Ray for years. He said he's never seen him so jumpy."

Connie fell silent and my mother took her hand and stroked it gently, with the same motion she'd used to comfort Nathan's dog.

"Can you say more about what Jag noticed?" I asked. "What exactly did he mean by 'jumpy'?"

"Jumpy, hypercritical. When they were hanging the show, if Jag said a painting should be hung here, Ray said it should go somewhere else. And not in a nice way apparently either, but like he was going nuts.

"Jag even wondered if Ray had started taking something."

Now we were all quiet, waiting for the rest of what Connie had to say.

"Is that possible do you think?" my mother finally asked.

With her lips clenched tightly, Connie shook her head. "I would know that—a wife would know." She sighed. "And somehow Ray found out I'd been at the gallery, and he asked me to stay out of his business. So that's the end of that."

I wasn't at all sure it would have ended there for me, but she was the one married to Ray, so I had to respect her choices.

As we signed off, Nathan and his brother-in-law, William, came into the kitchen from the backyard. They wore pressed khaki pants and matching green polo shirts that brought out the mossy color of Nathan's eyes.

"You two are adorable," Miss Gloria said. "Are all the teams required to dress as twins?"

I giggled as Nathan mugged a scowl.

"We tee off in half an hour," William said with a cheerful slap to Nathan's back. "Wish us luck."

"We'll need it," Nathan added, grinning at his brother-in-law. "And god forbid I should hit a ball into one of those steep sand bunkers. Even the pro golfers have trouble getting out of those. We might not make it home before dark."

I couldn't remember hearing my husband as excited about anything as he seemed this morning about playing golf on the

Old Course. And I couldn't help noticing the expression on his mother's face—bemused, bordering on astonished.

"Do you mind if we come down and watch you hit your first shot?" I asked.

"It would be ugly," he said, grinning. "You'd be disappointed. I never did play well with a gallery in attendance."

"We won't linger," Vera said, glancing at her watch. "We're due to meet the others, and it's an hour and a half drive. Could we watch from a distance?"

"Better still, come tomorrow when I've sanded some of the rust off," Nathan suggested. "If that's okay?"

"Sure. Miss Gloria said the cops were here?" I asked him. "Any new leads? Miss Gloria said something about digitalis?"

"In Glenda's stomach contents," he said, his cheerful smile falling away. "Which could mean everything or nothing at all. Apparently she does not take this medication routinely, so its appearance is suspicious. They've promised to keep me in the loop as a matter of professional courtesy. And that means my family and friends can stay away from trouble. Please."

"Of course," I said, wondering to myself whether Grace, the chef, had gotten this news. She would be distraught.

"Gotta go, partner," William said, patting Nathan's back.

I kissed him goodbye, and then we piled in Vera's car to drive to the local sites. Next to me in the back seat, Miss Gloria drifted off to sleep almost instantly.

"I never thought I'd see him play golf again," Helen said as we pulled out of town. "I can still remember the day he quit. He came home announcing that he'd chucked his clubs into the dumpster at the local supermarket. He was desperate to separate himself psychologically from his father, and hurt him if possible—and he did both by informing him that golf was an elitist game for rich men without enough athletic talent to play any other sport. He sounded so bitter. And that made his father so angry. And sad, though he never would have admitted to that." She had a pained look on her face, remembering what must have been a painful day.

"You know what his father asked?" Of course, the rest of us had no idea. "He said, 'Don't tell me you threw out your grandfather's putter too?' Nathan stung him hard with that move. The passing of that precious putter from grandfather to son to grandson had been a rite of passage. It meant everything about love and pride and hope that those silly men could not articulate any other way."

"Your husband was angry about everything in those days," Vera said, not even claiming her father as a relative. Her hands gripped the steering wheel hard, and she stared straight ahead. "You all were."

"We were mostly scared," said Helen softly. "We almost lost you. You know this family—when we're sad or scared, we don't know how to handle it. We're terrible at putting our feelings into words. The best we managed in those days was to act angry. And your father was trying to control the only thing within his grasp—our family." She glanced at her daughter, her expression full of regret. "I'm sorry."

Vera snapped on the radio and turned up the volume on the Celtic music so that further conversation became impossible. I must have dozed off, and I woke an hour later, hungry and droopy and needing a bathroom stop. "Is it possible we'll be near a restroom soon?"

"We're meeting Gavin and the others at the Falkirk Wheel, but first I'll drive you by the Kelpies. Gavin insisted on including these in our book. There's a restroom at the plaza and a little snack bar." With a tight voice, she added, "There isn't a whisker of a thin place for miles around. But I will have to leave that argument to the editors. Or the readers who trash the book because the authors persisted in including commercial sites with no real spiritual value."

"What are kelpies? What exactly are we seeing?" Miss Gloria piped up from the backseat next to me.

"They are a couple of giant horse heads made out of metal," said Vera grimly.

"Horseheads made of metal?" her mother asked.

"It's hard to describe them in any other way. A kelpie is a supernatural water horse that's supposed to haunt Scottish lakes and rivers. Legend has them appearing as horses but able to adopt the human form. Some of the local folks are quite proud of them, as they are meant to commemorate the role of horses in Scotland. They were designed by a well-known artist, and fans see them as powerful guardians of the gateway to the Forth and Clyde Canal." I could see her roll her eyes in the rearview mirror. "Obviously I'm not one of the fans. As metal horse heads, they are impressive. As a sacred site, not at all."

We visited the bathrooms and bought candy bars and cardboard cups of coffee and then stood outside with Vera, our necks craned up at the sculptures. "They're thirty meters high and built of steel," she said. "Honestly, they are marvelous creations, but they absolutely don't belong in a book of mythical places in Scottish history."

"Can't you put your foot down?" Miss Gloria asked. "Aren't you the lead author?"

"The tides have shifted on that. Gavin may be a major pain in the butt," she said, "but in addition to the fact that he's a brilliant photographer, our publisher adores him. He's desperately afraid that he paid too much for our book and can't possibly sell enough copies to get the money back, so he flails around, looking for new ideas to buff up the concept. Gavin is always happy to generate new ideas, no matter how ridiculous they sound to the rest of us."

Helen looked worried, as if she wanted to dispense advice or hugs or some kind of motherly comfort. But Vera's fierce and closed expression made it clear that none of that would be welcome.

"If we've seen enough of the metal horse heads, we're due to meet the others at the Falkirk Wheel," Vera said. We followed her to the car and got back in, and she resumed her travelogue. "You are about to experience a boatlift that connects the Forth and Clyde and the Union canals. There used to be a staircase involving eleven locks that took boats an entire day to transit. Now it happens in less than an hour, and tourists flock here for the chance to experience the ride in a glassed-in boat." She sighed. "The wheel was opened for business by the queen in 2002, which was a very big deal."

"This also sounds very different from the other sites you've mentioned," I said.

"You think?" She turned around to glance at me. "I suppose it is a modern feat of engineering, so I don't argue that point. And it's clever and brilliant as a solution to connecting the canals. But I can't believe anyone will ever have a spiritual moment while packed into a glassed-in boat and rotating around a wheel." She sighed again, more deeply. "You'll see."

Chapter Ten

My heart beat too fast and under my skin it felt mealy,
like an old apple.

—Lily King, *Writers and Lovers*

As Vera had described, the wheel was a multistory contraption made of concrete and steel. The tall central axle, which she told us was modeled after a Celtic axe crossed with a ship's propellor married to a whale's ribcage, allowed two boats to rotate at the same time, one up and one down.

"See what I mean?" she asked. "It's like the kelpie horseheads—amazing design and structure, but a zero as a place of Scottish spirit. At least not the kind of spirit that I find interesting." She headed for the office to purchase tickets, and soon returned to distribute one to each of us. We met Ainsley in line, waiting to board the boat.

"Where are the others?" asked Vera. "Is Glenda all right? And how about you? Nathan said the medical results showed signs of high levels of digitalis?" She squeezed her friend into a quick hug and then let her go.

Ainsley nodded and pointed down the pier to Gavin, who was taking photographs of the previous boatful of tourists as it descended slowly to the canal. A few steps past him, Glenda waited, watching him work. She looked perfectly healthy from a distance.

"She says she's fine," Ainsley said, pressing her hands to her temples. "But Gavin pulled me aside to tell me that she's all shook up. She fears that someone targeted her directly at the dinner, and she doesn't know who to trust—especially me. I have no idea how to talk to her about all this. She's freezing me out."

We all looked at Vera, who shrugged helplessly.

"Let's remember, we're friends first, and we've been through a lot together," Vera said to Ainsley. She kept her voice so low I had to strain to make out the words. "There's simply no way anyone would blame you for what happened."

Which made me wonder about what they'd been through. Vera, I knew, had experienced a terrible trauma before moving to Scotland for college. Had more happened after that? I reminded myself to try to corner Ainsley alone. Maybe she'd be willing to talk to me without an audience. I hoped she'd also talk about Grace, her talented chef. Had she had noticed Gavin's inappropriate contact with the chef or heard about it from someone else? Or could it be that Grace overreacted? Was there any possibility that Grace had intended for Glenda—or Gavin even—to get sick? I hated to think that because I liked her very much. But the question needed to be asked.

As the descending boat reached the concrete pier, workers began to unload the passengers onto the dock, and Gavin and Glenda returned to our queue.

"The light is exactly right this morning," Gavin said when he arrived. "The photos are going to be amazing—and from a perspective that most people don't have the opportunity to see. I climbed several meters up the structure before an ignorant and annoying guard insisted I come down."

Vera glared at him. "Sometimes rules are important."

At Vera's suggestion, Miss Gloria, Helen, and I took the three seats that remained open in the front of the boat, while the others headed toward the back. The captain explained the safety features such as where to find life preservers, and the importance of all guests remaining seated during the ride. "The landing area at the back of the craft is not safe and strictly off limits to our guests." The boat began to move slowly up, almost like a super slow-moving Ferris wheel.

As we were lifted higher, the Scottish flatlands spread out all around us: green fields, industrial buildings, the reedy canals that the Falkirk Wheel had been designed to connect, and way off in the distance the kelpies. Once we had almost reached the top of the ascent, out of the corner of my eye I thought I saw something fall. And then several people began to yell, and a woman in a seat toward the back of the craft screamed and then burst into tears. The boat rocked as everyone rushed to that side to see what was happening. The captain's crackly voice blared out from the speaker.

"Folks, please take your seats instantly," he said in an urgent tone. "We are going to be returning to the pier."

As we filed back to our original seats, Vera began to look around the boat, her eyes wild. "Oh my God, where's Gavin?

Has that fool gone missing! The authorities told him not to climb anywhere."

The wheel rotated in slow motion, the descent feeling twice as slow as our trip up. Off to the left in the canal, I could hear shouts. We watched the captain throw two orange life preserver rings into the water. Maybe there was the sound of splashing? I hoped so because that might mean whoever had fallen could have survived the fall.

"This can't be happening," said Vera. "I swear I will kill him if he fell out of this boat."

My surprise must have shown on my face, as she continued, "You have no idea how hard I've worked to get this project off the ground. And then Glenda sweet-talked the publisher into saddling me with her idiot husband. And first she thinks someone's poisoning her, and now he's tumbled out of this idiotic boat, which never should've been part of the book to begin with."

"I wouldn't assume it was him," said Ainsley softly. "He's a brilliant man who occasionally manages to make himself look like a clumsy fool. And he looks out only for himself, but he does that nimbly. He's not likely to take a dive from a high place."

Which sounded like an odd and unattractive description of a close colleague.

Vera was practically shaking with fury—or was it fear?— by the time we reached the bottom of the curve. Three men dressed in black, wearing train conductor hats with black and white checked bands, met us at the exit door and began directing the tourists off the boat and away from the figure that was splayed on the cement next to the boat. Scottish policemen, I realized, my horrified mind slow to grasp what I was seeing.

I glanced again at the shape on the pier, wishing desperately that this person could have landed in the water rather than on concrete. Hadn't the captain thrown out life preservers? Maybe it wasn't as bad as I feared. My head knew that no one could have survived plummeting from that distance onto an unforgiving surface, but my heart was having trouble computing that fact.

"Please wait over here next to the entrance," said one of the policemen. He pointed to the visitors' center where we'd planned to have lunch. "We will need to speak to passengers regarding what they might have seen prior to this individual's descent. Do not discuss this incident with the other passengers." He herded us past the motionless form. I couldn't help looking, but I could not see enough to tell me who it might have been. Besides, everyone I knew in this country was right here with me. Almost everyone.

The next thought landed with a jolt. Did all this police concern mean the fall might not have been accidental?

"Did you notice anything out of order before the captain began shouting?" I whispered to Miss Gloria as we were herded toward the cafeteria building. The cop surely hadn't meant I couldn't talk to my friend.

She shook her head. "I started to feel like I was getting a migraine on that thing," she said, gesturing at the wheel. "I don't like heights, and you know I'm a little claustrophobic. And I definitely didn't like the looks of that tunnel we were going to travel through once we got to the top. My whole head felt like it was squeezing into my brain, getting ready to explode.

"But I hope no one pushed him," she added, raising her eyebrows and tipping her chin in Vera's direction. "Is that what you're thinking? Like Vera?"

"Stop it," I hissed. "She would never hurt someone. She's Nathan's sister."

"She couldn't stand that Gavin," Miss Gloria said. "Didn't you notice what a buffoon he was at the party? And this morning too. He thinks he's too good for the rules that apply to everyone else in the world."

"Who didn't notice?" I asked, falling silent under the glare of the nearest policeman. Was the victim Gavin? Hadn't Vera been sitting cattycorner in the seats behind us when the ruckus began? Miss Gloria's comment was making me doubt what I'd seen or not seen, and what I thought was even possible.

As our turn with the police approached, Helen and Vera were the first in our group to be interviewed. Helen put her arm around her daughter's shoulder while they answered the authorities' questions. Helen seemed to be doing most of the talking, as Vera was visibly weeping. We shuffled a little closer to listen in.

"We didn't see anything," Nathan's mother insisted. "I'm a visitor from America, and we were looking at the amazing scenery. We have no idea who that person is or how he came to fall." She gestured at the figure on the cement pier, now draped with a silver space blanket.

Just then I noticed a man break through the police barrier, snapping photos of the police and the gawking spectators and finally even the figure on the cement pier.

"Sir, stop that this instant!" shouted one of the cops.

"It's Gavin!" said Miss Gloria. "He's alive and well. And still an idiot," she added under her breath.

Our turn came with the police. Miss Gloria explained that her headache and claustrophobia had kept her from noticing anything. I tried to report any details I could think of—how I'd hoped the person had fallen in the canal and how the only odd detail prior to the incident had been Gavin trying to climb the structure before we boarded the boat. "Honestly, I doubt that had anything to do with this. And we were sitting too far away to have noticed what happened before the fall."

By the time we had all completed the interviews and given our contact information to the police, Vera was barely holding herself together. Her teeth chattered, even though the temperature had to be near sixty degrees, and she took great gasps of air.

"Are you okay?" I asked. She waved her hand as if to flick my concern away.

"I'd like to ride in the back seat with her," said Helen once we reached the car. "Can one of you possibly drive?"

I thought of Miss Gloria lurching around Key West in her Oldsmobile, almost clipping gawking tourists and other cars with her big fenders while she warbled along with songs on her radio. Plus, this car was a stick shift, and it would require driving on the wrong side of the road.

"I can do it," I said, "as long as we put the directions in my phone."

Chapter Eleven

Of all the meatloaves, potpies, grilled cheeses and other comfort foods we have been using to self-soothe during this time of anxiety and perpetual sweatpants, the tuna melt I had last Friday was arguably the most important sandwich of my life.

—Judge John Hodgman, "Judge John Hodgman on Saving Leftovers From Your Leftovers," *The New York Times Magazine*, April 20, 2020

Once we arrived back at the house, Vera and Miss Gloria retired immediately to their bedrooms, and Helen called for a cab to take her back to her hotel for a bit. I was way too wired to rest, feeling as though I might never relax after an hour plus navigating Vera's car in the left lane and over strange roads. The backward roundabouts were the absolute worst. My fingers cramped from gripping the steering wheel and my mind whirred with fragments of conversation and images from that terrible scene at the Falkirk Wheel. I'd never be able to nap.

One thing might help settle my nerves: cooking. The repetitive motions of chopping and stirring, along with the smells of something delicious cooking, never failed to calm me down. I sorted through Vera's refrigerator and found a package of free-range chicken, plus leeks, parsley, celery and the packages of cheese I'd brought home this morning. Was that only this morning? It felt more like days ago.

Vera also had barley and chicken broth and flour and a box of prunes in her cupboard. On my phone, I pulled up a recipe for cock-a-leekie soup that looked similar to what Grace had served us at the dinner. I'd been meaning to try this anyway. That comforting stew, dished up alongside my best cheese scones, would make for a simple but appealing supper.

After placing the chicken in a pot of simmering water, I rinsed the grit from the leeks and began to chop, thinking about all that had happened across the day. Vera had appeared crushed by the accident at the Falkirk Wheel. She had hardly been able to share her observations with the police. I absolutely understood how awful it was to see the man splayed on the cement. I'd felt it too—a combination of shock and horror, and "this can't be happening." But she was even more distraught than the rest of us. More curious, she accepted the ministrations of her mother, whom, so far, she'd held at bay.

The more I thought about it, the more she reminded me of Connie's husband, Ray, the way he had been acting just before we left the country. My first impression of Vera had been that she was fine, psychologically solid—that her husband and Nathan were exaggerating about how emotionally fragile she was. But this incident, following closely on the illness of her friend at the dinner last night, had totally freaked her out.

I scraped the chopped vegetables into the bubbling pot of chicken and barley and began to mix up a batch of scones. I grated a hunk of sharp cheddar that Vera had stored in her fridge and added this to the dry ingredients along with a chunk of local butter, and a generous sprinkle of cayenne pepper. Once Vera's oven dinged cheerfully to announce that it had preheated, I popped the pan of scones into the oven, set the timer, and went to stretch out on the couch. Probably a cup of tea and a warm cheese scone were in order, after a brief catnap. I wished that my kitty, Evinrude, had been here to purr me to sleep, but Vera's big tom cat, Archie, eyed me from the back of the couch. I got back up to fetch a bribe of chicken scraps, thinking that with a little coaxing, he might be willing to serve the same function for me that Evinrude always did. Before I could lure him over, the oven timer dinged again, and I was back on duty.

By five thirty, the soup was ready, and both Miss Gloria and Vera emerged from their bedrooms. Miss Gloria looked well rested—she always bounced back after a snooze. Vera appeared not to have slept.

"Could I interest you ladies in a bite to eat?" I asked.

"I thought I smelled something delicious," said Vera, smiling, though the rest of her face did not look happy. "I was lying in there wondering what in the world I could serve my guests for supper. Somehow it doesn't seem right that you will be serving me."

"Hayley loves to cook," said Miss Gloria. "It's not a chore for her—it's therapy. She's wired differently than most of the rest of us, and this oddity serves her friends and neighbors and family very well."

I laughed. "It is like therapy, and I've been meaning to try Scottish cock-a-leekie soup, and you had all the ingredients that my pal Susan Hamrick uses. I'll be able to write about this in my weekly column for *Key Zest* as well, so it was a win–win situation." I glanced at my phone, hoping for a text from Nathan. Nothing. "Should we wait for the men?"

Vera said, "I think we'd be waiting for a long time. William informed me that they have to attend another official dinner that he hadn't counted on. God knows when they'll show up. How about if we have a little finger of scotch and then an early supper?"

"Perfect," said Miss Gloria, taking a seat at the table.

After we'd finished our drink out in the garden and then had a refill, we moved back into the kitchen, where I served up bowls of steaming soup and set out the platter of scones with more butter. We spent a few minutes eating in silence, enjoying the crusty scones, oozing with cheese, and rich chicken broth. Vera looked exhausted and worried but maybe more willing to talk.

"That was a horrible day," I said. "Following a dreadful night. You must be devastated."

She nodded slowly, set her soup spoon beside her plate. "Something is going on with this project that I can't quite put my finger on." She sighed and toyed with the placemat. "The last few days have made me question whether we shouldn't just quit now. Though the book isn't nearly done, and final photographs of some of the most marvelous places have yet to be added. We are supposed to be making one last pass around some of those featured sites so Gavin can take those photos and I can tweak the text and cut any unnecessary fat."

"It doesn't sound like you're ready to give up," I said.

She shook her head sadly. "We have all invested so much already. And we have a very tight schedule this week, and I was hoping we could all pull together. I was hoping for a magical ending."

"I wouldn't call the last few days magical," said Miss Gloria. "I hope having all of us here isn't throwing you off."

Vera sighed again but then forced a smile. "Oh no, we wanted desperately to meet Hayley, and you are absolutely icing on the cake. But if we don't come through with what we've promised by the end of this month, there's an enormous advance and a lot of prestige on the line." She covered her face with her hands, long slender fingers trembling. They had the same shape as Nathan's fingers, only more delicate.

"It's more than those personal things at stake; it's the future of our country's thin places. The places that are loaded with history and tragedy and lessons, if we only cared to try to learn." She dropped her hands to her lap and looked at me. "Maybe these two events are serendipitous, but I think not. I feel like somebody is trying to sabotage the project, but I can't think why. They have the same stakes in it as I do . . ." Her words trailed off, and she looked close to weeping.

"You seem to suspect that one of your friends is responsible for the troubles," Miss Gloria said. "But it could very well have been someone we didn't know who pushed that poor man. The boat was packed. He also could have been out on the landing by himself and simply lost his footing."

Vera could only shrug.

"If the fall today is related to what happened at dinner the other night, what could that connection be?" I asked gently.

"I have no idea." She threw her hands up in the air and began to breathe so fast I feared she was spiraling into a panic attack. Where was my psychologist friend Eric when I needed him?

"Well, let's start at the beginning," I said, trying to speak in a calm, level voice that might vibrate with confidence. "What were your friends like back when you first met them? Did you all gel right away, or did it start with a twosome, and later the third person was added? And what about the husbands? How do they fit into the mix? Are they friends? Do you have any old photographs from college that we could look at?"

Vera looked at me as though I was out of my gourd.

"What I'm trying to get at is whether you have some history that might be leaking to the surface now," I explained.

Miss Gloria was nodding as if I might be onto a good line of questioning. But Vera was still silent. Miss Gloria jumped in. "It's not as though all college relationships are smooth, because kids are trying to figure out who they are in those years. And so sometimes they choose duds, not people with the solid qualities that you'd want in a lifetime friendship. My sons got mixed up with some real doozies."

I waited a couple of beats to see whether Vera would pick up this train of conversation. Nothing. "I was lucky with my college roommate, Connie, because we hit it off right away," I added. "And we've stuck together all these years. We've changed—we've both gotten married, and she has a baby." I grinned. "We had her as the flower girl at our impromptu wedding. She is the cutest thing."

I held myself back from pulling out my phone to show her pictures of baby Claire toddling down the dock, clutching the posy of flowers. Or the rest of our wedding day. Those happy details didn't matter right now. Vera remained silent, so I kept talking.

"One other thing that drew us together was that her mother was terribly ill during our senior year. And horribly, she ended up dying of her cancer. My mother lived close enough that we were both able to go home and get comfort from her over that awful time. I will always be grateful for that. And Connie's good for me because she reminds me that even if my mother is occasionally a little annoying, I'm still very, very lucky to have her." I paused for a moment. "I think I'm trying to say that sometimes a traumatic event or a tragedy pulls people together. And sometimes it splits them apart."

I stopped yakking and looked at Vera, wondering if she'd take up any of the threads of conversation that I'd offered. I really wanted to hear about her relationship with Helen, but I wasn't sure that was most important to Vera right now either.

"You ask a lot of questions," Vera finally said after several minutes of silence.

I couldn't help laughing. "Nathan says the same thing."

"It makes me happy to see him happy," Vera said, reaching across the table to squeeze my hand. "And somehow you've won my mother over too, and that is not an easy task."

"I don't know if anyone told you, but your mother and I shared a near-death experience last year, and we bonded in the process."

She stared at me for a moment or two. "I had one of those too," she said, "and it did not work in the same way with me and her. In fact, it cracked our family into pieces. I'm pretty sure it was the cause of my parents' divorce."

I would have tried to reassure her otherwise, but I had no idea what had happened in their family, and she'd shrug off my attempts anyway.

Vera stood up and walked over to the bookshelves to pull a bulky book from the bottom corner. A family photo album? I would love to see more pictures of Nathan as a baby and a boy.

"This was our college yearbook," she said, handing the book to me. "I can't think that it will be helpful to you, but"—she shrugged—"at least you can look at the individual portraits of me and Glenda and Ainsley. Maybe you'll see the secrets we're keeping in our faces." She laughed weakly. "We can talk more about it later, see if it leads anywhere. But I'm doubtful." She put a hand to her temple. "Right now, I have the worst headache."

"I'll look it over. You go rest and take care of that headache—we'll clean up."

"Of course, we will," Miss Gloria said. "I usually have the KP job at home too. Or I did until Hayley moved next door with Nathan. It's only fair since she shops and cooks." She got up to carry plates to the kitchen sink. "Did you know that's why gay marriages are happier than straight ones? They don't have preconceived notions about who should be doing what, and so they're better at sharing the workload."

"I'm not surprised to hear that," I said, and then turned back to Vera. "One last question: Did you recognize the man who fell today?"

"No. But I wasn't close enough to really see." Now she held her head between both of her hands. "Tomorrow, we should all be ready to leave by noon," she added, straightening back up. "We're going to spend our first night in Peebles for the summer solstice festival. We'll grab a late lunch and watch the town parade before dinner—you two will love that. You are very fortunate to be visiting Peebles on the Eve of St. John's, the celebration of the birth of John the Baptist. William's ancestors considered the veil between this world and the next to be very thin on this day. Then the following morning, on to Glencoe." She grimaced and clutched her head again. "I'm sorry this is all isn't more relaxing, but I hope you'll find our itinerary well worth it."

"Go have a rest," Miss Gloria said, shooing her out of the kitchen. "We'll clean up." Once Vera had left the room, she added sotto voce, "I hope those weren't the same ancestors who massacred my people."

Once we'd finished the washing up and stored the leftovers in the freezer, Miss Gloria insisted on pouring us another finger of whiskey to sip in front of the telly. We watched the end of the BBC news, and there was not a word said about America or her policies or politics. Honestly, it was nice to have a breather from the problems that dogged us at home.

Deep into an episode of a TV series based on Ann Cleeves's *Shetland*, I heard a car outside in the driveway, and then somebody crashing into the garbage cans. Before I could panic about a possible intruder, Nathan and William clattered into the room, wearing kilts again—the full-dress version with what looked like animal pelts hanging from their waists and swords tucked into their skirts. This time, Nathan looked completely comfortable in his costume, as if he had grown up roaming the Scottish moors. For the first time, I could really understand why Claire went all wobbly seeing the redheaded Jamie in his kilt in *Outlander*.

I stood up to kiss him hello. "Who are you, you gorgeous hunk of manhood, and what have you done with my husband?"

"It is I, Nathan the conqueror, and I've come to sweep away a wee Scottish lassie," he said, sounding a little tipsy and absolutely giddy. He grabbed me by the waist and swung me into an embrace.

I couldn't help giggling once he'd released me. "And how much whiskey have you two had to drink? Because maybe Miss Gloria and I have some catching up to do. And I hope neither of you was driving."

"We cadged a ride from someone's wife." He flopped down on the couch beside our friend, and I perched on the other side of him and reached for his hand. "We've had the most amazing day. Do you have any idea what it's like to be playing the same course where Tiger Woods won the British Open? Of course, my drives aren't quite as long as his."

William cackled and brandished his sword. "No comment, my friend. Nothing you've got is as long as his." They both howled with laughter this time.

Then Nathan gazed around at Miss Gloria and me. "You ladies look a little glum. How was your day?"

"Kind of brutal," said Miss Gloria. "There was a death at the wheel."

Nathan looked horrified and sobered up in an instant. "What kind of death?"

"Is Vera all right?" asked William, getting to feet and looking wildly around the room as though he'd just noticed that his wife was missing.

"She's fine," Miss Gloria and I chorused. "She was exhausted and so she retired early."

"Who died?" Nathan asked. "Tell me you weren't involved or threatened in any way?"

"We weren't," I said quickly. "But it was a terrible shock to be as close as we were." I explained what had happened and that we didn't know the dead man, but how shook up Vera seemed by the incident, particularly in the wake of Glenda's illness at the dinner party the night before. "I made some Scottish chicken soup—are you two hungry?"

"Not at all, thank you," said William. "We've been tearing rare meat from bones with our teeth and that sort of thing. If you don't mind, tell me more about Vera."

"She was rattled," I said. "We didn't actually see the man fall, but the police were called, and they cancelled the rest of our boat ride, and then we all had to wait to be questioned. She did eat a few bites of supper, but then she went right to bed. Your mom has gone home too. Honestly, it was an exhausting day."

I took another quick look at Vera's husband. "I'd say she needs your support, but I'm not sure she'll be willing to talk about her feelings." I leaned toward William. "Nathan mentioned that Vera was feeling skittish before we arrived. Do you mind telling us a bit about why she was upset?"

"I wish she never gotten involved with this damn project," he said. "I really appreciate how much she loves Scotland and wants to do right by our history and our people and our special places. But at what cost? Her friends? Her sanity? Her life?"

"She isn't going to give it up, that's one thing I can say for certain," said Miss Gloria. "I know stubborn women"— she tipped her chin at me—"this one, for example. And your mother-in-law, for another example. Vera isn't quite so obviously obstinate, but scratch the surface and it's there."

"Takes one to know one," I said, winking at my friend.

But Nathan had lost all semblance of interest in cheerful banter, his party buzz gone, his expression stony. He turned to look at William and then me, his voice fierce and intense. "Let's stay focused here. Am I getting this right—you, or you and Vera, seem to think that the so-called poisoning incident and now this fall and subsequent death have something to do with her book project?"

"She didn't say that," I told the men. "I'm probably leaping to conclusions that shouldn't be drawn. She was distressed after today's incident, that's all."

"But she didn't know the man who fell to his death? He isn't involved with this project?" Nathan asked.

"I don't think so." I shrugged. "No one seemed to recognize him. And neither Vera nor the others in our party saw anyone that they knew while we were at the site. Maybe William can get more details from Vera than Helen or we were able to. In the end, I think it was a terrible coincidence."

"I don't believe in coincidences," Nathan said. "Coincidences point to a sloppy criminal, and it's not smart to brush them off. If there's any chance that these two events were connected, and possibly connected to Vera and her friends, I do not want you traveling off to the hinterlands tomorrow on your own."

"I wouldn't say that Peebles and Glencoe are hinterlands—certainly not Peebles," I said. I couldn't fault him for being worried, but Vera was troubled about the deadline for the project approaching. She would freak out if the guys messed up our plans. And honestly, my spidey sense was not tingling as I thought about our road trip. After getting involved in solving too many murders, my radar for danger was well honed. "And there will be a group of us going, and we won't branch out from everyone else, I swear."

"Can you put it off a day?" Nathan asked. "We could go with you day after tomorrow." He looked at William for confirmation.

"We have two more days to play," William said. "Then we're free. Vera and I talked about meeting you on the Oban ferry to go to Mull. If we don't make the same crossing, the plan would be to meet you at the hotel in Tobermory. From what I'm hearing, I'm no longer comfortable with that."

Miss Gloria put a hand on his forearm and shook her head. "Vera will never agree to postponing for two days or even one. They are on a very tight schedule. Everything has to be submitted to the publisher by the end of the month. The previous photos were not good enough for one thing. And for another, the solstice parade is tomorrow. We can't wait because we'd miss it completely. It's supposed to be incredibly special."

"We could skip the third day of the tournament," Nathan suggested to his host. "We certainly don't need another debauched banquet."

The two men looked at each other, and I knew they were thinking they would do whatever they had to in order to protect their wives and family. But I also hadn't seen Nathan laughing as hard as he had been minutes earlier, not in a long time. Maybe never. He was reveling in the company of his brother-in-law and enjoying the golf and the camaraderie of the other men, and I wasn't willing to take that away from him.

"I doubt very much that this incident had anything to do with us or with Vera's project," I said confidently. "You said yourself that Vera has been a bit jumpy lately. But I know you wouldn't be off playing golf if you thought either of us was in danger. The book project is on a super tight deadline, and you guys are having so much fun. And there's a whole caravan of us driving to Peebles. And we will be so, so careful, and we'll go to the police if there's any inkling of any trouble. Immediately. There are four of us, and we are strong women who will look out for each other. And we'll see you on the ferry in two days, right?"

The men agreed reluctantly, though both also seemed relieved.

Nathan fell asleep as soon as his head hit the pillow, but I was having trouble dropping off. I'd assured the men that we couldn't possibly be in danger, but was that true? I had no idea. Nathan was right: coincidences were rare except in badly written novels where the writers were desperate to wrap up loose plot points. I tossed and turned, punching the feather pillow and rearranging the blue quilt, trying to block out Nathan's soft snores. I gave up and rolled out of bed, heading for the kitchen. Maybe a half a scone and a cup of decaf tea would help me drop off.

While waiting for the scone to toast and the water to boil, I noticed the yearbook that Vera had pulled out of the bookshelves earlier in the evening. I poured hot water over the tea leaves and left them steeping for a few minutes. After slathering the scone with butter from a local dairy, I paged through the yearbook. It dated from Vera's senior year at St. Andrews. She looked young and beautiful in her graduation photo, if still a bit haunted around the eyes. I wondered if she'd ever share the details of her abduction with me. Or the ways in which she believed that incident had affected her and her family.

A Scone of Contention

There were candid photos at the end of the book, mostly the seniors all dressed up in their fanciest clothing—high heels and tight dresses with flapping graduation gowns layered over top. In one shot, Vera, Glenda, and Ainsley had their arms around each other, mugging for the photographer. They looked so happy, as though the great big beautiful world lay out in front of them, theirs for the taking.

Chapter Twelve

The smell of that buttered toast simply talked to Toad, and with no uncertain voice; talked of warm kitchens, of breakfasts on bright frosty mornings, of cosy parlour firesides on winter evenings, when one's ramble was over and slippered feet were propped on the fender, of the purring of contented cats, and the twitter of sleepy canaries.
—Kenneth Grahame, *The Wind in the Willows*

Nathan left for the golf course early the next morning, leaving me to cuddle with the two tiger cats, Archie and Louise, who'd slipped into our room as he left. Archie seemed to have extended his affection for Vera to me, though not if Nathan was nearby. He walked across my chest, back and forth, and finally circled into the crook of my elbow. Louise waited until he was settled, and then she stretched out alongside him. Their rough purring lulled me back to sleep. Sometime later I awoke at the sound of what I thought was a knock at the front door. I threw on Nathan's Key West Police Department sweatshirt over my pajamas and hurried out to check. I peered through the peephole: a beefy police officer with a round face and prominent ears waited on the stoop. He held up his badge, which I studied carefully. It looked authentic and so did he.

"I'd like to speak with Vera Campbell, Hayley Snow, and Gloria Peterson," he said once I'd cracked the door open. "It's about the death at the Falkirk Wheel."

"I'm Hayley. Please come in." I opened the door wider and waved him through. "Sorry to greet you in my PJs. I'm so embarrassed—I never sleep till nine o'clock. We had a very busy day yesterday, so we're having a bit of a lazy morning. I'll start a pot of coffee or water for tea, and then get the others."

I seated him at the kitchen table, noticing that one of the husbands had made coffee earlier. It would taste a little stale, but better than offering him nothing. I poured the man a cup of the strong brew and went to fetch the other women. First, I knocked on Vera's door and, in response to her muffled hello, told her a police officer was waiting in her kitchen. Then I trotted back downstairs to shake Miss Gloria awake. It wasn't too often that she slept later than I did, but the jet lag must have been wreaking some havoc with her system.

"Cop in the kitchen," I hissed. "He wants to talk with all of us."

She rolled out of bed, pulled on a robe, and stumbled down the hall behind me, with her hair standing up in cirrus cloud wisps. In the sunny kitchen, she blinked like a hedgehog who'd climbed out of his den after a winter of hibernation, like a character from *Wind in the Willows*. Within minutes, Vera followed us in and took the farthest seat from the cop.

I poured Miss Gloria a cup of coffee and made Vera a cup of tea, and joined them at the table.

"How can we help you, officer?" Miss Gloria asked.

"Following up on yesterday's incident at the Falkirk Wheel, we've identified the deceased. His name was Joseph Booth." He pushed a black and white photo to the center of the table. The man was dressed in formal suit and tie and stylish glasses, and his expression was dead serious, as though he'd been applying for an important position. Or possibly a passport. He had a square chin and laugh lines around his eyes so I imagined he had a nice smile too. Since I hadn't really gotten a good glimpse of the man yesterday, this face meant nothing to me except for feeling a whisper of sadness. He looked to be in his early forties, far too young to die.

"I'm sorry, I don't know him," I said. "Though we've only been in this country two days, so we hardly know anyone." I stopped myself from babbling off a list of every person we'd met on the trip so far.

"I don't know him either," said Miss Gloria, "though I'm very sorry for his family's loss."

We waited for Vera. After a pause, she shook her head. Her lips were pinched, which gave a grim cast to her face. Looking as though he didn't quite believe her, the policeman angled the photograph so it faced her directly.

"There is some question remaining about how the man came to fall from the wheel. Did any of you see this happen?"

Miss Gloria piped up, pressing her fingers to her temples. "I had the worst headache. I hate to malign one of your important Scottish monuments, but that wheel gave me a terrible feeling of claustrophobia. I'm afraid I wasn't paying attention the way I usually do. We've solved a few murder mysteries ourselves," she began to add.

Under the table, I tapped her foot with mine to cut her off. Our nosing into other crimes didn't seem like the kind of conversation we'd want to have with a foreign police officer. Nathan and Steve Torrence didn't appreciate our butting into crime solving, and they knew us well and loved us. *We should stick to the facts and keep our theories to ourselves,* I thought.

"Can I get you a refill on coffee?" I asked, noticing that he'd barely touched what I'd poured for him earlier. "Or tea maybe?"

"No thank you, ma'am," he said, fixing his gaze on me. "Did you see what happened?"

"No, we were at the other end of the boat, facing forward, away from the platform," I told him. "I didn't notice anything unusual before the fall either. Of course, we all shifted over to look out once the yelling began, but it was too late to understand what had happened by then. He'd already fallen."

"Same," said Vera briskly. "Only I was seated on the water side of the boat and saw even less than my friends did." She stood up as if to tell the cop the interrogation was over. He followed her lead, standing and collecting the photo after dealing out business cards to each of us.

"Should you remember any other details, please call me on my mobile or at the station." Vera thanked him for his time and closed the door firmly behind him.

Once he was gone, I pictured the scene on the boat after the man's fall, trying to visualize each of our party's positions.

Vera had said that she and Ainsley were seated across the aisle, a ways behind us. I didn't remember them moving to rubberneck. Glenda and Gavin would have been sitting together, but not near us, I thought. But I hadn't actually seen them, so I couldn't say for sure.

Why was Vera wound so tightly about this incident? Did she know more than she was willing to say? Did she really not recognize the dead man?

I would have liked to have questioned her about whether she told the cop the truth. The pause, the pinch of her lips, made me wonder. But I was a little afraid of her reaction, and she hustled off so quickly toward the hall leading to the bedrooms that I couldn't get the question out. I heard her footsteps on the polished wood of the staircase, going up. I exchanged a glance with Miss Gloria, and we both got up and trailed her down the hallway like puppies.

"Can we do anything for you?" I asked Vera.

"I need some time to prepare for our trip," she called back down the stairs. "When dealing with Gavin, it's best to have very specific instructions about what photographs must be taken. Otherwise, as he demonstrated so completely yesterday, he goes off on his own, and Lord only knows what the results might be. I will see you downstairs at noon, with your luggage in hand."

We watched Vera disappear into her bedroom from the bottom of the stairs. "She's a complicated character. Who in the world knows what's going on in her head?" Miss Gloria whispered. "I have a mah-jongg game online with Mrs. Dubisson, unless you need me for something?"

I shook my head at the wonder of her being technically savvy enough to set up and play mah-jongg on her iPad with her best Key West pal, time difference and everything. "No problem. I'll work on my articles and get ready to go."

As I was eating a bite of breakfast—cheese and toast with English jam—a text message arrived from chef Grace: *I know you're leaving for Peebles today, but any way we could chat for a few minutes before then? I can meet you at the statue in the center of town? Would prefer to talk in person.*

Another mysterious missive. *Be there in 20*, I texted back.

I pulled on my most comfortable black jeans, a turtleneck, and my jean jacket and sneakers, and headed outside to meet Grace. The day was turning out to be glorious, sunny with puffy white clouds, but cool and not a bit humid, so you knew it was Scotland and not Key West. Vera's flower garden looked lovely in the morning light, some of the buds beginning to unfurl into a pale lavender. If it wasn't for the stressful events of the last couple days and my sister-in-law's distress, I would have reveled in the free hours and taken my time exploring the town. As it was, I checked the map on my phone to be sure I was headed in the right direction and walked briskly to meet Grace.

She was pacing around the statue.

"Thank you for coming, I know it's an imposition. But I didn't know who else to turn to." Her eyes were blinking furiously, from the effort of not crying I suspected.

"It's okay. Tell me what's up."

"The police were at the house again this morning," she said. "They reported that there were traces of poison in

Glenda's plate at the dinner the other night, but only her food." At this point in the narrative, Grace lost her battle with tears. They flowed down her cheeks as she said, "How in the world could they figure this out if everything had already been scraped into the trash? Wouldn't everyone's leftovers be mixed together?" Suddenly a look of horror crossed her face.

"Do you mind walking that way? I totally forgot that I have a cake in the oven. Mr. Dougal will need tea while you lot are off in the countryside."

I pinched my arm to keep from asking what kind of cake. It didn't matter right now. What mattered was one death that was possibly a violent murder, and another possible poisoning attempt. At the house, maybe I would also get the chance to talk to Ainsley, be able to ask her about the conflict behind the scenes in this book project.

I trotted across town behind Grace, who had set a quick pace, wondering how such a talented and experienced chef could forget something as basic as leaving a cake in the oven. The answer had to be that she was distracted by something that felt even more important.

Once we got to Ainsley and Dougal's building, she unlocked the door and hollered behind her, "I am going to take the stairs, the elevator is so slow."

I vaulted up behind her, huffing and puffing and thinking I needed to up my exercise game. My gym trainer at home in Key West would agree. By the time we reached the fourth floor and burst into the hallway, I could already smell the scent of well-done, bordering on burnt, cake. Grace darted into the kitchen, slammed the oven door open, and grabbed the pan with two blue oven mitts. "I may or may not have saved it," she said.

She slid the cake on to the cooling rack that was waiting on the counter. Thin slices of sugared lemon covered the top, slightly caramelized by the heat. The crispy sugary citrus smell was incredible.

"It's stunning," I said. "I think you got it out in the nick of time."

Grace went to the door and cracked it open to be sure no one was listening. "Sorry to bring you out this morning with my cloak-and-dagger act," she said in a hushed voice. "It's just that Blair reminded me that I told him I'd seen a man I didn't recognize come out of the apartment the day I was preparing for the party."

Blair, I remembered, was the cheese vendor we'd met at the farmers market. I had wondered what their relationship was. "It wasn't Blair who saw this man, it was you?"

Grace nodded slowly but said nothing.

"Okay, what did he look like? And did you get a sense of who he came to see? Why he was here?"

She looked distraught. "Maybe medium height, reddish-brown hair, wearing tortoiseshell glasses. That's hardly any help is it? It could describe fifty percent of Scottish men."

Including the dead man, I thought but didn't say. "What do you think he was doing in the house? Any idea?"

"After Blair stopped in the kitchen to deliver the cheese, I walked him out. On the way back, I saw this man rushing down the hall from Ainsley's office, apparently in a big hurry to leave. I called to tell Blair about the party when

I got home that night because I was so upset. And then I remembered this man, wondering if he had some connection to their book. But after that, I was worried to distraction about what happened at the dinner, and so busy that I never thought of it again."

"But you must have thought of it if you remembered to tell Blair."

She shrugged. "I tell Blair everything. Besides, you remember what a difficult night that was. With Glenda collapsing and then the accusations that someone had tried to poison her—it went by in a blur after that. It was a bad night to be the chef who'd catered the party. I was pure done in."

I nodded my agreement. "Have you asked Ainsley who this person was?"

She shook her head. "She's hardly speaking to me. She's left a few notes about what to prepare for her husband while she's away, but that's it. I'm afraid she thinks I really did poison her friend." Her lips quivered. "I know you're wondering, but honest to gosh I didn't. Not on purpose anyway."

Then I noticed the time on her kitchen clock. "I need to dash. I haven't even packed. Please text if you remember anything else—I'm certain we'll get this all straightened out soon." I smiled warmly. "I think that cake will be perfectly lovely." I started out of the kitchen but turned back halfway. "Does the name Joseph Booth mean anything to you?"

"Sorry, no," she said and returned to her stove.

I hurried back across town to Vera's home, puzzling over what could be going on with this group of friends. All three of them seemed on edge about something. The yearbook photo haunted me—the promise radiating from them compared with the horror of the past few days. I hadn't had the chance to talk with Ainsley or Glenda, but hopefully I could get each of them alone over the next several days.

My mother-in-law Helen had already arrived at Vera's home, and was installed at the kitchen table having a cup of tea and reading the paper. Her suitcase waited by the door.

"You're up and about early," she said, her eyebrows quirking with curiosity.

"Yes, and I'm not packed so I better get moving. Have you talked to the police this morning?"

"They came to the hotel," she said. "I suspect they showed you the same photo, Joseph Booth?"

I nodded. "Miss Gloria and I certainly had never seen him before, and Vera said she didn't know him either." I paused, biting my lip, wondering whether to tell her my concerns about her daughter and her friends. I hated to align myself too tightly with Helen because I was afraid that would sour things with Nathan's sister. But I could ask questions.

"Did you meet Vera's friends when they were all in college? They seem lovely, Ainsley especially."

Helen looked pained. "We came over to visit twice a year—that's all she allowed. It was so hard to have her far away and wonder how she was coping. She was holding us at such a distance that I didn't dare ask too many questions. We took those girls to dinner each time we visited, at Vera's request. I think that was another way of keeping us away. We couldn't very well quiz her about personal issues with guests at the table. And Nathan's father and I weren't getting along well, so I suppose dinner with us must have felt a bit like living through a cold war."

A nightmare, I thought, imagining his father—a man like Nathan, but more intimidating, because he'd be even more distant and cool—sparring with Helen. Helen had opened up to me after the trauma we'd suffered together, but sharing difficult emotions wasn't her natural inclination. "That must have been so hard."

"Indeed. Vera insisted she was fine," Helen continued, "but she struck me as so fragile still. She was very sensitive to us hovering, and always scanning our faces and voices for a reason to shut down. That's why I hate so much to see this sort of thing happening. Again." She sighed, her shoulders drooping.

"We'll figure it out together," I said, smiling with encouragement.

Miss Gloria clattered into the kitchen, dragging her wheeled suitcase, with the two tiger cats tagging behind. She would always be the Pied Piper of pets. "Ready to rock and roll. And ready for a second breakfast," she said, glancing at the scones and teapot on the table.

"Yikes, it's late. I better get ready."

I retired to our room and took a quick shower and then threw some clothes into my small bag, thinking over the events packed into the last couple of days. Something definitely felt off with Vera. She felt brittle, in the way her mother had described her in her college years. Was the problem really with the book project?

For an instant, I wondered if she was having the same problem with me that I suspected her mother had faced when she first heard of Nathan's plan to marry me. Was she still close to Nathan's first wife and not eager to welcome number two? I pushed that thought away; it didn't fit. It felt more like Vera was reacting badly to the weight of her project, the events of the last two days, and maybe recurring themes in her history with her mother.

Maybe they were simply different animals—her mother had a backbone of steel, while Vera was a reed.

Chapter Thirteen

Her idea of fun was putting cake frosting on a bran muffin.
—J. Ryan Stradal, *The Lager Queen of Minnesota*

Exactly at noon, we all met in the kitchen, then trooped out to Vera's car and loaded our bags in the trunk.

"Hayley," Vera said, "Why don't you ride in the passenger seat next to me so we can have a proper chat?"

I turned to my mother-in-law to be sure I wasn't stepping on maternal toes. Helen insisted this seating arrangement was fine, but based on the expression on her face, I suspected her feelings were a little hurt about the backseat assignment.

Vera turned the radio to a station playing Scottish folk music, and we set out north through the rolling hills. "You're going to love Peebles," she said. "The town sits along the banks of the River Tweed and Main Street is just adorable. The hotel we're staying at is a bit dated but within walking distance of town."

She glanced over her shoulder at Miss Gloria. "I hope you all don't mind sharing a room. Because the town is flooded with tourists who come in for the solstice, there were only two rooms left. We'll have more space to spread out when we get to the Highlands and the islands."

It took me a minute to realize that she had arranged for the two of us to be in one room, and Miss Gloria and her mother in the other. She really did not want time alone with Helen. And that made me feel a little sad for her, and grateful for my own mom too. I'd felt a teeny bit crowded when she first moved to Key West, but now she had her own catering business, her own husband, her own life. Now it was more a matter of making sure she could fit me into her busy schedule.

"We are not fussy," said Miss Gloria. "We're used to the tiny spaces on our houseboat. And we sure hope you and William will be visiting us soon so we can show you around properly. It's honestly hard to understand Key West until you've been there. Isn't that right, Helen?" she asked my mother-in-law.

"That's for sure," said Helen, with a bit too much heartiness. "And I was there at what Hayley says is the busiest time of year and not exactly representative for visitors. You wouldn't believe the Christmas decorations. That town does not hold back."

"Not in any way, not ever." I laughed. "We'd love to have you and William for the holidays soon."

Vera nodded as if they'd consider it, but we shouldn't hold our breath. "This town was built at the confluence of two rivers," she continued as we drove. "The River Tweed and the Cuddy. I wouldn't describe Peebles itself as a thin place, in spite of the battles which were fought here. But it is a glorious place to watch the solstice festivities. Fun fact: the coat of arms of the Royal Burgh of Peebles shows three salmon on a red background, two facing one direction and the one in the middle facing the other way. The motto is *Contra Nando Incrementum*, meaning 'there is growth by swimming against the stream.'"

"Could just as well be your motto," Helen grumbled.

"Will you tell us about what we're going to see?" I asked.

"It's the festival of the summer solstice—the longest day of the year. The solstice is the moment when the sun is closest to the earth, so it's a festival of fire. Like the sun. The big event is the parade through town, with bagpipe bands, and kids singing and dancing, and special flags hand-sewn by local women. It's hard to describe, but it's all very quaint and very Scottish, and I know you're going to love it."

She glanced over at me, and I imagined she was going to talk about the spiritual meaning of the festival. Maybe she was sizing us up to see how much of that talk we could handle.

"I'm dying to hear how you met my brother," she said.

I heard Miss Gloria snicker in the backseat.

"It's not a pretty story," I said, twisting my wedding band around my finger and looking out the window. "I've grown up a lot since then. And he has too."

"He's still Nathan, but he's not emotionally impenetrable the way he used to be," said Helen. "I would say you've worked a miracle with my son."

"Don't tell him that." I laughed. "He thinks he was just fine before I met him. Anyway, I had recently moved to town and was living in a tiny houseboat with my college roommate, Connie, and working in her cleaning business. My room had been her storage closet, so it smelled like bleach."

"Tell her the dirt, not the boring facts," said Miss Gloria, leaning forward to poke my shoulder blade with her finger. "She might as well hear it now."

I could feel my face color. "I met a guy in a bookstore in New Jersey, and we kind of fell for each other. Though since we didn't know each other, we fell for the idealized version of what we hoped each other would become. Not the best way to choose a mate," I added. "Anyway, that lasted about ten seconds and Connie took me in. End of story."

"Except," said Miss Gloria, "there was a murder, a poisoning by key lime pie. And Hayley was a logical suspect, since the victim was her former boss who also happened to be the woman who stole her boyfriend away."

"That's awful," said Helen.

Miss Gloria nodded. "The murder was tragic, but on the other hand, we're grateful that woman did steal Hayley's boyfriend, because he was a loser, and my friend didn't have enough sense to notice that at the time."

Everyone laughed. "Whose story is this?" I asked. "Anyway, because of those connections, as Miss Gloria said, I became a suspect. And Nathan came to Houseboat Row and questioned me. Over and over, I might say, in a very fierce manner. I thought he was utterly gorgeous, but also a major asshat." I glanced over my shoulder at Helen. "Oops, sorry."

Miss Gloria was giggling hysterically by now. "You're probably wondering how Hayley and I became family," she said, leaning forward again to be sure Vera could hear every word. "The real key lime pie murderer conked me on the head and left me on the dock like a piece of trash. Hayley found me in a crumpled heap and sized me up as an old lady, one foot on the proverbial banana peel, the other buried deep in the Key West Cemetery. But she was W-R-O-N-G, wrong! The closest I have come to that location is giving historical tours of the most interesting gravestones."

Vera looked a little stunned by the onslaught of Miss Gloria's storytelling.

"That's hardly a fair description of what I thought," I said. "And once I got to know you, I discovered what a tough old bird you are." I reached back to squeeze her hand. I loved this woman to pieces—she'd brought so much vibrant color to my pastel life.

"And then, to continue with the rocky path of their love story," Miss Gloria added, mimicking a drum roll by slapping the back of the front seat with her palms, "Nathan and Hayley had a date. However, he stood her up because of the murder of someone dressed as a drag queen—this is Key West after all, and then his former wife came to town and swept him off his feet for another go at their marriage."

"Aha," said Vera. "The effervescent Trudy."

"Were you and she close?" asked Miss Gloria. I could have kissed her, because that was exactly one of the things I wanted to know.

"Not really," said Vera. "Their romance began after I moved to Scotland, so I never got the chance to know her well." From the set of her jaw, I suspected that was all she intended to tell.

"She was a nice enough girl," Helen said. "She was lively and attractive, but not a spark plug like you, Hayley."

Which was probably as close as she was going to get to telling me she preferred me as her daughter-in-law, though I'd come to believe that was true.

We left the countryside and Vera drove us into town minutes later. It was just as charming as she'd promised. The brown and white stone buildings of Main Street showcased small shops with window dressings that made me want to visit each one. There were turrets on the rooftops and flower-beds along the sidewalks in front of the shops. Banners made of red and white cotton cut into triangular pennants floated above the street, part of the solstice celebration, as Vera told us. "We'll come back for lunch, and you'll have a chance to stroll the shops," she added.

The Peebles Hydro Hotel, a sprawling white brick structure with a red roof, had stunning views from its high vista looking out across the rolling hills and forests of the border-lands. Flat gorgeous, and a world away from the palm trees, busy streets, and ocean-hemmed Key West.

"They are in the process of renovating this place," Vera said after she parked in front of the steep steps leading to the lobby. "We can leave the luggage here and get some help once we have our keys. Please excuse any worn velvet. I think you'll find the hotel magnificent, but parts of it are still slightly shabby." She smiled. "I suggest that we check in and wash hands and faces, and then pop into town for a bite to eat. That will leave us time for a rest or to catch up on some work before the parade starts."

A soaring portico with white columns and dentil mold-ing details led to the reception area, which bustled with customers. Under tall white ceilings in the foyer, a collection of tufted furniture was covered in red and gold velvet. We signed in for our rooms, with a plan to meet back in the lobby in fifteen minutes.

Vera and I walked to the end of the left-hand hallway, and she inserted a key card into the slot and pushed open the door. The room was papered in gold and had red curtains and bed covers on the twin beds pushed close together. It had been a while since I had roomed with anyone other than my husband. I hoped I didn't turn up with snoring or other unpleasant habits.

"Do you want to go first in the bathroom?" she asked.

"Go ahead," I said. "I'll stretch out here for a few minutes and try to do some thinking."

She looked puzzled but did not inquire any further. Why did I have the sense that she didn't want me to press on any of her mysteries? That impression of course made me all the more curious.

Half an hour later, we met up with the others and hiked down a short hill that led into town. The most adorable shops mushroomed alongside the road as if we were in an Agatha Raisin mystery. We settled into a small coffee shop on the edge of Main Street. Within minutes, a waitress in a frilly white apron and red hair pulled into a ponytail bustled over to our table to welcome us.

"If you haven't been here before, and from the looks of you, you haven't, we've two local specials on our luncheon menu. Our coronation chicken consists of roasted chicken dressed in a sauce of mayonnaise and whipped cream with curry spices, mango chutney, and apricots mixed in. And our Scotch pie was a runner-up in the World Scotch Pie championship. Questions?" She held her order pad up with pen poised.

At her suggestion, I ordered the coronation chicken over a jacket potato, aka baked potato, which would not be on anyone's diet list. But what was the point of vacation if a girl didn't splurge? Miss Gloria chose the prize-winning Scotch pie stuffed with meat, promising that I could taste it.

"Kitchen's a little backed up as you can see. I'm guessing it might be fifteen minutes until lunch is on the table." The waitress gestured at the other tables filled with diners and then buzzed away to get our drinks. I quizzed Vera about the roots of the chicken dish.

"It was designed to be served at Queen Elizabeth's coronation in 1953. I can't imagine why this dish was chosen for her big celebration, but perhaps she asked for it," Vera said. "Perhaps it was a taste of home in a very turbulent world when she was about to take on massive responsibility."

While we were waiting for our food to be delivered, Helen took Miss Gloria to the shop next door to peruse gifts for her friends back home. They seemed to have bonded in the biggest way.

"Anything with *Outlander* on it, Mrs. Dubisson will go crazy for," I heard her telling Helen. "She watches that over and over, and then we discuss the characters."

I met Vera's gaze and snickered.

"She herself is a big character," said Vera with a wide grin. "When Nathan told me you were bringing your octogenarian housemate on your honeymoon, I admit to being puzzled. But she is completely lovely. Like the grandmother I never had. And Nathan seems to feel the same."

I could only nod in agreement. Inhaling a deep breath, I braced to ask the question I had been dying to launch. There was a blanket of tension between Vera and her mother, and I didn't believe she'd reveal anything with Helen at the table. I worked hard to keep my voice friendly and level so she wouldn't feel like I was pushing too hard or, even worse, accusing her of something.

"The photo that the police officer showed us this morning. Are you certain you didn't recognize him, this Joseph Booth? Your face had a funny expression, so I couldn't tell for sure."

She began to rearrange the silverware that our server had brought to the table, knife next to fork next to spoon. "He looked like a man I knew in college," she admitted after a beat of awkward silence. "The Mr. Booth I knew was a teaching assistant, but there was some kind of scandal, and he left the university unexpectedly, and I'm quite certain he moved to Canada. I don't see how it could be the same person at all. Hearing the name took me by surprise, that's all."

"You didn't recognize him?" I asked.

"No. But it doesn't actually matter, does it? Even if I'd met the man years ago, none of our group had anything to do with the tragedy. It was a horrible coincidence. Still, a man died violently in our proximity, and that's hard to accept. It shook me up, that's all." She looked greatly relieved when the waitress returned with our lunch. At the same time,

Miss Gloria and Helen burst back into the café, laden with packages.

"You won't believe the cute things I found, including a scarf made from the MacDonald tartan. Not that there will be much use for a wool scarf in Key West, but I bought one anyway since it's family history, and one for each of my sons too. They live in Michigan," she explained to the others. "With their long winters, a scarf is always welcome."

"It's the first shop you visited—hope you saved room for some other treasures," I said.

"I'm counting on lots of space in Nathan's suitcase," she said with a wink. "He's not much of a shopper." She leaned back so the waitress could slide our orders onto the table.

My plate was piled high—a mound of creamy chicken salad loaded onto a baked potato, with a green salad on the side. The usual eyes-bigger-than-stomach problem. I would need all my food critic skills to eat with moderation, enjoying the dish enough to describe it and remember it, but not one bite more. Miss Gloria was equally delighted with her pie. The meat stuffing steamed as she broke into the crust, filling the air with a delightful oniony scent. I took a few quick photos before we destroyed the perfect arrangements.

As we were tucking into our lunches, I saw the other members of Vera's book team walk by outside. Ainsley noticed us and beckoned the others into the café and over to our table.

"Good morning. Or good afternoon, I suppose I should say. Hope you all had an easy drive up and a pleasant morn-ing." She pasted on a smile that could not make up for the fact that her body was tight as a wire and that Glenda and Gavin were hanging several feet back.

"Won't you join us?" Vera asked, gesturing at the table nearby, where diners appeared to be finishing up. "We could ask the waiter to put the two tables together?"

"Oh, we made a little lunch stop on the way up," Ainsley said. "Gavin wants to scope out the best views to take photographs of the parade."

"He has the most amazing shots in mind," said Glenda, tucking her arm into her husband's and gazing up at him.

"And we're meeting for dinner, right?" Ainsley asked.

Vera said, "Yes, I made the reservation for eight o'clock at the hotel."

Ainsley winked at her, smiled at us, and followed the other two out the door to the street.

"I hope no one kills anybody before this project is over," said Helen. She spread her white napkin on her lap and picked up her fork and knife.

"Why in god's name would you say something like that?" Vera asked, glaring at her mother.

"I didn't mean it literally," said Helen. "I was merely commenting on the obvious tension." She looked as if she might add more, but instead sighed and cut into her sandwich.

We ploughed through our lunch in silence until Miss Gloria brought her packages out from under the table and began to show each of the gifts she brought and tell us why she'd chosen them.

"The *Outlander* cookbook is for Phyllis," she said. "She's the only one of our mah-jongg group who does any serious cooking—aside from Miriam, and she's in the loony bin for poisoning one of our pals with peanut butter cookies." My in-laws looked horrified, but Miss Gloria rattled forward. "She sort of had it coming, even though the murder was definitely taking it too far. I'm a big fan of talking things out if you're mad about something." She wrapped the cookbook back up in its polka-dotted paper and turned to me.

"I figure Phyllis can whip up a Scottish dinner for the whole group and then we'll watch a couple of our favorite *Outlander* episodes again. Hayley, maybe you can help, because some of the recipes look complicated and the print is tiny for an old lady's eyes." She cackled with delight. "The stuffed sheep is for Mrs. Dubisson. She desperately wants a cat but she's allergic. She comes down the finger to visit our boat at least once a week, but by the end of tea time, she's wheezing from Sparky and T-bone and Hayley's Evinrude. And of course, as I mentioned, the scarves are for my boys." She held up the packages of plaid wool.

Once everyone had finished lunch, we walked back to the hotel to rest before the evening celebration, as Vera suggested. In our room, she took her shoes off and stretched out across her bed.

Now or never. "I'm sorry things feel tense between you and your mom," I tried.

"Do you know," Vera said after an uncomfortable silence, "it sounds like you and your mother have a lovely friendship. But mother–daughter rifts tend to accumulate over a lifetime until finally the weight of miscommunications begins to fray and sometimes severs the tie. In our case, that happened after my so-called 'incident' as my parents referred to it. I'm sure they meant not to upset me, but by not calling it an abduction, they only made me feel more alone."

"I'm so sorry," I said. "If it helps, she did talk to me about it. I think she's open to—"

Vera cut me off. "You didn't see her after the abduction. It was all chipper, chipper, let's get back to life as normal, and so on. Except I could feel the waves of anger radiating underneath. When there are problems in my life, she's not the person I feel I can turn to in order to talk them out."

She curled up into a little ball and pulled the sheet around her shoulders, and I got the message. She needed some alone time. And she did not need me crowing about my developing friendship with her mother.

On my way out, I heard her voice again, muffled by the bedcovers. "Don't worry a bit about Trudy. She was a girlie girl, and Nathan has always been attracted to that kind of thing, taking care of her, watching her whirl in social tailspins, and all that. Even if he was drawn to her, they weren't a good fit, and it wasn't sustainable in the long run."

Chapter Fourteen

Beauvoir had never liked dark chocolate. It seemed unfriendly.

—Louise Penny, *The Beautiful Mystery*

Since I was not feeling sleepy, especially after Vera's last comment, I carried my iPad to scope out a library or other comfortable spot for reading. Did Vera mean Nathan wished I was a girlie girl, that's what he really wanted? I hated feeling jealous of his ex-wife, because he'd assured me over and over that he had moved on from that relationship and chosen exactly where he wanted to be. With me. The lingering jealousy left me feeling unmoored, insecure, and a little silly.

Afternoon tea was being served in the lobby, but in spite of my best intentions, I had finished off my plate of coronation chicken plus a baked potato the size of a Highland cow, and all that sat a little heavy in my gut. And eight o'clock would come soon enough for dinner. I did pause by the door of the restaurant to check out tonight's menu, which was front-loaded with salmon starters, a mackerel pate, duck and chicken terrine, and an Arran whiskey cheddar beignet that sounded irresistible.

I settled in a little nook in the lower level, in a comfortable upholstered chair near the Gin Palace aka bar that served hundreds of kinds of gin, but far enough away to avoid distraction by the cocktail chatter. First order of business: google Joseph Booth. I had suspected this would be a common enough name that the search would not be very helpful. There was a Joseph Booth, Dublin master clockmaker; a Joseph Booth, missionary in the early 1900s; and a small news item about the fall from the Falkirk Wheel.

I clicked on that link and began to read.

Mr. Joseph Booth of Glasgow, England fell to his death from the Falkirk Wheel in Falkirk on Tuesday. Mr. Booth, 43, was employed as a senior software engineer. He is survived by his mother Mrs. Joseph (Violet) Booth Senior, and an aunt, Bettina Booth, of Peebles, England, who were known for winning the British Baking Show, Scone Edition, last fall. Said Bettina Booth, "he was clever and fit and never would have taken such a risk, nor suffered such a fall without some help." She called for the local police to treat this as a criminal incident.

Police are investigating the fall as suspicious and encourage anyone who observed the incident or has any information to call the station.

The fact that Joseph Booth's relatives lived right in this town was simply too much of a tempting coincidence to ignore.

The signs that Vera was somehow in trouble were mounting up, starting with what Nathan had told me about her husband's concerns before we even came to Scotland. And culminating in the fall from the Wheel. My instinct told me that Joseph Booth was an important part of the mystery. Vera had definitely recognized him when the police officer showed her his photo. Or to be more specific, she had startled as though he was someone she knew. And she did tell me that the man reminded her of someone she'd known in college, but that that Mr. Booth had moved to Canada, so she didn't see how it could be the same person. I thought it was possible they were one and the same. Didn't people move from Canada to the UK all the time?

Perhaps his family would be willing to share more about why he'd left the university and why he might have shown up at the Wheel the same day and time that our party did.

The most difficult problem was how I could explain stopping into someone's home to ask questions of recently bereaved relatives about his murder. The answer, I thought, might lie with the prize-winning scones. I Googled "Bettina and Violet Booth scone recipe" and learned from the *Peebles Observer* that although the sisters had declined to share their prize-winning recipe for cinnamon scones, they'd alluded to the secret lying in very cold butter and eschewing cinnamon chips. There was an adorable photo of two older women with matching gray bobs, arms around each other's waists and grinning, in front of a pile of fluffy scones. A big blue ribbon lay on the table next to the baked goods.

I easily found the address for Violet Booth, then clicked on the maps app on my iPhone and put in the location. The app told me her home was about a mile and a half from the Peebles Hydro, on the other side of town. I didn't see how I could get to the house and back to the hotel in time to meet up with the others for the solstice festivities. But I would be able to trot across town, visit with Joseph Booth's family, and then join Vera and Miss Gloria and Helen downtown.

I was starting to type this plan into an e-mail—only my plans to meet in town, not the reason for the change—when I felt a tap on my shoulder. I startled, feeling guilty as though I was doing something wrong. The tapping finger belonged to Ainsley.

"So sorry," she said, with a friendly and apologetic smile. "I didn't mean to scare you. I'm interrupting something, aren't I?"

I surely wasn't going to tell her what I was planning without knowing whose side she stood on, if in fact there were sides. The relationships between these old college friends who were working together felt like a big snarled ball of ominous awkwardness.

"Not at all," I said, waving at the club chair angled next to me. "Come sit for a minute. I was reading about that poor man who fell from the wheel yesterday. It was so unexpected and so tragic, and poor Vera seems torn up about it."

A series of expressions flooded over her face like fast-moving clouds: surprised, distressed, worried. And then she pulled on a cheerful mask. "Yes," she said, "that was a terrible, terrible event. I can't think what that man was doing up there. They clearly asked visitors to remain seated while the wheel was in motion."

Either she knew nothing or I was being stonewalled. "The police came to Vera's home this morning to ask if we knew the man or had seen anything in the moments leading up to his fall." I waited for a few seconds to see if she was going to chime in without being pushed. She wasn't. "Did they also interview you?"

"They did. But I had nothing to enlighten them with." Her face looked stony.

"Did you recognize Mr. Booth?"

"I did not," she said, adding a small smile. "But it appeared to be one of those early photos, so it was difficult to judge how old he was in actuality—what he would look like today. So tragic." She reached over to lay her hand on mine, gazing steadily at me. It was hard to think she was lying about anything. "I'm only sorry that your visit is not more relaxing," she said. "I know that Vera was looking forward to meeting you very much."

"And I her. And it's also lovely to meet her old friends. Sounds as though you've known her since she moved to Edinburgh."

She nodded thoughtfully and pulled away to lean against her chair back. "We were so young. She didn't know a soul and was so brave to move alone to a new country. I'm glad we connected, because sometimes when you're that young, you don't choose the friends that could last a lifetime."

"That's exactly what I was saying yesterday," I said, and then moved doggedly forward with my questions. "Have there been any developments with Glenda and the food? Grace was terribly distressed about someone thinking she would try to hurt one of your friends. And she was sad about the wonderful meal getting ruined, though that of course is not nearly as important as Glenda's health."

Ainsley smiled and crossed her hands in her lap. "Grace is a real treasure, but she gets wound up about entertaining. Rightfully so, as she's a professional and wants everything to be perfect. She will probably be grateful and relieved to have only my husband to cater to for a few days." She smiled again, which I took to mean that she was done talking about Grace and the poisoned dinner.

"Tell me about Glenda," I said. "Were you and Vera instant friends with her as well as each other? I hope you don't mind me saying that it seems as though there's a fair amount of tension between all of you right now."

She sighed and smoothed the fabric of her skirt across her lap. "I'm afraid it's the book. It's starting to wear on us as we get closer to the deadline. Glenda's a bit of a drama queen, as you saw at my dinner party. And managing a husband, especially her Gavin, is not so easy." Her eyes twinkled. "That sounds so old-fashioned, doesn't it? I still believe that marriage is an art and that one must be a dedicated student. I'm sure you're learning your Nathan's ways."

I smiled in return. Nathan would hate that description. And I was determined not to get derailed from my questions about Glenda. It felt like I was knocking on each door and window in her house. I could see her inside, but she was opening none of them.

"Do you mind saying more about the tension?" I asked. "I'm worried about Vera. And I know that she's concerned about both the dinner and the terrible fall. But like her brother, she's not a big talker."

She slumped back in her chair and closed her eyes, as if too tired to keep up the cheerful pretense that everything was fine.

"We all met during her first year in Scotland, in a class on the history of Edinburgh. For Glenda and me, it was the same stuff we'd heard in school for years. But Vera was fascinated and horrified with the violence. I suppose every country has its low moments, but she was appalled at the battles between clans—people against people, and between Scotland and England, Scotland and Ireland, Scotland and France." She focused her gaze on my face. "I always wondered whether her strong reactions and her intense desire to write this book were related to her own trauma. Isn't that often where art is born? Anyway, she has been interested in Scottish history ever since she arrived. And as I'm sure you've heard, she wanted to showcase it in a way that would be unique. I was all in favor of that."

She glanced at her watch. "Goodness, it's getting late. I'll see you at the parade—I need to run to my room and grab a sweater."

Chapter Fifteen

A pound of best butter—that's what you told me to ask for, and I did, but I kept wondering whether there was such a thing as second-best butter, or worst butter— Brianna was handing over wrapped packages to Fiona, laughing and talking at once.

—Diana Gabaldon, *Voyager*

Once Ainsley left, I tucked my iPad into my backpack and left the hotel, retracing our steps down the hill and into town. Whatever was going on between those friends, they were not going to share it with me. Not yet. But I wasn't finished digging.

The streets were busier now, beginning to fill with excited children, townspeople, and musicians carrying instruments, dressed in full dress red plaid kilts, white shirts, and black vests, with tall knee-high white stockings. Some women wore red sashes over black tops.

I had about an hour before I had promised to meet the others outside the café where we had lunch. Much as I yearned to browse in each of the shops along the road and chat with the local shopkeepers, I had to hurry to squeeze in the visit with Joseph Booth's family. The cottage I was looking for was almost at the end of the village along the road, and overlooked the river in back. A pretty garden brimmed with red geraniums and some of the flowers that had been blooming in front of Ainsley's building. Hollyhocks, I thought Grace had told me. Or was it foxglove? The cottage was built of white stucco, with brown shutters and a glorious pink rose bush that climbed up the stucco and cascaded over top of the door to the other side. I took in a big breath of air for courage, climbed the steps, and tapped the door knocker, which was made of brass in the shape of a sheep. A couple minutes later, a woman whom I guessed to be in her early sixties, came to the door.

"I'm Hayley Snow," I said quickly. "I am so very sorry for your loss. When I read your son's obituary in the paper earlier today, I could not help noticing that you are the author of prize-winning cinnamon scones. I'm a food writer, working on an article about Scottish specialties. I realize this is terrible, clumsy timing, but I am only in town this afternoon, and I wonder if we might talk for a few minutes? I simply could not resist stopping in to express my condolences and to meet the winners of the baking contest." This was pushy even by my standards, but it felt so important to understand what had happened on that wheel.

"Aunt, I'm his aunt," she said. Her eyes narrowed as she looked me over, as though she couldn't believe I had the gall to come calling about scones at a time like this.

"Sadly, I was on the Falkirk Wheel the other day when your nephew fell, and I am so terribly sorry for your loss." That sounded so blunt and cruel, but I couldn't think how else to get them to talk to me about Joseph.

"I'm Bettina. Come in." She opened the door wider and waved me in.

"I'll only stay a few minutes. I imagine you are getting ready for the parade. Or maybe not much in the mood for a parade," I added quickly. "Which I would completely understand." I did a mental forehead thunk to remind myself not to babble. It was a miracle that she'd let me in, and I didn't want to ruin the chance.

She led me to the back of the house, into a small kitchen with a rustic wooden farmhouse table overlooking the backyard and the river. The tabletop was covered with baked goods, delivered I supposed by concerned neighbors and friends. An old brown dog woofed, then struggled to his feet from his plaid bed in a patch of sunlight and shuffled over to snuffle my hands.

"Good dog," I said, smiling. "You must be smelling my sister-in-law's cats. Archie and Louise. They're gorgeous gray tigers, but not fans of dogs."

"I'll put the kettle on," said Joseph's aunt. "You sit," she said, glancing at the crowded table. "Push a few things aside, and I'll see if my sister is willing to speak with you. She might wish to hear what you know. And she might enjoy a distraction, much as the pain will return after."

I sat in a wooden chair with a rush seat, near the window, listening to the river that burbled along the bottom slope of their lawn. The old hound butted my hand out of the way and placed his head in my lap. He smelled comfortingly musty and doggy, and I rubbed his ears and felt my anxiety drop. "I wonder if you miss him?" I asked. "Did he live here? Or visit often?" The dog said nothing, only swished his tail, whap, whap, whap against the wooden post of the table and then stinging my calf with each wag.

The two sisters appeared in the kitchen shortly after, Joseph's mother, Violet, pale to the point of almost gray. Her shoulders were stooped and her eyes drooped, the picture of sadness. She would certainly have imagined her son outliving her many years after her death, perhaps attending to the two of them as they grew older. I felt a little sick about pushing my way into their grief.

I stood up to greet her. "I'm so sorry for your loss," I said in a quiet voice. "Thank you for agreeing to talk with me."

"And you are here to tour Scotland?" Bettina asked. "Please, sit down." She pressed her sister down into the chair across from me and took the seat nearest the stove.

I explained about Nathan and his sister and our honeymoon, and then stammered a bit about how much I was enjoying the Scottish food so far. How in fact I wrote about it for a living and was at this moment obsessed with scones. All of which was true.

In the background, the tea kettle whistled. Bettina held a finger up and hurried over to get mugs, tea, and sugar from the cabinet. After quickly fixing three drinks, she folded her sister's hands around a warm mug of liquid. She placed another in front of me along with a small china plate rimmed with pink roses, and a fork and knife.

"Now, you do not sound like you are from Scotland or even England. New Zealand perhaps? America?" asked Bettina.

"America," I said, smiling. "I live at the end of the state of Florida on a small island called Key West. As I said, I'm writing an article focused on scones . . ."

The two women looked at the baked goods covering the table, each plate and pan centered on a hand-tatted doily. "Then you absolutely must try some of these," said Violet. "I can't fathom why our friends and neighbors think we could eat all of this or have any appetite for it, but I suppose it's the best one can do under the circumstances. Unfortunately, we haven't had the nerves to do our own baking, but some of these are not awful."

Bettina took me on a whirlwind tour of the sweets on the table, the shortbread, the tablet, the Dundee cake, the raspberry almond scones, and the black bun, or currant loaf, which she explained was more traditionally served at New Year's. Without waiting for me to choose, she cut pieces of each offering and loaded the plate in front of me.

"Will you tell me about your cinnamon scones? To have won such a prize, there must be family secrets." I smiled at the women, sipped my tea, and nibbled on a piece of shortbread.

"As we clearly said in that article," Bettina said, emphasizing her words with a brisk nod of her chin, "we don't intend to share the recipe. Scones look so simple, but the truth is, they can be easily transformed into tough and tasteless lumps of dough."

"One secret is frozen butter, grated into the dry ingredients," said Violet. "Don't skimp on good cinnamon. And work the dough as little as possible." She sat back with a small but satisfied smile, her hands folded in her lap. "That's as much as we are prepared to share."

"I understand," I said, feeling a bit disappointed. Even if my original goal for visiting had nothing to do with the prize-winning scones, they would have been the pièce de résistance of my article on Scottish delicacies. Maybe I could wangle something similar from Grace once we got back to Edinburgh.

"What will your tour cover?" asked Bettina.

I listed off the places we were going—and then took my chance, mentioning the Falkirk Wheel.

"Bettina said you were with him when he fell?" Violet's lips trembled, and she pinched them together to contain her distress. "Did you see him fall? Did someone push him?"

I glanced at my phone. It was fifteen minutes before six, and I was bordering on late. Obviously, I couldn't leave yet. I took another sip of strong tea and told them the story of the fall in the broadest possible terms.

"Unfortunately, we were seated at the front end of the boat, so I'm unable to report on how it happened. There were screams and everyone was on their feet trying to figure out what had happened. And then the captain instructed us to take our seats because we were returning to the pier. Once we disembarked, police were everywhere, and your son was on the ground, though I didn't know it was him, of course. It all happened so quickly that I'm quite certain he did not suffer." I added that last bit thinking how awful it would be for them to imagine the scene.

Violet covered her face with her hands, and Bettina stroked her back.

"I know the police are investigating, because this morning, they came to my sister-in-law's home and showed us your son's photo." At this point in my recitation, I realized there was no logical reason to explain me visiting their home and pressing them about Joseph, if I didn't want to tell the truth—the truth being that Vera and her friends appeared unusually tense and that all or some of them were hiding something, possibly related to Joseph Booth's death. Or murder.

"I'd really love to help sort this out if I could. Had you talked to him recently?" I asked. "The newspaper piece said you wanted the police to pursue this as criminal. Did you have a sense that Joseph believed he was in danger?"

"He called me every Sunday," Violet said, "isn't that right?" She asked her sister as though she wasn't sure of anything these days. Bettina put a hand over her sister's clenched hands and nodded.

"He never missed, not once. He was a lovely young man and devoted to his mother."

Violet snuffled at her sister's words.

"And devoted to me too, as he knew I had no children of my own," Bettina added.

"He was exactly as always this last visit on the phone," Violet said, straightening her shoulders. "He asked about the garden club and the dog and whether I've been taking my constitutionals every evening. And he naturally wondered if we had thought about entering next year's baking contest and what recipe we would consider submitting. He was so proud of us. Nothing out of the ordinary. One day he was there and the next, gone." She began to weep a little, and I took bites of each of the baked goods on my plate, to give her a moment to gather her composure.

"Would you tell me about Joseph?" I asked. "I understand that he was a tutor at St. Andrews for a while and more recently worked as a software engineer. Did you get the idea that he was involved in something difficult at work, something dangerous?" Which I'd sort of asked already, but it hadn't been answered. And it seemed important. Because I'd love for there to be another reason that he might have fallen, unrelated to my sister-in-law and her friends.

Bettina dropped her gaze to the table. "If he did, he didn't share it with us. But he wouldn't have done, wouldn't have wanted to worry us."

"I understand. Do you know why he left the University suddenly some years ago? Or was this something he preferred not to talk about?"

"He wanted to teach," said his mother in a firm voice. "He always wanted to teach from the time he was a boy, when he used to gather the neighborhood kids to play school." She gave a sweet but sad laugh, as if remembering. "He was a whiz at mathematics and computers and history, and he loved each one of those subjects. But then he left abruptly midterm, and we were so surprised, but he refused to tell me why. He said that it was done and best not to discuss it. But it seemed to me that he lost something after that, a spark. Would you say, Bettina?"

Her sister nodded. "We wondered if it was a love gone sour," she said. "We couldn't think why else he would abandon the work he was so excited about."

"I do believe it was a broken heart," said Violet, nodding in agreement.

"Do the names Glenda or Vera or Ainsley sound familiar?"

They looked at each other, and both shrugged. Their kitchen clock chimed six, and I felt the pressure to ask everything and wrap up my visit. "The paper said he was a software engineer most recently? Was that going well? Was he married? Any children?"

"Never married. No children. His job was fine, as far as he told us," Violet said.

She was so sad and I was so late, I knew it was time to go. I pushed back in my chair and stood up, causing the old dog to struggle to his feet too. I left my *Key Zest* business card on their table between the currant loaf and the shortbread.

"In case you change your mind about sharing that recipe. I would be so thrilled. Or remember anything more about Joseph. Thank you for speaking with me and for all the delicious goodies. Again, my deepest condolences on the loss of your son."

Bettina walked me to the door and closed it behind her so we were standing on the stoop together.

"I don't truly understand why you are the one to ask all these questions," she said. "You're not affiliated with the police?"

I gulped and crossed my arms over my chest, determined to tell the truth as I knew it. "No. As I mentioned, we were on that boat, and we all felt so terrible about what happened. And then it turned out that some of my friends seemed to have known him from school, which made the loss even more shocking. And my husband is a detective back home, so asking questions comes naturally." I paused to take a breath. "When I read in the paper that you weren't satisfied with how the investigation was going, I hated to think about you suffering with no answers. That's it, mainly. I hoped I could help."

She stared at me for a moment, then gave a quick nod, as if I'd passed a test. "He was tense about something, Sunday," she said, emphasis on the *was*. "I didn't like to say anything in front of Violet, but he had an angriness in his voice that I'd seldom heard. Except perhaps when he first left Edinburgh. He did fine in his career, but he lost the spark he'd had as a teacher. He was going through the motions of his life, I'd say."

"Did your sister notice the difference in his voice as well?" I asked.

"Violet is a kind soul who prefers to see the good in every situation and hates to make waves. So she never did press him too hard. But something bad happened before he left St. Andrews, and last Sunday he sounded exactly like that."

She looked away and plucked a couple of brown leaves off the climbing rose. "Violet would be devastated if she began to think we should have noticed and done something to help him before that terrible fall. That somehow if we'd paid more attention, we could have saved him." She grabbed my hand. "You'll tell us what you learn?" She pressed a scrap of paper into my fingers with a phone number on it. "Call my cell."

In the distance, I heard the mournful wail of the bagpipes and the rhythmic tap-tap-tap of drums. "I will," I said. "I promise."

Chapter Sixteen

*It wasn't very nice of me, but I hoped the pickles gave him
heartburn.*
　　　　　　　　　　—Jenn McKinlay, *Buried to the Brim*

I hurried back toward town, hoping I hadn't missed the
parade highlights. As I got closer, the crowds grew bigger
on the sidewalks, and I had to weave through the villagers to
make my way to my friends and family.

A traditional bagpipe band led the parade, consisting of
about twenty pipers and half that many drummers behind
them. They set off down Main Street, playing "Scotland the
Brave." The crowd around me was clapping and cheering, and
several of them began dancing a jig, dipping and whirling,
with joyful faces. Behind the bagpipers trailed the women I
had seen earlier in the day, with sashes across their chest—
town officials maybe? Children dressed in red sweat suits followed them, who I guessed belonged to a sports team of some
kind. A breeze had come up, causing the white and red pen-
dants strung across the street to flap. And the sky overhead

roiled with big white and gray clouds. When had I experienced any scene quite so beautiful? I wished Nathan could have been here to share it with me.

As the musicians moved on to the melancholy notes of "The Skye Boat Song," I spotted my group gathered in front of the café.

"I hoped you weren't going to miss this!" cried Miss Gloria. "Isn't it the most amazing thing you've ever seen? Can you imagine a more festive way to welcome summer?"

I gave her a quick hug. "I love it. I'm speechless."

Helen grabbed my hand firmly and drew me a yard away from the others. "How was your afternoon?" she asked.

"Fine," I said, feeling surprised and slightly ambushed. "I did some work, though not nearly enough. I need to rough out my thoughts about lunch, so I don't get it mixed up with dinner. If the meals start piling up, I won't remember what details go with what. And I still have the scone and cock-a-leekie soup recipes to write up." I grinned, suddenly aware that I was talking too fast—and all about food, which I knew didn't interest her that much—and generally acting guilty. "And then I walked to the end of Main Street to stretch my legs."

She shot me a look of stony disbelief that reminded me completely of Nathan. "I know you know something is going on here"—she tipped her head toward Vera—"and I know you well enough to know you aren't just letting it go."

I could tell a small stretcher from time to time as needed, but I couldn't flat-out lie to my mother-in-law. I beckoned her to move a little farther away from the others, and explained about the article I'd come across about Joseph Booth and how, in utter synchronicity, his mother and aunt lived right here in Peebles. "I know we're busy this evening and leaving in the morning, so this seemed the only chance to talk with them. They are just adorable—two sisters who look like peas in a pod. I assume they must have married brothers, because they share the name Booth."

She cut me off. "I wish you wouldn't shoot off places by yourself," she said, a sober look still on her face. "Nathan would have a coronary. I don't think I should need to say it, but there have been two possible murders, or one murder and one attempt, and we have no idea who is behind them. And everyone who might be a suspect is right here on this trip with us."

"I see what you're saying, I do," I said, nodding my agreement. "Probably not everyone." That was supposed to be a joke, but it fell flat. Not even a ghost of a smile. "And I hadn't planned this at all. It's just that I googled Joseph Booth and noticed that his family lives right here in town, and I couldn't see when else I would get the chance to talk with them."

I explained about the prize scones and how I'd thought they would be a perfect cover for my questions. Then I smiled, knowing I was repeating myself and possibly sounding dizzy, but wanting her to understand the strong urge I'd felt to gather this information. She still looked grim.

"Point taken. I won't go off alone again."

I wanted to say more, such as "I didn't want to wake you or Miss Gloria," and "I am quite capable of taking care of myself," and "You are my mother-in-law, not my mother." But in the end, she had a good point. Nathan would not be happy. Nor did I want to put myself in danger.

Then her face seemed to soften. "What did you learn?"

"We know that Joseph Booth was teaching at University the same time that your daughter and her friends were there. He left suddenly, for unknown reasons, even though his mother said he'd always wanted to be a teacher. His relatives believe that it had something to do with a broken heart." I sighed. "Actually, that's what his mother thinks. She was so sweet and so devastated."

Helen looked sad too—she would understand the horror of almost losing a child.

"I started to wonder as I was walking back to meet you," I said, "whether it's possible that Vera or one of her friends could have dumped him, and that's why he left his teaching position."

"Maybe," Helen said, "but why would they then all deny they knew him? I don't remember Vera mentioning that name, but she wasn't telling me much of anything back in those days."

I nodded. "Joseph's aunt pulled me aside as I was leaving, to say he sounded angry about something, both back at University and also in the last conversation they had with him this past weekend."

"Why would he be angry now about being dumped in the past? And why would that old news become cause for his murder?" Her expression showed a mixture of annoyance and concern. "Next time," she said, "please don't hesitate to wake me up. I would have gone with you, and sometimes it helps to have a second observer. And then I wouldn't have to report to my son that once again you went off half-cocked and put yourself in danger."

She forced a little laugh, and suddenly I realized that her feelings had been hurt that I hadn't invited her to go along. And that she was seriously worried about my safety.

I gave her a hug, quick enough to surprise her. "I will."

In front of us, the parade appeared to have wrapped up, and the participants had begun mingling with the crowd, accepting their congratulations. The temperature felt as though it had dropped ten degrees, and I was no longer dressed appropriately. I began to shiver.

Vera said, "We should start back up to the hotel so we're not late for our reservation."

*   *   *

The dining room was simply decorated with plain blond wood tables, wooden chairs with patterned blue fabric seats, and no tablecloths or rugs. I liked the clean lines, though it was not what I would have expected for a grand old hotel. The waitress showed us to a long table with a name card at each place. Someone, Vera, I suspected, had already arranged the seating.

I found my place toward the end of the table, seated between Gavin and Glenda. Across the way, Nathan's mother winked as if to say, 'Don't worry about getting stuck with the duds, I am in this with you.' When the waitress returned, she was carrying a tray of drinks, which she described as Simmer Dim gin on the rocks, ordered by Gavin for everyone.

Vera opened her mouth as if to protest, but Gavin headed her off.

"They don't have to drink it, but it's the perfect toast to solstice. And it's on me. This gin is made in Shetland, to celebrate the midsummer light," he explained to everyone. "You will notice hints of orange peel and licorice root, with a spicy finish." He lifted his glass and said, *"Slàinte mhath."*

I took a sip and choked a bit as the strong drink burned my throat. I took another, paying attention to the flavors he'd described. Meanwhile, the alcohol rushed in two directions—straight to my belly and right to my head.

"That parade was a spectacular event," I said, glancing down the table at Vera. I lifted my glass a third time. "Thank you for including us on this visit. We couldn't have imagined something so special."

"Yes, thank you all," said Miss Gloria, and then drained the gin in her glass and grinned at me. "It was positively glorious, an experience that we will never forget."

"And this," said Gavin, "is exactly why people will be so excited about the way we've woven my concept into the new book. It's the difference between watching a sport like rugby from the stands versus actually dodging players on the field."

"It's the difference between watching a television show and sitting on the couch chatting with those same characters," added Glenda. "My husband can take videos and photographs and post them all over the internet, but he can't videotape something that's happened in the past. That's where the virtual reality brings history alive."

"But I'm confused. I thought this project was to be a book," said Miss Gloria.

Glenda opened her mouth as if to explain, but her husband waved her off.

"Imagine," said Gavin, "if I had told you about this parade. Or even showed you a few snapshots. I could tell you about the bagpipers and maybe even play a snippet of the music and show some photos or a little video. But how would that compare to attending the event?"

"It wouldn't be the same," Miss Gloria said, nodding yes to the waiter who hovered behind her with a bottle of white wine. He splashed her a full glass, even though I tried to catch his eye and motion that she only needed an inch. "Don't pay any attention to that lady at the end of the table," Miss Gloria said to the waiter, pointing at me and winking. "She does not speak for me." Then she turned back to Gavin: "So many amazing details would be missed."

"Yes!" Gavin pounded a fist on the table. "It cannot possibly be the same in a two-dimensional experience." He explained that there would be two ways to access the book. One would be the old-fashioned way of reading. The second would be by also purchasing the specially made goggles, and this would allow the consumer to access the virtual reality component of the chapters.

"Access?" I heard Vera mutter. "Books are meant to be read, not *accessed*."

Then the waitress reappeared and our orders were taken; for me, the whiskey cheddar beignet with onion and leek puree that I'd been thinking of all afternoon, and a grilled salmon with local vegetables to counteract an onslaught of Scottish carbs.

"Now what did you say you did for a living?" Gavin asked, once the waiter had collected the menus and shaken out the napkins on our laps.

"I'm a food critic. I taste food and then write about it to help people choose where they will dine and what to eat once they get there." Two waiters appeared and slid our appetizers in front of us.

"Perfect example," Gavin said, holding up a homemade roll that he'd carefully buttered earlier. "Reading about food can never compare with the experience of actually being in the place and tasting it yourself. You can and do write about it, I'm sure, with finesse and detail, but how can you capture that first moment where the food hits your tongue and the flavor bursts forth?" He bit into his roll. "For that moment when you realize the butter is probably made of milk pumped from a local cow and churned by the farmer's wife, you must have your knees under the table."

"You have a point," I said, surprised that he'd understood exactly what I was trying to say about my work and the limitations a critic faced. "But I can't think how your process could replicate that."

"No," he agreed, "we can't do taste, though new techniques are always trying to push those boundaries. But we do have a way to include smells. And history is different. We can definitely amp up the sounds and sights until they become so real that a person suddenly understands the history of that place in an entirely new way—and then begins to imagine more, even feeling the emotions of the people who lived through it."

As we continued to chat, I did not get the feeling Gavin was trying to overwhelm me with his knowledge. He truly wanted me to understand his excitement. He seemed charming and lively, not the buffoon I'd assumed him to be. Maybe I'd been too quick to judge. I was surprised to be warming up to him, getting the sense that he felt unappreciated and maybe even edged out of the project by the women.

Though, on the other hand, at Ainsley's house, he'd struck me as an insufferable boor. Maybe he'd been wound up about something personal and stressful that had nothing to do with the book?

As the appetizer plates were cleared, I turned my attention to Glenda. Her husband had not once looked away from our conversation, and I was afraid she would be feeling neglected. And possibly annoyed with me.

"This is such an astonishing and complex project," I said. "What is your role in getting it accomplished?"

"Gavin needs me—it's that simple." She dropped her voice. "The others constantly nag him or argue, and it's positively draining. He knows I'm a hundred and ten percent on his side of the ledger, both emotionally and financially. He's so brilliant, but the small things sometimes slide right by him." She glanced at him with an expression both irritated and adoring.

"He's so lucky to have you," I said. "I've not even been married a year, so we're still finding our way."

She let loose a peal of laughter. "Oh that first year, doesn't it plummet from peak to valley?"

As we chatted, I noticed that she pushed her food around her plate without eating much of it. From the tiny size of her, I suspected this was not uncommon. But it also could be a sign of physical or emotional distress.

"How are you feeling?" I asked her, lowering my voice so Ainsley wouldn't overhear the question. "You had quite a scare the other night."

"You know, it was terrifying," she said. "At first, I thought perhaps I'd eaten a bit more than normal or that some of that heavy food didn't agree with me. But then the stabbing pains got worse, and I was afraid I'd die." She closed her eyes and pressed the back of her hand to her forehead. She blinked them open. "I know Ainsley thinks the world of her, but I do not trust that cook, not for one moment. Plenty of times my stomach has been upset after leaving a meeting at their home. Everything she makes is overdone to the point of nauseating."

Based on my small experience of Grace's cooking, I did not agree with Glenda's assessment. Did she actually believe that Grace put something in her scones to make her ill on visits before the party? That seemed unlikely, but I made a small noise of sympathy to keep her talking.

"And furthermore, she does not like me," Glenda added. "I think she fancies my husband."

"Is that so?" According to Blair, it had been Gavin who fancied Grace, not the other way around. I wanted to ask her straight out if she thought that Grace had intentionally tried to harm her, but here at the table was not the right place. "Were you acquainted with Mr. Booth, the man who fell from the wheel?"

She shivered and clutched her arms to her chest. "Why, oh why would they come around flashing that dead man's photo at us when we had nothing to do with him?" She glanced at her husband, her cheeks flushed with worry. "I, for one, cannot wait until this work is completed. It's been very hard on my Gavin."

After we'd eaten our main courses and been served a potpourri of Scottish cheeses and shortbread cookies to finish, Vera stood to get the attention of the table. She looked drawn and pale. "If we could wrap up breakfast by nine in the morning, we will start off for Glencoe. We plan to spend the rest of the day there so our team can consult on photos, and then travel to Loch Long for the night, where we'll be having dinner with our publisher, who is driving in from Glasgow. I wish you all a pleasant evening." She sounded like a tour guide at the end of a long trip that had been oversubscribed with difficult travelers.

As we started back to our rooms, I checked my phone and noticed that I had missed a call from Nathan. "I'll see you in a bit," I told Vera. "I'm going to the lobby to chat with your brother."

"Tell him we're taking good care of you," Vera said. "He need not fret."

Nathan picked up on the second ring. "How was your outing?" I asked, so happy to hear his voice. "Did you play like Tiger?"

Nathan snorted. "I can't even describe how bad it was. It was as though I'd never seen, never mind touched, a golf club. It was as if you were playing instead of me." We both laughed.

"Thanks a lot," I said. "For all you know I could be the most coordinated person in the world."

"I'll say one thing, I miss you like crazy," he said, sounding more mellow than usual, which I attributed to the whiskey and having nothing to worry about but bad golf. His job as a senior detective in the Key West Police Department was super stressful, both physically and mentally—especially during these times when a few bad apple cops made all of them look potentially bad. He had needed a break from our island and its troubles for a while.

"Vera's two cats have taken over our bed and left me only the smallest knife edge of space. They lie on my legs, and it feels as though I'm wearing a lead apron. And the purring is so loud, it's like being back on Miss Gloria's houseboat. And I can't tell one from the other."

I felt a quick stab of homesickness—for him, for Key West, for our animals. "That sounds so lovely. It's easy to tell them apart if you look. Archie has more white on his face than Louise, and she's much more outgoing and chatty. Are you having a good time in spite of the golf?"

"I'm enjoying my brother-in-law, and we had the most amazing bagpipe performance and whiskey tasting."

"That sounds an awful lot like our evening." I gave him a summary of lunch and the parade and then dinner, and my new assessments of Gavin and Glenda. As I talked, I wondered whether I should tell him that I'd visited Joseph Booth's family home. I decided I'd better, so I spilled that news quickly. Even more quickly, I segued from his possible dismay by wondering aloud whether I should tell Vera about this too. After all, I had shared this information with Nathan's mother, and I thought Vera might resent that I'd kept it from her.

"There is something going on between these people who are supposed to be old friends, and I have no idea what it is. Why won't any of them talk about it? Why would they even do this project together if there are that many problems? That much tension?"

I realized that I didn't truly understand the relationships between these three women. "They've been friends for a long time and now work together on this book, but how have things changed over time? Ainsley appears to be keeping her distance from Vera. Glenda distrusts everyone. Is it possible that she thinks of Gavin as a rock star, maybe a little bit out of her league? Maybe easily tempted by other women, including these two?"

"Wait, let's back up a minute," he said, sounding a lot less sleepy. I pictured him sitting up in bed and shoveling Archie and Louise over to my side. "Why in the world were you making a house call to the Booth family? And who went with you?"

I explained that I had discovered his family living right in town, and this had been my only chance to chat with them, and no one else was available. "It was two sad ladies plying me with baked goods on doilies. And they won the best scone in the country contest recently and I hoped I could get their recipe. Alas, not to be. But I swear I was in no danger. And they think he left the University because of a love triangle."

"And this has become your problem because?"

"Because it's your sister, and we are her guests, and we were right there when these incidents happened. And I swear she knew Mr. Booth, and I'm worried that she herself could end up in danger. And you know perfectly well that it would go against my human nature not to ask questions."

"And it would be deeply embedded in my human nature to worry about you. And I wish you would leave the poking and prodding to the professionals." I heard him sigh. "I should never have agreed to this tournament. I should be right there watching over all of you." Another big sigh. "I'm going to stop at the local police department tomorrow before we tee off and see what I can squeeze out of them. What does Vera say about it?"

"Vera is so tightlipped that I'm surprised she can eat."

After we both said, "I love you," and he had made me swear that I would absolutely stick with the group, especially Miss Gloria, Vera, and his mother, I hung up, stood up, and stretched. The bar looked appealing, light sparkling with flashes of blue and pink through the bottles arranged on the counter, the people laughing, those lovely Scottish accents. Gavin, Glenda, and Ainsley were sitting at one table in the back, heads close together. Which totally surprised me after the scuffle following Grace's dinner the other night. But I had promised Nathan no more solo butting in, so I returned to the room. Vera was in bed but said a muffled hello.

"Nathan sends his love," I said. "Do you mind if I ask one question?"

"If it's not too hard to answer," she mumbled.

"Your friends don't seem to enjoy one another or see eye to eye. I'm just so curious about how and why you all agreed to work on this project," I said.

"Oh, that's not an easy question," she said. "That's a lifetime of complications." She rolled over and put a pillow over her head. "I'll think about it and maybe get back to you tomorrow."

Which sounded like a polite way of saying "mind your own business."

Chapter Seventeen

No matter what you write about, you're writing about food. It's what brings us together, and sometimes separates us, but we've all got to eat.

—David Lebowitz

After a filling Scottish breakfast of eggs, bacon, and assorted scones, we set out in Vera's car again. As we drove, the scenery grew only more fantastic, with sweeping green vistas and, off in the distance, mountains peeking out of clouds of mist. The land was largely empty except for sheep and the occasional tour bus pulled off the road to allow its occupants to stretch their legs and take photos.

"Sounds like you have a busy day ahead," I said to Vera.

She grimaced, glancing at me. "An understatement. If you don't mind, I'm going to leave the three of you to explore the site on your own. I really need to walk the land with Gavin and the others to make sure we get the photos we promised."

"That's fine," I said, looking over my shoulder at the others, who also chimed in with their agreement.

"We weren't expecting a full-time tour guide," Helen added. "It's amazing enough to have you escorting us to your favorite places. What should we expect to see?"

Vera flashed a tight smile. "The most amazing views ever. Plus you'll learn about the sorrowful history of the glen. Don't skip the short movie in the visitor's center—they did a wonderful job capturing the historical background. You'll see in living technicolor the heart of the conflict that gave me the idea for our book."

"Looking forward to this," Helen said from the back seat.

Vera added, "If you're still looking for souvenirs, you will enjoy the gift shop very much, though it's not inexpensive. They carry tartan scarves and other clothing and local jewelry—things like that. And of course, the shop is loaded with requisite Harry Potter and *Outlander* gifts." She let out a sigh that sounded exasperated. "You'll probably recognize the scenery from the opening credits of *Outlander*. And if you've seen *Harry Potter and the Prisoner of Azkaban*, you might recognize the backdrop for Hagrid's Hut. This is the kind of thing that irks me about tourists today. We will be visiting the site of a horrific massacre, and yet people are skipping over the historic displays and browsing for souvenirs based on fiction."

Which sounded a bit harsh, considering that while Miss Gloria was definitely searching for *Outlander* and Harry Potter keepsakes, she would also be tuned into the tragedy of the area. But Vera was under a lot of pressure, so I realized it would be best to keep my mouth zipped.

We chatted a little more about the ecology of the glen, and then I checked my visor mirror to see what the occupants of the backseat were doing. Miss Gloria had dropped off to sleep, and Helen was quiet, listening to something through her earbuds. I took this chance to ask the question I had tried last night without results.

What I wanted to say was "Why in the world are you working with these people, when the tension is thick as frozen Irish butter between all of you?" I tried to frame it more gently.

"How did your thin places project get started? And what are you calling it?" I asked Vera.

She let out another big sigh, glanced over at me, her green eyes wide. "Interesting that you should bring up the title, because that summarizes exactly the problems we are having." She fell silent for a few minutes, then said, "Maybe five or so years ago, William and I went on a road trip and visited some of the same places we are taking you to. At many of them, I felt a physical jolt, a sense of something luminous that words could not describe. We were traveling in the off season, when there weren't a lot of other tourists to distract us. And I believe that relative emptiness of the landscapes helped me realize what was under the surface. I literally felt as though I was communicating with or almost stepping into a different space and time."

She stopped speaking, as though remembering that trip and what it had triggered.

"I'd never heard of thin places before coming here," I said. "But I believe that Miss Gloria feels these things while she's leading tours at the cemetery. And my friend Lorenzo has mentioned something like this too. I think he experiences life the way you're describing. He talks about Key West having a special energy, and the current of energy running around the perimeter. He thinks our island is being ruined, overrun by tourists and the money-hungry politicians and businesspeople who want to take advantage of it."

Vera looked sad. "This is a problem. People crave the experience of beautiful, spiritual places, but that very experience can be destroyed by mobs of visitors." She tapped out a rhythm on the steering wheel with her fingers. "When we returned home from that trip, I began to write about what I'd seen— but more importantly, felt. This might sound a little wacky, but it was almost as if something spiritual had filled my mind and heart and taken the lead. I had also taken masses of photographs. In some of them—though I didn't even see this at the time—you could hardly tell where sky ended and land or sea began. And slowly the idea for the book emerged: thin places, where the veil between heaven and earth is lifted."

"It sounds like the original idea you envisioned has gotten a bit distorted as it's developed?"

"Yup," Vera said glumly. "It was a bit of a Hobson's choice because I knew I couldn't pull it off alone. Who would believe an American claiming to be an expert in Scottish history? It certainly wouldn't sell in Scotland."

I clucked sympathetically.

"One day while having tea with Ainsley," she continued, "I wondered aloud whether and how it would be possible to help visitors connect with the thin places in this country. She loved the concept right away and said she knew an editor at a press that might be interested. This editor, whom you will meet tonight, was excited about the idea, with some caveats. As I'd predicted, he was not thrilled with me being a transplant from America. And he wanted gorgeous photographs, sexier than any I had taken. Or had the skill to take. I have a pretty good eye, but I'm certainly no professional photographer. Ainsley was happy to work with me on the project."

"What exactly is her role?" I asked.

"She's the business manager, my sounding board, my first reader—she's good at all of that. And she has a beautiful sense of design." She made a face. "And for better or worse, she brought in the other talent. Of course, I knew Glenda and Gavin from college days, but I wouldn't necessarily have chosen them as collaborators." Another grimace.

I wanted to know more about these relationships, but I'd ask her all in good time. "What did you end up calling the book?"

"I never had a perfectly satisfying title, but I was thinking something in the realm of *Tearing the Veil: Rediscovering the Thin Places of Scotland*. Or should it be 'piercing the veil'? Or maybe *Thin Places: A Walk in Two Worlds*. Anyway, that's how I pitched it generally."

"What did the publisher ultimately choose?"

Her lips tightened. "They chose Gavin's working title. *Bloody Blades: Crossing the Thresholds of History*."

"Ugh. That's hideous, nothing like your versions, which were all lovely. Tell me more about how everyone got involved."

"Ainsley got very excited and suggested Glenda might be interested in investing. Next thing I knew, Glenda called me and said her husband would be thrilled to participate. I knew him a bit from university days. He was a brilliant lecturer and had published before, and he had the kind of name that could raise the project into another league. Unfortunately, the further we got into researching and writing, the clearer it became that our visions were not aligned."

"There's no way to compromise or split the project up?" I asked. From my experience with my first boss at *Key Zest* magazine, I knew something about trying to work with someone you weren't getting along with. Especially if the other person held most of the cards. That relationship had ended poorly.

"It's a little late now to adjust. Absolutely everything is due on Martin's desk at the end of next week. My fear is that Gavin has won the publisher over and that they will market this like a video game, which is absolutely anathema to experiencing the spiritual nature of these natural treasures."

I thought she might cry.

"Honestly, this trip is an attempt to resuscitate my original vision. Especially here in Glencoe, but also Tobermory and Iona. I'm hoping their beauty and spirit will be powerful enough to pull Gavin into their orbit. Because I don't think I can persuade him alone. He's very stubborn and very much fixed on his expanded-reality idea. And where he goes, Glenda follows. With her family money. And I'm beginning to think Ainsley follows too."

She bumped off the road into a parking lot nestled in a stand of trees set back against the mountains. Murmuring noises of people waking up came from the back seat.

"Are we there yet?" Miss Gloria asked, and then giggled, fluffing her tousled hair with her fingers. Helen stretched and retrieved a small brush from her purse. She ran it through her hair so her bob fell perfectly into place. We got out of the car and walked toward the welcome center. Up ahead, Gavin, Glenda, and Ainsley waited in front of the wood, stone, and glass visitors' center.

"This is lovely," Helen said, pausing to absorb the building, which looked like a big tree house set against the mountains in the background.

"Everything was designed to reflect the setting, and every inch made ecologically cognizant," Gavin said. "I was gobsmacked when I first visited. It used to be a cramped little shack that did nothing to enhance the experience."

"What's up next?" Miss Gloria asked, and I saw Vera wince.

"As I was telling Hayley, I need to do some work with the others for an hour and a half or so. That will give you time to visit the center and walk some of the nature trails, and then we can meet up for tea. Is that okay?"

"Right-o," said Miss Gloria, with a wide grin. "Tea is always welcome. Until then, we'll be absolutely fine."

I took her arm and we headed for the building, Helen right behind. Inside the vestibule, I stopped to admire the dappled light let in by the soaring ceiling and floor-to-ceiling windows. High above the welcome desk a motto had been painted: "Living on the Edge." Which perfectly described this perch on the edge of the mountains, as well as Vera's powerful urge to go deeper into her adopted country.

"We should start with the movie," Helen suggested. "Then maybe hike one of the nature trails? And certainly take a spin through the gift shop, and after that a scone and a cup of tea for your article, Hayley?" She sounded all jolly and seemed to have forgiven me for leaving her behind yesterday.

We sat through the short film, which was an overview of the ecology of the glen and then the history of the clans in the late 1600s. Having watched all of the seasons of *Outlander*, I thought I would have been better prepared for the battles. The creators of the film had done a good job of explaining the falling dominos that had led to the Glencoe massacre. But they hadn't sugarcoated the violence. In a nutshell, the MacDonald clan chief had been slow to swear his allegiance to King William of Scotland and England. In retaliation, soldiers who'd been billeted to the homes of these Highlanders were instructed to murder many of the men and boys. Women and children fled to the mountains and froze to death in blizzard conditions.

"Excruciating to watch," I said once the lights came on and we were filing out of the little auditorium. "I don't know what is wrong with people."

"I suppose the fights in the western world happen more on social media than on battlefields these days," said Helen. "Equally vicious, but not as physical."

Back in the lobby, I spotted a large section of books in the gift store, and they were calling to me. "Do you mind if we take a quick peek in here and then go on our walk?" I suggested.

"Fine," Miss Gloria said.

"I'll wait outside on the bench," said Helen. "I could use fifteen minutes of sun on my face. It's not so easy to get vitamin D in Scotland."

"We'll see you there," I said.

Inside the shop, I was drawn immediately to *Outlander Kitchen: The Official Outlander Companion Cookbook*, with a woman holding a basket of bite-sized chocolate and strawberry tarts on the cover. I leafed through pages of gorgeous photos, snippets of text from the *Outlander* books, and droolworthy recipes.

I was torn. I loved the photos and the connection to Scotland and the TV show we enjoyed, but as I lived on a houseboat, stark choices had to be made. I did not own shelves and shelves and shelves for cookbooks in my new kitchen; I had one small ledge. If I brought a new cookbook in, something had to go out. I turned the page and found Fiona's cinnamon scones—a layered pastry laced with cinnamon and topped with a drizzle of white icing. My stomach growled. Though I had gone to visit the Booth sisters looking for clues to Joseph's death, I'd left their home with a serious craving for scone recipes.

I made a decision to buy the cookbook, based on the cinnamon scones and a recipe for a fish pie, crammed with fish and scallops and shrimp in a white sauce and topped with cheesy mashed potatoes, that made my mouth water. I thought this fish pie would translate well to my Key West kitchen. Key West pink shrimp and either yellowtail or grouper fish would be amazing in this presentation. Even my newish boss, Palamina, who stayed thin as pipe cleaner because she held back from eating anything too delicious, would be tempted.

And there were several recipes that I thought my mother would love for her catering business, including an onion tart that could be cut into bite-sized pieces and the tiny chocolate pies in a flaky crust I'd seen on the cover. In the end, I overcame the thought of Nathan's eye-rolling when he discovered that I had slipped the books into his luggage, and bought two copies, one for me and one for her. I fitted the books into my backpack and went outside to look for the others. Helen was waiting for me on the deck in back of the building, but there was no sign of Miss Gloria.

"Is she coming?" Helen asked, looking behind me and adding a laugh. "I've never seen anyone so excited about choosing the right gifts for her friends. She is such a treasure. I hope I have half of her energy when I get to her age."

"I lost track of her," I said, peering around the deck and getting an uneasy feeling. I was the one who'd been fooling around in the gift shop, not Miss Gloria. I hadn't noticed her in there at all. I tried to think where she would've gone. "Maybe she started off on the nature trail on her own? Or maybe she saw Vera and went with her? Or probably she made a stop in the restroom."

"I'll wait here so we don't lose each other," said Helen.

I checked the ladies' room, calling for her in case she was in one of the stalls, and then the gift shop again as I knew Miss G was excited about bringing presents home.

But the slight uneasiness I'd noticed was developing into a sick feeling in the pit of my stomach. My friend had been quiet all morning, never so quiet as during and after the little film that described the massacre of the MacDonald clan. I should have stuck closer to her, not spent so much time perusing recipes. I should have noticed signs that she might be troubled.

"She's probably gone looking for the ruins of the cottage," I said. "And that worries me because she takes these emotional things so hard."

We studied the map describing the various nature trails, and took a narrow path carpeted in grass in the direction of the ruins, where the farmers of the MacDonald clan had lived in the late 1600s. As we drew closer, we saw piles of stones covered in moss and lichens that would have been the foundations of their cottages.

My heart rate began to rise as I heard a terrible moaning noise. In the distance near the green stones, I spotted Gavin trotting toward the noise from the opposite direction. But no sign of Miss Gloria.

Finally, I saw her, crouched in a stand of ferns next to the mossy stones, keening like an injured animal. I tore up the path, vaulted over the rocks, and squatted nearby so I didn't startle her. She was wearing some kind of big black goggles and had her hands clapped over her ears.

"Look out! Look out!" she yelled as I edged closer, and pointed at something that I could not see or hear. "They're coming—oh, be careful!" She looked around wildly, emitting little squeaks of fear.

"It's okay," I said, touching her hand so she'd sense it was only me. "It's me, Hayley. We're all okay." I put my arms around her and rocked her gently like a baby. "Can I take these?" I asked, touching the sidepiece of the goggles.

She nodded without seeming to recognize me. I slid the eyepiece off her head, and handed it over to Gavin, who was standing helplessly beside the path, a few feet away. Glenda, Helen, and Vera waited behind him, looking horrified.

Miss Gloria's eyes grew wide and distant again. She was breathing quickly and started to whimper. "Oh no, oh no, I'm so cold." And she began to shiver.

"It's okay," I said. I realized that she must be, in some way I did not quite understand, experiencing the massacre of her people. And whatever had been shown on Gavin's goggles was part of what had set her off. "Everything's going to be okay. You're here with me right now, and that history has already happened. Years ago. It's all over."

The tears began streaming down her face. I reached into my pocket to find a tissue and pat her cheeks. I didn't know whether this was like a night terror, where you weren't supposed to startle the person awake, or whether I should somehow try to snap her out of the place she had found and bring her back to safety. Helen marched over to us.

"Let's go get a cup of hot tea," she suggested. She reached for Miss Gloria's hand and pulled her to her feet. "The world always looks better with a hot drink and maybe a buttered scone, don't you think?" She circled her arm around my friend's shoulders and steered her down the path toward to the visitor center. I dropped back a few feet to talk to Gavin.

"What the hell was that?" I hissed. "Why did she have those on?"

Vera glowered at him from the other side of me. "What the hell were you thinking?"

He shrugged, hands in his pockets. "We were chatting, and she said she was strongly getting the sense of her ancestors. And she wished she could be there, that she felt so helpless not being able to live with them in those moments. Maybe warn them what was coming. I offered her a few minutes to try the glasses—that's it. How was I to know she'd wig out?"

"It wasn't his fault," Glenda said, a sharp edge in her voice. She stepped in front of her husband and turned to face us. "We were scoping out the extra photos that you insisted we needed, which, by the way, is a lot of unnecessary work. And then she interrupted—barreled right up to us and begged to borrow his goggles. Next thing we know, she is screaming to us to get out of the way, that someone is coming for us. She went bat-shit crazy. We tried to help, but she wouldn't let us anywhere near her."

At that moment, I wanted to strangle her, but I knew it was mostly because I hated witnessing how upset my friend had gotten. And I felt guilty for not looking out for her. We all should have paid a little more attention to this old lady who was more sensitive than most people and primed to feel overwhelmed by the ghosts of her ancestors in this glen. I paused, took a deep breath, and turned away from the others to look back at the tumble of mossy stones. I listened for voices, for the sounds of battle, even for the sounds of ordinary, peaceful farming life. But I heard nothing.

I trudged behind the others, who were still arguing about the use of the goggles. Vera ignored Glenda, focusing on Gavin, and obviously working on sounding reasonable while still angry.

"Let's set our competing artistic visions aside for a moment. If this tragic interlude has shown us anything," Vera said to Gavin, "it's shown us that we need to understand how in the world you intend to include these as a part of my book without putting us all at great risk for legal action. How many people would react the way Miss Gloria did?"

"*Your* book?" Gavin asked. His voice was calm, but his expression told me he was furious too. "You would not have a contract if it wasn't for me. Or perhaps, you'd have a little book with a little press that no one outside of your cultish followers would read." He steamed off down the path, with Glenda stalking behind him.

"This project is nothing like what I had envisioned," Vera called after them.

Glenda turned back to holler, "It's a good damn thing we are not following your vision because it was a losing proposition. Everyone could see that except for you."

Chapter Eighteen

The March Hare took the watch and looked at it gloomily: then he dipped it into his cup of tea, and looked at it again: but he could think of nothing better to say than his first remark, "It was the best butter, you know."
—Lewis Carroll, *Alice's Adventures in Wonderland*

We retired to the cafeteria for a quick sandwich and a cup of tea. My mother-in-law insisted that Miss Gloria order soup even though she said she wasn't hungry.

"You'll need to keep up your strength after a shock like the one you've had," Helen told her, and practically spoon-fed her the cream of celeriac soup and the miniature cheese scone that came with it.

Vera was silent as we ate and so was Miss Gloria, so I chattered mindlessly about the cookbooks I had bought and the recipes I planned to try first. I felt like an idiot, but this trip seemed to be spiraling out of control, and I didn't know how to fix it. Finally, we finished our light meal, gathered our trash, and carried our trays to the rubbish cans.

"Are you sure you don't want to see a doctor?" Helen asked Miss Gloria on the way to the parking lot. "We could get you checked out and then meet the others at the lake? I'm sure it wouldn't be an inconvenience." She glanced at her daughter who nodded.

In fact, I was sure it would be an inconvenience, but Vera would certainly want to do the right thing.

Miss Gloria shook her head and flashed a small smile, a pale shadow of her usual chipper self. "I'll be fine. All I need is a little cat nap and I'll be ready for the next adventure." Then she set her lips into a firm line, which I knew meant there would be no point in arguing. Nor was she ready to talk about what she'd experienced.

I sat in the back seat with her this time, and she fell asleep holding my hand before we even left the parking lot. I felt the comforting warmth of her head as it hit my shoulder. I stroked her wrist and her fingers, freckled with age spots, the skin thin enough that I could almost see the blood beating in her veins. I had to remember—and help the others remember—that she was more fragile inside than she let us see on the outside.

"Tell us about what to expect for the rest of the day and the evening?" Helen asked her daughter.

Vera heaved a big sigh. "I am so sorry to have dragged you all into this drama. I never should have brought you on this trip. I was dreaming when I thought this would go smoothly." She glanced in the rearview mirror at my sleeping friend. "Instead, all hell's broken loose, and I've wreaked psychological havoc on your dear friend."

"We wouldn't trade this trip for anything," I said in a low voice, because that was mostly true and I didn't want her to feel worse than she already did. "We are seeing things in a different way from any tourists. Miss Gloria will be fine—she's just tired. I'm sure she would say the same thing." I stroked a wisp of white hair off her forehead. "She's an emotional soul, and it's my fault that I didn't stay with her."

"I hardly think it's your fault," said Vera. "Any fault can be centered squarely on Gavin, who is too self-absorbed to think past his own greedy fantasies." She shook her head. "Tonight, we are having dinner with the publisher, Martin. That should be a barrel of laughs." She barked out a snort of laughter. "Those of us working on the book need to meet with him before dinner. We will see you in the bar for a drink. And then everyone will retire to the restaurant for dinner. One of their restaurant's specialties is fried fish and chips with mushy peas."

Miss Gloria popped awake. "Fried fish and chips, yes! Mushy peas, the jury is out." Then she dropped back to sleep, a big grin on her face.

Vera forced a return smile. "After we eat, you'll hear some fabulous local musicians, including pianist and folk singer Alan Reid, and Jack Beck who plays the guitar and sings. He lives in America now but was born in Scotland and toured here with a folk band for many years before he married an American. It should be a very special evening."

Helen cleared her throat and glanced at her daughter. "I don't suppose you'll want to talk about what's going on with the publisher."

"I don't suppose I do," Vera snapped.

In silence, Vera navigated a series of roads winding through the mountains. The Loch Long Hotel finally appeared in the distance, a four-story white stucco building set against the mountains and across the road from the end of a narrow lake. I shook Miss Gloria awake. "We're here."

"Everybody's got their own room this time," Vera explained as she pulled into the parking lot. "I didn't want us to get on each other's one last nerve. And that was before I even knew what was going to happen at Glencoe." She chuckled but didn't sound happy. "I asked for Miss Gloria to have a room on the ground floor because their elevators can be wonky."

Miss Gloria blinked her eyes wide open. "I'm quite capable of stairs. In fact, they help me get my daily steps in."

"If I'd realized you were such a live wire, I wouldn't have worried," Vera said, glancing back in the rearview mirror.

We dragged our bags out of the trunk and into the lobby, which had an old-fashioned flavor, with tan plaid upholstery on the backs of black leather banquettes, and faded gold curtains framing the windows that overlooked the lake.

"The bar is in that direction," said Vera, pointing to the left. "If the barkeep isn't behind the bar when you show up, holler into the back room to put out an alert. But don't worry, they are loaded with Scottish whiskey and beer and anything else that strikes your fancy. We'll try to join you for cocktails, but definitely dinner at seven with music to follow."

My room was located on the top floor in the far back corner of the building, overlooking the mountains. I dragged my bag through a warren of narrow hallways and staircases to reach it, wondering if I should have left a trail of crumbs to find my way back to the lobby. The room was furnished with blond wood built-ins and more plaid pillows, plain but functional. I had just about enough space for me and my luggage, so I had to admit a sigh of relief that I wasn't sharing the night with Nathan's mother, or even Vera, much as I liked and admired them both. I needed some time to unwind from the events of the last few days. And despite her protests that she was absolutely fine, I was certain Miss Gloria did as well.

I carried my toiletries into the small bathroom, delighted to notice a hot towel rack. I could swish out some undies and socks and be sure they were dry for the next day. I flipped off my shoes, peeled back the coverlet, and stretched out on the bed, hoping I could catch Nathan. I texted him about our arrival.

Call me if you get a minute in the next half hour or so, or don't get in too late tonight. We had kind of a wild day. Everything's okay, I just want to hear your voice. It is our honeymoon after all. I added some laughing and crazy-face emojis to let him know I was mostly joking.

Then I called my friend Lorenzo, hoping it wasn't too early for his night owl schedule—I'd known him to sleep until almost noon. His voice sounded a little fuzzy but also happy to hear me.

"Are you home already?" he asked. "I can't wait to hear about the trip. Did you bring me a cute redhead in a kilt?"

We both laughed. "Not yet' to both your questions, but we have enough time for me to keep looking. I need to float something by you." I paused. "I'm a little worried about Miss Gloria."

I described the devastating scene in the Glencoe ruins. "I've never felt anything like that, not even little tremors of old spirits. Not the way you do. But obviously she was experiencing something terrifying. I'm wondering if you have any advice on how to help her. Is she going to be all right?"

The words kept pouring out of me. "The worst of it was with those dratted headphones. I would like to strangle those people for inflicting that much distress on a sensitive soul." I made myself pause and take a deep breath. "I don't know how much to press her to talk about it or whether I should leave her alone to sort things out for a while in private? Or what?"

"That sounds so painful," he said. "I'm so sorry she went through that. It's a blessing and a curse, this ability to see through the veil between the worlds. I can tell you, from my own experience, the worst thing you can do is tell her she didn't feel those things or see them. Which I know you wouldn't do," he hastened to add. "After she's rested, invite her to tell you about it. If it seems like she's disappearing back into the battle, sometimes a touch on her arm or shoulder and a soft word can help anchor her in the present."

All that felt reassuring and exactly right. "What else is new in Key West?" I asked, feeling the same spike of homesickness that I'd felt talking to him last time. Scotland was beautiful—stunning in fact—but it wasn't home. I could only imagine how hard the transition between countries might have been for Vera as a traumatized teenager. "Have you heard anything new about the incident with Ray?" I asked.

"What's new in Key West is that my tree is chockablock with ripe mangoes," he said. "Your mother came over yesterday and carried off a couple dozen. She's catering a mango madness dinner, and she promised to save me a plate. She's making a bourbon-marinated pork roast with spicy mango salsa, a green salad with walnuts and mangoes and some kind of fancy cheese, and an almond cake with mango puree."

"That sounds like heaven," I said. "I hope there will be a few left when we get home."

"Definitely. Nothing really new about Ray." He paused, making me think he was either thinking hard or figuring out how to share difficult news. Though he never labeled bad news "bad news," he always described it as "a life challenge."

"Your mom brought Connie to my booth at Sunset last night," he continued.

I waited for the bad news, thinking that's truly what it had to be.

"She's distraught," he said, more blunt than usual. "The more he won't talk about what's going on, the bigger the problems he must be experiencing, or so she imagines. Your mother convinced Connie to let me read three cards." An ominous silence. "She drew the ten of swords, death, and the three of swords."

I pulled these three cards up in my mind's eye. They were on my top ten list of six you don't ever want to see in your reading. The ten of swords was a horribly shocking card, a man on his back with ten swords stabbed into him, often interpreted as a pending unwelcome surprise. The gravity of its meaning could depend on whether Lorenzo saw Ray's "surprise" in the future or the past. The death card—enough said. As often as my friend told me not to take this card literally, it was hard to avoid the visceral fear that spiked in me every time. The three of swords I wasn't that familiar with, but how could swords mean anything good? I waited to see how Lorenzo would spin this selection.

Lorenzo said, "It's not as though what's in his heart and his life has been brought on by the cards, you know that, right?"

This was going to be bad. "I know that. Go on."

"I told her that if he was sitting in the chair across from me, I would advise him to remember that the cards help him prepare for what's in his life, what's coming. And that knowing what's coming helps a person prepare in advance, both emotionally and literally. If someone is stabbing him in the back, wouldn't he want to know that?"

A text came in from Vera, reminding me that the group was gathering in the bar. *Are you coming? Miss Gloria looks like she could use some support from a friend.*

I said goodbye to Lorenzo and thanked him for talking with me. "I'll keep you posted, and I know you'll do the same."

Chapter Nineteen

Mr. Scott was a pale, thin man. A stick of forced rhu-
barb said Sally's mother, who had seen him at a parents
meeting.

—Ann Cleeves, *Raven Black*

I wended my way back down four levels of stairs and went directly to the bar. On the wooden counter sat the biggest collection of whiskey bottles I'd ever seen. Remembering how delicious the cream whiskey had tasted at Ainsley's welcome dinner, I requested a small glass of something similar, even though the bartender warned me this was a dessert libation.

Drink in hand, I turned around to find my people. The two musicians were setting up their instruments in a small alcove one step up from the lobby. They were older fellows, with graying hair and slightly weathered faces, who laughed and talked together like longtime friends.

"They look like a couple of elves, don't they?" Vera came up behind me, and we shared a grin. "Wait until you hear them play and sing. You'll think you're back in old-time Scotland."

She leaned in to whisper: "I'm a little worried about Gloria. I'm glad you're here."

She tipped her head in the direction of my friend, who was perched on a couch next to Helen. She was holding a glass filled with ice and a clear liquid, but her face looked pale and tired. The others in the group sat nearby, and the division between them was palpable. Gavin, Glenda, and Ainsley were seated on one side of a man who must be their publisher, and on the other side, an empty space where I imagined Vera had been sitting.

"Come say hello to Martin before dinner," Vera said.

"Perfect," I answered, making a beeline for Miss Gloria. I leaned in for a hug. "Everything okay?"

"Great," she said raising her glass in a toast. "I am abstaining tonight, on account of risky whiskey overload this week. Sometimes an old lady is too tired to tipple."

"I've never heard that from you before," I laughed, and rubbed my hand across her bony shoulders.

"Martin, this is my new sister-in-law, Hayley," said Vera, "and Hayley, this is my esteemed publisher, Martin. He puts out absolutely stunning books."

"Why thank you, my dear," he said, and shook my hand with great enthusiasm. Martin was not what I would've expected had I put much thought into it. I would've imagined an introvert with stooped shoulders and reading glasses, gray-haired, quiet, and wise. Martin was none of that, though it was too early to judge about his wisdom. He had a shock of black hair; a round, bordering on rotund belly; and a laugh to match it. "I adore your sister-in-law and her team, and couldn't be more excited about this project."

Vera announced that we'd been called to dinner, and we followed the others into the dining room. The room was decorated in more blond wood and plaid upholstery. I wondered whose clan was represented by all this tan plaid.

As we reached our table, Vera once again took charge of the seating. "Hayley and Mom, I thought you might like to sit next to Martin since you've not met before."

Was she being polite to her guests, to make us feel included? Because it almost felt as though she needed to marshal her troops around her boss. I wondered what had already happened in their meeting and whether she was afraid she was going to be dumped. I refocused on the conversation at the table, where Martin was expressing his powerful desire to visit the states, even in spite of our recent political turmoil.

"It's so funny, isn't it, that my friend Vera was desperate to write a book about the special places in Scotland when she comes from the wild and wonderful world of America?"

"America is all well and good," Vera said, "but here you have thin places and astonishing history, and craggy mountains, wild seas, and windswept islands. And now the rest of the world knows that because of the amazing fiction that's coming out of this country." She smiled warmly, and I suspected that she was still trying to stay calm and win him over to her perspective on their project. "Ann Cleeves, Diana Gabaldon, J. K. Rowling—Scotland exactly as she is couldn't be a hotter topic."

"It's all been done," said Gavin, from his place on the other side of Helen. "No one wants a quiet book anymore. And that's why we're expanding our horizons."

"He does have a point," said Ainslie, glancing at Vera with a pleading look on her face. Which made me realize that I'd hardly seen Vera's friend all day.

"And I must say everyone at the press is thrilled with the way the final photography for the book is shaping up," Martin said. "Ainsley shared the proofs from the Peebles parade and Glencoe—magnificent!"

The waitress made her rounds, and I wavered over what to choose—steak and ale pie or fish? In the end, I ordered the fried fish and chips with mushy peas that had been calling to me since Vera had mentioned them earlier. Raised voices from the other end of the table snapped my attention back to our party.

"It makes no difference how lovely your photos are, what you are doing with the goggles and the bar codes and whatever else you might come up with is wrong." Vera was hissing now at Gavin, her face red with outrage. "It is not right to capitalize on the tragedy and hurt of other people's ancestors for the purposes of your financial gain and reputation."

"Can we defer this discussion until after dinner, please?" Ainsley asked, her voice pleading. "It's going to give us all indigestion. I'm sure we can come to some kind of arrangement that will be satisfactory to everybody."

"I hardly think that's possible," said Gavin. "Some of us believe the book should be quiet and boring in order to sell as few copies as possible, and others of us want to separate this book from the slavering pack of wannabes."

Martin held up his hand, as if to intervene, as the waitress came around with a bottle of red wine in one hand and white in the other. She filled all of our glasses, and the publisher proposed a toast.

"To my fiery team, and the magnificent product they are in the process of producing. *Slàinte mhath*." He raised his glass and then downed half of it in one swallow. Between Helen and me, we were able to steer him into talking about the other titles his company published and what it was like where he lived and worked in Glasgow.

Not long after, our dinners were delivered, saving us from more possible unpleasant discussion. I focused on tasting the tender white fish, wrapped in its thick batter crust, and the crispy potatoes piled all around it. I snapped a few photos and made notes in my phone. Situated as it was in the middle of the ocean, Key West was well known for seafood, though the preparation was not often fried. This was something special, and iconic to Scotland.

"You should at least taste the mushy peas," I teased Miss Gloria, who had eaten very little of her dinner. "As vegetables go, they sound awkward, but they're actually the perfect addition to the fried food."

She gave me a tremulous smile and pushed the green mush around with her fork. The waitress returned to clear our plates and announced that dessert would be served in the lounge, where the musicians would entertain us.

Miss Gloria leaned over to whisper to me: "I'm beat. I'm going to bed early."

"No dessert? Really?" It wasn't like her to turn down a sweet, but it also wasn't like her to pick at her dinner. I worried about the lasting effects of the incident in the glen and

whether all this tension among the publishing team was taking a toll on her, maybe even amplifying her trauma.

"Too much food, too many scones, too much excitement,"
she said. "Plus, I cannot wait for Iona, and I have to stay
rested." She stood up from the table and excused herself.

Helen watched her leave the room. "Is she all right?" she
asked me.

"Just tired," I said, not sure I sounded convincing, because
I didn't believe it myself.

"Is there a problem?" Martin asked.

"My friend tried Gavin's goggles today and found the
experience disconcerting." Which was to say the least, but
I didn't know him well enough to go into detail about her
trauma. And it should be her call how much to tell him. "You
headed off the conflict at dinner rather adroitly," I added.
"How did all these folks end up working with you? They don't
seem to have an easy fit."

He laughed heartily. "I've known Glenda's father for years.
He's been involved with a number of projects. She insisted
on showing me her husband's photography portfolio, which
was spectacular. And the goggles were ingenious. Exactly the
boost the project needed."

"Ainsley and Vera were happy with this?"

"They had no choice," he said flatly as he folded his napkin and got to his feet. "Between her money and his talent,
their book was able to come off life support."

We followed the others to the section of the bar where
the musicians had set up. I slid onto a banquette next to
Helen and turned down the waitress's offer for another drink.

"What about dessert?" she asked. "Our local specialties are the cranachan which is made in a tall glass with raspberries, toasted oats, and whipped cream, or the sticky toffee pudding. Though we also have apple pie and ice cream."

"I'll take the two specialties, please." I thought about explaining that I was a food critic, not a glutton, but smiled instead. She had surely seen worse. She continued along the table, taking orders, as Jack and Alan began to play Scottish folk songs with the easy repartee of old friends. Though I loved the music, my mind couldn't stop worrying about my friend. Once the dessert was delivered, I leaned closer to Helen.

"I'm going to check on Miss Gloria. It's not like her to skip her favorite part of a meal. Be back in a jiffy." I picked up the plate with the cake floating in what looked like a caramel sauce topped with a generous blob of whipped cream, and grabbed two forks. At the end of the hallway, I tapped on Miss Gloria's door.

"Come in if it's Hayley," I heard her say.

The room was dim except for a beam of light from the bathroom, and my friend was rolled up in a ball under the covers. "I'm fine," she said, her eyes blinking open. "Please don't worry. Go back to the party."

"But I am worried," I said, putting the cake on the nightstand. "You never miss dessert. I've never seen that happen, ever. And this looked too good not to share."

She sat up and straightened her flowered flannel nightgown, then turned on the bedside lamp.

"I'm a little tired, that's all." She took a bite from one side of the cake, as I dragged my own bite through the caramel on the other side. "Tasty," she said, depositing the fork back on the plate and returning to her bedcovers.

This was not right. At home in Key West, she was my top taster, game especially for eating anything sweet and a fan of almost anything I made or served. And a card-carrying member of the clean plate club. "Do you feel like talking to me about what happened today?" I asked. "You don't have to, of course, but I'd be happy to share the load."

"If you insist. What I was hoping to do was sleep it off." She heaved a great sigh and fingered the satin edge of the blanket that was wrapped around her.

"Take your time," I said, "but I really won't be able to enjoy anything unless I know you're okay."

She nodded. "Don't laugh, but I was feeling my people the minute we arrived at that visitor center." She pressed her hand to her chest. "It was like I had a rope tied around my waist, and they were reeling me in. That's why I couldn't wait for you when you were in the shop. Those women and children and animals and men were calling to me."

I nodded in return and took her hand in both of mine. "That part sounds very special."

Her eyes looked a little glassy, but she continued to talk. "At first, maybe because I was alone on that walk, I felt that I was walking on sacred ground. I was sensing the quiet spirits of those who had gone before. You remember how sometimes I feel that way in the Key West Cemetery? If I'm quiet and centered, it can happen. I hear the deceased people talking. Or even see them in a gauzy way."

I stroked her fingers. "You and Lorenzo have special spiritual connections that most of us don't."

She looked across the room, her eyes not focused on anything I could see. "I had no feelings of fear or panic at that point. It was almost like they were explaining that this was where they lived and worked and raised their families. I felt a sense of sadness yet quiet acceptance from these spirits that echoed in the whispering of the leaves. It was emotionally overwhelming and a memory that will always remain with me."

She sighed and frowned. "But then he came tromping along with those damn glasses. And you know me. Of course, I asked if I could try them. I was so curious about how they could possibly change my experience.

"And once I put them on, I could see those awful soldiers staying with my relations, sleeping in their homes and eating around their fires and patting their dogs and flirting with their daughters. That morning, well before dawn"—her voice had dropped to a whisper now—"there were gunshots and a clash of swords and blood everywhere until the snow turned red. I hardly know how to explain it because it makes me sound like a kooky old woman, but I felt every moment of that massacre. And I was screaming at them to watch out, run to the mountains, they're coming after you. But no one could hear me."

Tears were streaking down her cheeks, and she began to shiver, almost as if I was watching her experience a rerun of her trauma earlier in the day. I didn't want to stop her— Lorenzo had warned me against this, but I hated seeing her so distraught. I tucked the blanket around her shoulders and held her hand, praying that encouraging her to talk was the right thing to do.

"And the worst of it was knowing the marauders had been taking advantage of the MacDonald hospitality for almost two weeks before the massacre," she said. "Can you imagine that? People that you had welcomed into your fold and cared for turning on you in a most vicious way. Only the night before, those soldiers had sat around the home fires, dining on mutton stew and homemade bread and drinking the wine of my people. And yet now, there were bodies everywhere, with blood on their nightshirts. I'm not sure I will ever recover from seeing all that."

"That sounds so terrifying," I said.

"On top of all that noise and horror," she added in a very small voice, "I felt so very, very cold."

That detail made me remember the story of what happened after the massacre, as told on the video we'd seen in the welcome center. It was winter then, and the few survivors escaped into the surrounding mountains, into the snow and frigid cold. Some made it to the next village, but most perished in the blizzard. That matched exactly what Miss Gloria was saying she'd felt. I had to believe she had really seen this because where else would that level of detail come from? But what had she seen? Was it something in the goggles? Or real spirits from the past lurking on that site of carnage?

"Anyway," she said, shuddering deeply, "I feel so tired, and I simply cannot sit through another evening listening to those people fighting."

"Would you like me to stay in your room tonight?" I asked. "I wouldn't mind sharing a bed. You don't take up as much room as a cat."

A quick smile flickered on her lips. "Nope. I'll be fine tomorrow. I promise. This helped a little, talking to you. And you know how I bounce back once I've got my beauty sleep. Leave the cake right there. I'll probably be starving in the middle of the night."

I smoothed the covers over her shoulders, pretty sure she was giving me a whitewashed version of how she felt. And guessing that she wouldn't be up in the night snacking, like the old Miss Gloria.

"Text me if you need me," I told her. "I don't mind any-time, night or day. Promise?"

"I promise," she said, her eyes fluttering closed.

I turned off the light and shut the door quietly so I wouldn't jar her awake. I started down the dimly lit hall and nearly screamed when a black-clothed figure popped out of the shadows.

Chapter Twenty

An unhappy chef will make unhappy food. That's simple science.
　　　—Juliet Blackwell, *The Vineyards of Champagne*

"Shh," the person whispered. "It's only me—Grace. The cook? I have to talk to you. Can you meet me down by the dumpster at the bottom of the driveway in ten minutes?"

I hesitated. What in the world was she doing all the way out here in the wilderness? Did she mean to harm me? That seemed melodramatic. But WWND: What would Nathan do?

"Honest to gosh, it's urgent," Grace said. "Please? I don't know what to do."

"Okay, give me ten minutes." Nathan would kill me if I went off with her alone in the darkness without telling a soul.

I returned to the bar, where the musicians were wrapping up, telling our little group what an honor it was to perform and how they had one last song that they thought would be familiar to the Americans in the company.

"Not very many people realize that this song was based on a poem written by our own Robert Burns," said Alan as he played the opening notes on his keyboard. Jack stood behind him and they began to croon "Auld Lang Syne." Several of Vera's group, who by now had consumed a river of whiskey, joined in.

I tapped Helen on the shoulder and leaned in to whisper. "I'm stepping outside because Grace, Ainsley's chef, drove all the way here to talk to me."

"Wait, what? No way you're going out there alone." She bolted to her feet, her eyes flashing, and I beckoned her to follow me to the far end of the room.

"I know she's not dangerous. But I'm telling you just to be safe. I'll meet you back here in fifteen and we'll chat? I would really love to have another ear and another mind to help me sort through everything that's going on."

"I still don't like it. I'll go with you," she said.

"We'll scare her off," I said. "How about you watch from the front porch, and I'll scream if I need you?" She finally nodded, making me glad I had asked. I felt absolutely certain that if I didn't reappear in minutes, she would send out the dogs.

I walked down the short, steep driveway toward the dumpster, located next to a clothing collection box similar to our Goodwill and Salvation Army boxes; though out here in the sticks at a small hotel frequented by tourists seemed an odd place for the box. Grace stepped out of the shadows again, causing my heart to leap. I clutched a hand to my chest.

"What are you doing here? How did you get here?" I asked. "Has something else happened?"

"Blair drove me up. Not exactly. I felt like I needed to tell you this in person." Grace bit her lip, and a quick puff of wind brought the scent of rotting vegetables and fish wafting by from the garbage bin. The temperature had dropped twenty degrees since our arrival, or so it felt to me. I rubbed my arms briskly and waited for her to continue.

"I've been thinking and thinking, trying to reconstruct what happened at the dinner. You know the police found traces of digitalis in Glenda's food?"

"Yes, you told me that before we left. You said that you had no idea how that happened because you'd already scraped the plates into the trash."

She sucked in a breath of the bracing Highlands air and let it out in a sigh. "I'm pretty sure that the problem was in the salad. Remember how we served a green salad at the end of the dinner?"

I remembered. We had eaten and drunk so much by then and were also woozy with jet lag. I wouldn't confess this to Grace, but I'd been grateful to reach the end of the offerings at that point. "The salad was lovely, but I was kind of full and you'd mentioned cheese was coming."

A smile flickered over her face. "It was a lot of food, wasn't it? But Ainsley insisted we serve the salad because it acts as a kind of palate cleanser before dessert." The smile fell away, leaving a pinched look in its place. "Those plates were still on the kitchen counter after Glenda fell ill. I hadn't had time to scrape them because I was busy serving dessert. I suspect that salad carried the poison."

"All the salad? Why didn't everyone get ill?" I waited in silence because it looked as though she had more to say, even if reluctantly. "Wouldn't someone have had to come into your kitchen and poison a specific salad plate? And what did they use? And why wouldn't they worry that this would be discovered?"

Finally, she shook her head, seemingly overwhelmed by my questions. "Not all of the plates contained the substance. I'm wondering if it's possible that Ainsley switched some of them around before I delivered them. And that would mean that she was the one who either put the poison leaves in Glenda's plate or made sure that she received them."

"Ainsley?" I felt shocked with this new information. "She tried to kill Glenda right at her own dinner party?" From the pain on Grace's face, I thought she must have been horrified to even imagine that her boss would be capable of such a thing, because she obviously thought highly of her. "What exactly did you see when you returned to the kitchen? Tell me every detail that you can remember."

Grace pressed her palm over her eyes for a moment. "Ainsley was in the kitchen when I returned from clearing the dinner plates. She pointed to one of the dishes and said something like 'Make sure Glenda gets the one without the celery. She's allergic. Or so she says.' Glenda had come into the kitchen a few minutes earlier, fussing about what she could and couldn't eat, and I assured her that we remembered and that would not be a problem.'"

"Both Ainsley and Glenda were in the kitchen while you were clearing dinner plates?"

"Not at the same time." She paused. "I can't be sure I remember everything correctly. Definitely not at the same time, though. And then I finished putting the nasturtium garnishes on all the plates and brought them into the dining room."

I tried to make sense of this new information. Ainsley had the opportunity to set up the poisoned plate, but what about the motive? Even if her friend was the most annoying person in the world—which she possibly was—murderers didn't usually try to bump someone off because they were a pain in the neck. "Why would she want to poison Glenda? And why do this in her own kitchen?"

Grace nodded again, slowly this time. "It's difficult to fathom, and I wouldn't ever imagine her doing something like that. But she had easy access to digitalis, and that's what they think it came from—foxglove leaves."

Oh lordy, I could picture those tall purple flowers planted in front of her condominium. The same plants that were slow to bloom in Vera's garden.

Grace's eyes seemed to glisten in the dim yellow light of the lanterns affixed to the hotel entrance, and I thought she might be about to weep. "Are you okay?"

"There's something more. When Ainsley got home from the Falkirk Wheel after that horrible fall, she was devastated. She told her husband that she was going to bed and taking a nerve pill. She said she would sleep in the guest room so as not to bother him."

"We were all so upset after that incident, especially Vera," I said, thinking that Ainsley's collapse into her bedroom hardly provided a murder clue. "All of us took a nap, or tried to."

Grace nodded. "Understood. And going to the other room was not so unusual either. Sometimes one or the other of them sleeps apart if they stay up late or if they have an early morning planned." She fell silent, fidgeting with the scarf around her neck.

"But," I said, "it sounds like there's something even more."

Grace dropped her gaze and rubbed her hands together. "Before leaving for the night, I was going to tap on her door and see if I could bring her anything. A cup of tea, a bit of chicken soup—anything. But when I got to the hallway, I heard her sobbing and sobbing. I didn't want to intrude, so I left without knocking. In the morning, when she came in for breakfast, I asked if she was okay. And she insisted she was fine, only shaken up—it had been such a shock to see that man fall. She said she'd be fine and that the time away with friends would do her good."

"Can you think of a specific reason why Ainsley would want to hurt Glenda?"

"No one really likes Glenda all that much. She's a plain pill. But murder?" Her pale eyelashes brimmed with tears, her face completely stricken. She threw her hands up, as if hopeless about understanding any of it.

One more question popped into my mind, though I didn't know if it meant anything or if it would be smart to mention it when I was down here in the dark and only Helen knew where I'd gone: *And why did you only now remember what happened?*

"Even worse, if it was Glenda who did this, rather than Ainsley, I worry that she meant the poison for Vera."

A new twist and very confusing and unwelcome. "Wait— she meant to poison Vera but fed it to herself instead? That doesn't make a lot of sense."

Grace pressed her hands to her face. "I have no idea what actually happened. But that thought came to me, and now I'm afraid for your sister—she's the stick in the wheel spokes who could make the whole project grind to a halt. I've seen that every time these people get together."

Unfortunately, I too had seen that in action from the beginning. Vera had a different vision of this book than at least two of the others, Glenda and Gavin. I wasn't sure where Ainsley stood—she was doing her best to play peacekeeper. Though I had seen the three of them powwowing in the Peebles bar the night previous. About what? And then when we visited Glencoe, she'd pretty much disappeared.

Grace had begun talking again while I was lost in nonsense theories. I pulled my attention back. "I heard her fighting with her husband before she left town. He accused her of still being quite in love with someone. And she said he was acting ridiculous, and stormed out."

"Ainsley? In love with Gavin?" I asked, incredulous.

"I have no idea what he meant. The more I think about it, the more confused I am." Down on the road below the hotel, a car flashed its headlights, causing the light to flicker on the lake's surface like an SOS. "That's Blair," she said. "I have to go. I'll text if I think of anything else."

By the time I got back inside, the musicians were packing up their instruments and chatting in their charming Scottish brogue about friends they used to know and play music with. On the far side of the lobby, I spotted Helen. She waved at me and beckoned me over. Before I could approach her table, my phone buzzed. I had missed a call from Nathan. I held up a finger to let her know I'd be a minute.

I backed into the lobby to listen to his voicemail.

"Headed to bed. Can't wait to see you tomorrow. Some romantic honeymoon! One day we are going on a trip without any friends or in-laws. Deal? We checked in with the police investigating the Falkirk Wheel incident. Short story, several witnesses claimed to have seen someone with Mr. Booth before he fell and possibly heard an argument. Some saw a man, others a woman. As you described, the seats were facing the other direction; so far no one has identified the second individual with any certainty. *Be careful.* I love you."

I returned to the bar and found Helen sitting in a corner by herself with an inch of whiskey in a glass on the table in front of her. "You look tired," she told me as I slid into the booth beside her. "In fact, you look awful."

Which was not a kind thing to say, even if true.

"Last call. Tipple of whiskey?" the bartender called.

"Why not? It's my honeymoon after all." Nathan's mother's eyes widened, and we both began to snicker. After the bartender delivered my glass, I gave her the short version of what Miss Gloria had told me, and also filled her in on my conversation with Lorenzo. I worried about whether it was right to break Grace's confidence, but I'd already told Helen half of it; she wouldn't rest until she knew everything.

"What in the world is going on with these people?" she wanted to know, once I'd finished telling her about the conversation.

Then I told her about the message Nathan had left, that he'd been in contact with the police and that several of the passengers on that boat reported either seeing or thinking they'd seen someone with Joseph Booth, and that this person could have been responsible for pushing him over to his death.

"That's distressing, though not surprising," Helen said. "Unfortunately, we weren't in a position to identify the perpetrator."

"We were not," I said glumly, wishing we could rule out the people we knew—at least the ones we liked. "Although, now that I'm talking, I'm quite sure Grace said that Ainsley was upset about *seeing* the man fall. Maybe she knows who pushed him and why, but isn't willing to say."

"Do we have any reason to doubt the veracity of Grace's report?" Helen asked.

"Lots. She's a suspect in the attempted poisoning and would be thrilled to move someone else to the hot seat. And she has accused Gavin of molesting her in the past, which, as far as I know, he denied."

"One thing we do know for certain: Grace couldn't have been the person who pushed Mr. Booth to his death. She wasn't at the wheel." Helen swallowed the last of her whiskey and stood up. "I think we must be missing something big. Who is this Joseph Booth? Someone on this trip must have known him. Personally. And more recently than college."

"Maybe tomorrow on the ferry, we'll have the chance to interview each of these people in the project separately," I said. "My feeling is we should start with Ainsley. Her name keeps coming up."

"Yes, but keep in mind that it's her chef who is bringing the name up, which makes me wonder if she's trying to divert the blame from herself to her boss. Make sure you lock your door behind you tonight. I'm going to text Vera right now and tell her the same thing." She marched off with a grim look on her face. I wondered if she was thinking about how she hadn't been able to protect her daughter as a teenager and she wouldn't make the same mistake now.

I trudged off to bed, my mind whirling with questions and worries and whiskey. My brain kept returning to Lorenzo's warnings about Ray as well. Had he known the people at the gallery as long as Vera and her friends had known each other? Were their current projects fraught with competition and envy carried over from the past, the way Vera's work seemed to be? If I hadn't felt so exhausted, I would have started madly googling Ray and his coworkers.

One thing I knew—this hotel had flimsy-looking locks for their guest-room doors. And no loose furniture to wedge under the knob. I'd have to sleep with one eye open, as my grandmother used to say.

Chapter
Twenty-One

His Susan had always been a lovely baker. There was no sweetness in her nature these days and Percy had the sudden notion that it all went into her cakes and puddings.

— Ann Cleeves, *The Moth Catcher*

The next morning, the phone trilled, waking me from a deep sleep. For a moment, after patting the bed beside me, checking for Nathan's familiar and comforting form, I had no idea where I was or why I was alone. Slowly the events of the last few days filtered in. Though I didn't recognize the number on the phone's screen, it was definitely Scottish. I punched "Accept."

"Hayley? Hayley Snow?" asked a quavering woman's voice.

I mustered a firm response. "Who's calling?

"This is Bettina, Bettina Booth of Peebles?"

The picture of the two sad old women materialized in my mind. "Of course," I said, sitting up and gathering the bedclothes around me. "How can I help?"

"We were up in Joseph's room yesterday, to find something from his college days to put in the casket, and we got to talking about how to tackle ridding out our poor Joseph's belongings, which just about broke my sister's heart, I tell you. We had to stop and rest so she could have a cup of tea. But then I found something in his briefcase that looked important, and I thought to call you. It was an article in the Sunday arts section of *The Scotsman* a few weeks ago. Something about a new book expected to come out early next winter. He had underlined lots of sections and put exclamation points and written "You've got to be kidding me' along the margins."

"What was the book about?" I asked, although I had a sinking feeling I already knew.

"It's to be called *Bloody Swords* or some such cod swaddle. And it's supposed to pertain to experiencing the thin places of Scotland through technology. Double-speak all of it, you want my opinion."

"Had your nephew been involved in anything like this?"

"No," she said slowly, "but he was always good with computers. He was very proud of a project he dreamed up about making the past seem more like a film than a book. We never exactly understood it because he was so smart, and his ideas were over our heads. A wizard, really. Shall I read you the paragraph that he had circled and highlighted?"

"That would be wonderful. Let me get a piece of paper." I rolled out of bed and grabbed the notepad supplied by the hotel.

She read through a paragraph describing my sister-in-law's project. "Here's the part he seemed to have some objections to. And I quote:

Gavin Findlay, professor of computer science and photography at the University of Saint Andrews, is the lead author on the project. Others in the field have described him as an intellectual powerhouse.

She paused and I could hear papers rustling. "Next to that he scribbled something that I can't quite make out. Along the lines of 'thieving scum bastard.' And I apologize deeply for the bad language."

"No need. I'm not sure what it means, but it may turn out to be helpful," I said. "Thanks for ringing me back. Did you by any chance have any more thoughts about his broken heart? Maybe you've remembered a girl that he mentioned from time to time?" I thought of asking about a boy, but if that would make the women more distraught, what would be the point? "Did you ever hear him mention the name Ainsley?"

"There was a girl he talked about, Anne maybe? It was so long ago. I couldn't say for certain."

I thanked her again and dressed quickly, then packed my belongings into my suitcase and headed downstairs to breakfast. This new information made me worry that Gavin had killed poor Mr. Booth. He was definitely invested in his version of reality and quite capable of giving someone a push off that wheel. And if Ainsley was an old friend of Booth's, she might be in danger too. Would that explain the poisonous leaves in the salad the night of her dinner party? Grace hadn't mentioned Gavin coming into the kitchen, but Glenda had been there for sure. And she might be the kind of woman who'd do anything for her husband.

Miss Gloria was already at our table, tucking into a big plate of eggs, sausage, fried tomatoes, and baked beans. Ainsley and Helen had settled in on either side of her and were peppering her with questions about how she was feeling.

"A good night's sleep and a big breakfast cures about all ills," she said, though I thought the dark smudges under her eyes suggested something different.

Ainsley stood up to leave as I sat across from them. "The ferry from Oban leaves at noon for the Isle of Mull, our second-to-last stop," she said. "It will take an hour or so to drive from here to there. And Vera will need to be in the automobile loading line at least an hour ahead. There's a lovely bookshop and plenty of fish and chips to be found in town while you're waiting. We'll see you on the ferry?" She pointed to Glenda and Gavin as they rolled their suitcases to the lobby.

Our car was quiet on the first part of the way to Oban, where the ferry would carry us to Mull. I had hoped we would be able to get Vera talking, but so far, she had batted away any attempts at conversation as if she were playing badminton and my questions were plastic birdies. Why wouldn't she talk about what she thought was going on? She was clearly bothered by something.

"How did you feel the meeting with the publisher went?" her mother asked, as if hunting for a neutral subject. Which this clearly was not.

Vera glanced over, her lips set. "Unmitigated disaster. With a dash of full-blown hysteria thrown in. He's worried, as he should be, about Gloria's bad reaction to the goggles. Gavin tried to assure him that her response was idiosyncratic because she feels such a powerful connection to her tribe."

"So true," said Miss Gloria. "I'm sensitive that way. I truly have no plans to sue. Our society is lawsuit mad, and all that does is line the pockets of the lawyers."

Vera nodded, perhaps looking a bit relieved. "He's loath to change anything because preorders have already been so high. People are not traveling lightly these days—they choose their destinations very carefully and travel less frequently than they might have in the past. He is convinced that providing the goggles along with the book will give readers a sense of real history and real place. Or should we call them 'gamers' rather than 'readers' in this case?"

"Have you changed your mind about Gavin's concept?" I asked, a bit dumbfounded to hear her describe it as a done deal. Had she given up trying to change the direction of what she hated about the project? Although referring to readers as 'gamers' would not support that theory.

"Trying to be realistic," she snapped back, her voice seething.

We drove a few more miles in silence.

"Will you tell us about the Isle of Mull?" Miss Gloria asked.

I watched as Vera made a conscious effort to relax her shoulders, which were hunched up around her ears. This trip, which should have been delightful, was turning into a nightmare. And I regretted that this was my first introduction to Nathan's sister and hoped that she wouldn't refuse to either visit us or have us return to Scotland under less stressful circumstances.

She smiled at Miss Gloria in her rearview mirror. "It's the most beautiful, tranquil, glorious place, though often windy and wet this time of year. I checked the weather, and it seems we may get lucky."

"We already are lucky," said Miss Gloria, gesturing at the green fields we were passing.

"True," said Vera, smiling again. "The only way around the island is crossing on a one-lane road. You will see that tomorrow when we drive to the tiny ferry that takes us to Iona. The locals know when to pull over to let others pass. There are enough designated pull-offs, but unfortunately the tourists don't know the etiquette. And if you don't know the ropes, it can be a little hairy. Other than that, you'll see thousands of sheep, and animals that the locals call 'Heilan Coos.'"

"*Koos?*" Miss Gloria asked.

"Rustic long-haired Highland cows, in normal English. They are shaggy and reddish-brown and have big horns and big brown eyes. We'll spend tonight in the town of Tobermory, which is absolutely adorable. You'll see. It almost looks like a Scandinavian town, with the brightly painted homes and shops curving around the shoreline. And with any luck, you'll meet the orange tomcat who owns the village."

Once we reached the port of Oban, Vera queued up with the other drivers waiting to be loaded on the ferry. The rest of us walked the short distance to town. The day had turned blustery and cool, making our first plan of sitting out in the sun on the benches overlooking the harbor seem less appealing. Instead, Miss Gloria browsed a gift shop with Helen while I circulated around the stacks of books in the store adjoining. I chose a romantic comedy by Jenny Colgan that took place in the Highlands, thinking a happy love story, instead of a real murder mystery, would be relaxing.

I met them outside on the sidewalk. "A spot of lunch?"

"Do either of you get seasick?" asked Helen. "Because fish and chips might not be the best choice in that case."

Miss Gloria and I snickered, and I assumed that she too was thinking about the meals we'd downed in all kinds of weather on Houseboat Row.

"We have iron stomachs," she said, pointing at the sky. "Onward."

We ordered three boxes of chips and fish cakes from a carry-out shop and stood at a bar facing the water to gobble them down. A pair of seagulls landed next to me, eying my scraps.

"Do you think we should have saved something for Vera?" I asked looking at the few chips left in my box.

"I checked. She insisted she wasn't hungry," Helen said. "We did have a substantial breakfast, but I think she's worried about this week and her book."

"Since when is hunger the criterion for choosing a meal anyway?" Miss Gloria asked, grinning, her lips shiny with grease.

"What's our plan of attack on this ferry ride?" asked Helen.

"I think we have to play it by ear, depending on who we can find alone," I said. "No one's going to tell any secrets if the others are around." I explained to Miss Gloria what we learned about Joseph Booth from his family and from Nathan. And then I told both of them about the phone call from Bettina this morning, including Joseph's notes in the margins of the article about the book, and my suspicions about Gavin's involvement.

"You were certain you didn't see anything right before he fell from the wheel?" Helen asked Miss Gloria.

"Nothing," she said. "And yesterday, after that stunt with the goggles, I was preoccupied. I haven't been paying attention to the interactions in this group the way you two have."

"Obviously," I said, putting a hand on her shoulder. "We would never expect that. Do you mind telling us about the glasses again? How did you happen to be trying them on?"

"Take your time and tell us as many details about what you remember as you can," Helen added. "Even if they seem silly. Where were you standing and where were they?"

"I was standing right beside the mossy stone wall that was part of a MacDonald clan home. It was such a strange sensation because I felt as though I had a foot in each world. The lady who used to live in that house was welcoming me at the same time the others were squabbling about . . ." Her words dropped off.

We waited a few minutes, and then I nudged her gently. "Squabbling about?" I left the question open, hoping she could fill in the blanks.

"Wait, I remember overhearing something said between Glenda and Gavin right before they offered to let me try the goggles on. I wasn't listening because I was so wrapped up in my sensations. And then those goggles derailed me completely."

"Of course," said Helen. "And you don't have to tell us if it makes you uncomfortable."

"I had the sense that Glenda wanted him to cut the other two loose. But he was balking, insisting that Martin, the publisher, loved Vera's writing. And then he said that without Ainsley the project would disintegrate from lack of organization. And aside from all that, it was way too late in the publication process to make major changes. And Glenda got annoyed. More than annoyed—outraged. And she asked if there was something between him and Ainsley again that he hadn't bothered to mention. That's when he noticed me and asked if I wanted to try the goggles."

"Was Ainsley with them?" Helen asked.

"Honestly, I did not see Ainsley all morning. Not that I was trying to keep track of her, so I wouldn't go to the bank with that memory," Miss Gloria said. "And the rest was history. Ugly brutal history." She dabbed her face with a napkin and carried her empty box to a nearby trash can.

The alarm on my phone went off, reminding us to return to the ferry. "I'm going to try very hard to talk with Ainsley on the ride over. It shouldn't be so difficult, because she seems to be putting a little distance between herself and the others."

Helen said, "Fine, I'll keep working on my daughter, though heaven knows that is unlikely to produce anything useful." She lowered her voice as we approached the line for the ferry. "Do not go off alone with Ainsley, because I don't like the way things are adding up. Or at the very least, pointing in her direction. Last thing we need is someone else getting thrown overboard."

I thought she must be mostly joking, but the warning struck me hard. I couldn't wait to rejoin the guys and share the load of worry with Nathan. We managed to score a bench seat on the top deck at the front of the ferryboat, from which we'd be able to see a grand panorama of the scenery. I went to the snack bar to get cups of tea for all three of us. As I carried the cardboard carton back, I spotted Ainsley sitting by herself in the far corner.

I was about to approach her, when the captain's voice sounded over the loudspeaker, instructing passengers to take their seats as the waters were expected to be slightly choppy. I returned to my group with the drinks. We pulled out of the harbor, enjoying the wide vista of gray-blue seas and passing clouds. Once we had settled into the rhythm of the slap of waves against the boat, the captain spoke again, explaining that the ride would take approximately forty-six minutes and that the snack bar would remain open until the final ten minutes of the trip.

Having finished my tea, I got up to use the ladies' room and try for a chat with Ainsley. She was absorbed in reading something on her iPad, with headphones on. Her message was pretty clear: do not disturb. I slid into the seat next to her anyway.

She looked up, annoyance flitting across her face, and then she mustered a smile.

"Are you enjoying the trip so far?" she asked.

"Other than the kerfuffle with Miss Gloria and the head-phones, it's been absolutely lovely. Spectacular. You live in the most stunning country."

"We think so as well," she said. "I'm very sorry about Glo-ria. I wish I could have been close by to head that off. Is she all right this morning?"

"She'll bounce back," I said. "She's a sensitive soul." It was difficult to decide what and how to ask her next. So many bits and pieces of the project were going off the rails. How could I possibly get her to confide in me?

"I hope you don't mind me saying that you seem tense. If there's any way I can help smooth things over, I'd be happy to." Now I was simply yammering about whatever came to mind, hoping something would catch her attention. Why in the world would she ever think I could help with her col-leagues? I plowed onward.

"I hate meeting Vera for the first time and seeing her so worried as well. And your dinner was utterly amazing—it was criminal to have that ruined."

She pressed her lips together, gazed at her lap. "It's been very hard," she said finally. "I suppose one never quite knows what it will be like to work with someone when one starts out as casual friends. And I certainly did not realize how rivalrous Glenda was."

"Rivalrous?" I repeated, trying to sound interested but not nosy.

"She sees competition for Gavin everywhere she looks. Has she looked at him lately? He's let himself go and get fat." She snickered. "Though with men it's different, isn't it? Sex appeal comes from success and power, which is not true of our fair sex. We must remain willowy or risk being cast aside. Anyway, that fat comment was a rude thing to say, and I retract it."

"Do you suppose she's worried about him as a man or him as the writer, photographer, and leader of the pack?"

Ainsley laughed again. "I suppose I haven't actually spoken with her about that question to be able to tell you accurately, but from the way she sticks so close to him, I'm going to say all of the above. But to be fair, this is a stressful time for all of us. We are down so close to the wire with the due date, and there is so much undecided."

"In a nutshell, Vera wants to cut out the virtual reality part of the project? And Gavin and Glenda want to beef it up? Is that fair to say? Where do you stand?" I asked.

She straightened her shoulders and sat up taller. "Vera is a very dear friend, but I'm trying very hard not to take sides. I am not on the artistic end of the project. I am focused on logistics."

"Logistics?"

"Organizing, editing, designing the layout—like that." She tapped the iPad that she had been studying before I sat down.

And I took that to mean she needed to get back to work. Fair enough.

"One last thing: you mentioned Glenda being rivalrous. I'm curious about what Glenda dreamed of becoming while she was in college? I have a good image of you as an artist and Vera the writer, but I haven't figured Glenda out."

Ainsley looked surprised. And uncomfortable. "To tell you the truth, we weren't close in the last couple years of college, so I can't answer that. She came from family money, and I don't think that helped her focus. Then she hitched her star to Gavin, and she seems quite content with that choice. We only got back in touch because of this project."

"If I could ask you one last, quick question, did you know the man who fell to his death? Mr. Joseph Booth?" I thought a look of pain passed over her face. But she hid it just as quickly.

"We all knew him at least a little bit back at University."

Which was not what Vera had said.

Ainsley continued, "I don't think he had what it took to become a professor, and it was difficult for him to realize that. So he left—or was asked to leave. I couldn't say which. End of story as far as I knew it."

I simply didn't believe she was telling the truth. But on the other hand, I had poked and prodded and gotten not much in return. Time to retreat and maybe try again from another angle later.

"I really hope that our presence has not made the project harder. We will do our best to stay out of your way over the next couple days."

"Oh no," she said. "Vera is thrilled that all of you are here. And honestly, I think it shores her up to have friends and family around. She probably hasn't told you, but this is around the anniversary of the attack and abduction. She always falls apart a bit at this time of year. And unfortunately, that makes her judgment suspect too."

"Judgment?"

She shrugged. "I've said enough."

I thanked her again for talking with me and pulled open the heavy side door so I could step outside to get a breath of fresh diesel-scented air. The engine was loud, and I let the noise wash over me as I watched the water rush by and the spit of land approach in the distance. This gave me a few moments to absorb both what Ainsley had said and how she'd said it. Someone was flat-out lying, either Grace or Ainsley. Either Joseph Booth had come to Ainsley's home, and then she'd spent the evening alone sobbing, as Grace had told me last night. Or he hadn't and she didn't. As for Vera, now I had to wonder why she'd lied about not knowing Joseph Booth. And I also wondered why she was willing to talk to Ainsley about her traumatic abduction years ago, and yet say nothing to her family.

By the time I returned to our seats in the front of the ferry, my mind was pretty much made up. Ainsley was lying. If Joseph Booth had really visited her home as Grace described, then she had to have known him in a more personal way than merely as a washed-up teaching assistant. Maybe Nathan could have a heart-to-heart talk with her once we got to the town of Tobermory. He was a real detective, after all, and had his clever and sometimes scary ways of squeezing information out of people that I did not.

Miss Gloria and Helen waited for me at our spot, and my friend was vibrating with excitement.

"I had such a good chat with Glenda on the way back from the ladies' room," she said. "I didn't plan on it, because I know you wouldn't have approved, but we met up at the sinks at the same time. She was so solicitous about how I was doing and also quite interested in what my experience had been like. She said that Gavin felt dreadful about how distressed I was and that they both would love to hear more about exactly what happened to me so they could make a proper decision about the project. She said the last thing they wanted was to be reckless." She paused to look at me. "Bet you never expected something like that from her, did you?"

"No, I did not. I thought they would have control of what a person experiences using their goggles, but it doesn't sound like it worked that way for you," I said.

"So true. I told her it's like their instrument set off a time travel experience for me, which was completely unexpected and quite traumatic. Then she wanted me to explain this to Gavin, I suppose so he can fix it. So we walked back to where Gavin was sitting with their stuff, and I ended up telling them everything about the Campbells and the MacDonalds. They were fascinated about my special connection to Scotland. Even though they've known for over a year, and maybe more, that they're writing a book about thin places, it's like in some strange way they didn't really understand what that meant. Can you imagine?"

"No, I cannot," Helen and I said in unison.

Something seemed fishy with this conversation, but we'd have the whole afternoon to sort that out. The captain announced that we'd be docking shortly. All walk-on passengers should gather their luggage and be prepared to disembark and meet their vehicles and drivers on the road. I offered to take Miss Gloria's bag, but she insisted she could handle it.

We started toward the exit and filed down the stairway, our rolling suitcases thunking behind us on the metal steps.

"And Gavin told me about a big and bloody battle involving John MacDonald and his son Angus that happened near the harbor where we're headed, so I shouldn't be surprised if I feel some twinges there as well," added Miss Gloria once we'd reached the bottom of the stairs. "And as I was leaving, I said I appreciated their concern, and maybe it would be the right thing to pause the development of the goggles in order to conduct a scientific test to somehow make sure people aren't damaged by the experience."

A smart idea, but I very much doubted they would go for it. Not from what I'd been observing. In my mind, Gavin and Glenda were a pair of steamrollers flattening every objection on their path.

"Meanwhile, what were you up to?" Miss Gloria asked.

Luckily, we were distracted by our arrival at the gangplank before I started to answer, because then I noticed that Ainsley was right behind us. It would have been a horrible faux pas and a total bush league move to talk about her while she was in earshot. Particularly if she had in fact been involved with Mr. Booth's murder—if it was a murder. That would be dumb, rude, and downright dangerous.

"See you in Tobermory," she called cheerfully when we exited the gangplank. "You are going to adore the Tobermory Hotel. We'll meet you in the bar after six."

We waved her off, then trotted to Vera's car, parked further up the road. The sky had turned gray again, and gusts of wind blew needles of rain into our faces. As we loaded into the car, Miss Gloria and me in back and Helen up front with her daughter, I wondered whether we should discuss my questions about the murder on the way to Tobermory. I wanted to talk more with Helen and Miss Gloria; the question was whether to mention anything in front of Vera. As Nathan had warned me before we left for the trip, she seemed fragile. Which did make sense considering Ainsley's comment about the anniversary of her abduction. And to be quite honest, I was a tiny bit afraid of her, same as I still was of Nathan's mom. Even though I was growing to admire and possibly even love my mother-in-law at the same time, the whole family was a tiny bit intimidating.

They were clearly cut from the same cloth as my Nathan, with their careful Southern coolness masked by a veneer of friendliness. Although something had gone awry in this family with that Southern trait; they behaved more like New Englanders than anything else. Like my father's parents, whom we'd visited twice a year in Boston. Once you broke through the thick layer of coolness, the love and the fire and protectiveness underneath were powerful. But breaking through? Not so easy.

Looking back over our short history, I had to wonder what had led me to choose Nathan. He was not an easy match for me. Though to be honest again, who was? Big loser Chad Lutz who invited me to move in with him and six weeks later booted me to the curb with my stuff and my cat? Or how about slightly milquetoast Wally, who couldn't decide whether he was in or out, while I was foolish enough to stick around to watch him waffle? Miss Gloria had helped me out of that mess. And now that she might be in a mess, I needed to return the favor for sure.

I felt the weight of her head drop onto my shoulder and then heard a faint snore. That answered the question—we could discuss what I'd learned from Ainsley later.

Chapter Twenty-Two

One time I asked him if he was one of those people who'd take a pill instead of eating, and he looked at me like I had two heads. Of course, he told me.

—Belle Boggs, *The Gulf*

Miss Gloria woke up when we were about five miles outside of Tobermory.

"Wait, are we here already? What did I miss?" she asked, eyes blinking furiously as she looked right and then left. The hair above her forehead stood up in a little white cowlick, and I thought for a moment that I couldn't have loved her more.

"Not much. Sheep and a couple of those Highland cows aka Heilan Koos," said Helen. "But Vera says we'll see them all again in spades tomorrow. You've seen one big hairy brown beast with horns, you've seen all of them."

We all laughed. From what I'd seen of her so far, Helen was missing the pet gene, with no urge to fuss over animals the way Miss Gloria and I did.

By the time we arrived at the town, the weather had changed again. The sun was out and the bay running along the main street was mirror still. And that allowed the multicolored attached houses and stores to be reflected perfectly in the sea—red, then pink, followed by yellow, occasionally broken up by a stone façade. It was take-your-breath-away stunning.

"This may be the most beautiful place yet," said Miss Gloria. "Maybe even the most beautiful place I've ever seen. Vera, we can't thank you enough for showing us your favorite Scottish haunts."

A smile lit up Vera's face, which I hadn't seen much in the past few days.

"It's my pleasure, of course. I wish it wasn't so hectic and stressful." She pulled her car alongside the curb. "If we grab our hand luggage from the boot, the folks in the hotel will help with the rest. The plan is to meet in the bar at six, and then we will have dinner together at seven," she added, muttering, "a lot of togetherness, I know."

We lined up at the tiny check-in counter and received our metal room keys. "Knock on my door when you're ready and we'll walk through town?" I suggested to Miss Gloria.

The bedroom that I would share with Nathan was on the second floor, overlooking the main street and the water. The wall behind the bed was covered with a beautiful inlaid wood façade. The bed covering looked like an actual animal skin, furry with white and brown stripes. I would try not to think about where it really came from. The bureau was made of metal, with leather handles that reminded me of an old-fashioned trunk. And red plaid curtains hung in front of the windows, draping a white wooden bench seat that looked like it would be perfect retreat for reading. If I ever had a spare moment. A text came in from Nathan at the same time someone tapped on my door.

Almost there, my husband said. *Can't wait to see you.*

Same here, I wrote back, and told him we were going out for a short walk. *Meet you in the bar.*

Miss Gloria was waiting outside the door. "How's your room?" she asked.

"Glorious," I said. "Come in and take a look."

Once my friend had admired the view and the window seat and the faux-chest bureau, we left the hotel and wandered down the street, exclaiming over the seaside panorama and peering into shop windows. A large orange tiger cat with a thick neck and a square head strolled out from a doorway to meet us, then flopped down on the sidewalk in front of us.

"Tobermory!" I said. We both crouched down to cluck at him, and stroke him, and admire his stripes. "Don't tell the other cats, but you're a very handsome guy." He flicked his tail and scrambled off. "I wonder if he minds being named after the town?"

"He's a cat," said Miss Gloria. "Probably not. Most likely he thinks the town's named after him."

We crossed the road to lean against the white metal rails that overlooked the harbor. "You know how I mentioned that Gavin and Glenda said there was a bloody battle near here?" Miss Gloria asked. She looked very serious, her eyes focused on the horizon, and I nodded for her to continue. "I don't know quite how to explain it, but I kind of feel that battle in my bones right now too. A little bit like what was happening in Glencoe."

I felt instantly alarmed and reached out to put my hand on her arm.

She chuckled. "Don't worry. It's nothing scary or dangerous and nowhere near that intense, not right now. But let me put it this way: if someone offered me the use of their virtual reality goggles, I would say, 'No thank you' before they even finished asking."

I felt a surge of concern. "Are you really okay? Do you need to rest a bit?"

"I'm fine," she said. "Nothing needs to happen. I only wanted to share how I'm finding these thin places astonishing, exhilarating, tragic, exhausting. Let's head back. It's almost time to meet the others for a drink."

"I hope you don't regret coming," I said as we crossed the road.

"Not in the slightest. And look, it's your Nathan!"

Nathan and William were disappearing into the hotel, and by the time we arrived, they were already sitting at the bar, sipping pints of Guinness. I had never been quite so happy to see anyone as I was him. I trotted across the lobby to throw my arms around my husband.

"I missed you something fierce," he whispered in my ear, holding me tight in a bear hug. He let me go and turned to hug Miss Gloria, though more gently. She looked so small wrapped in his arms.

"Are you all right?" he asked, looking into her eyes. "Hayley said you had quite a shake-up."

"Everyone keeps hovering, but I'm fine. Turns out thin places are not for the faint of heart," she said. "Not when you're the original divining rod. But it's been amazing, and really, I'm in top-notch form. I may look old, but I'm sturdy." To prove her point, she hopped onto the barstool next to Nathan without an assist. "My friend and I will have a wee dram of your finest sipping whiskey," she told the bartender, who looked slightly surprised and then amused. "And tell us about your golf match," she said to the men.

William laughed, his teeth white against his golfer's tan. "I'll leave that to my brother-in-law. I'd better reacquaint myself with my wife. We'll see you shortly for dinner."

"The less said about the golf, the better," Nathan said, turning back to us. "I'd rather hear about Glencoe, if you're willing."

I leaned into Nathan as Miss Gloria talked, feeling a sense of safety that had been missing for the past few days. After we'd chatted about our time apart, the rest of the group clattered into the bar, and a waitress escorted us to the long table nearest the fireplace. A fire crackled in the hearth, throwing out a good amount of very welcome heat in the cool of the evening. Vera sat at one end of the table, with her husband by her side and her mother across from her. Nathan, Miss Gloria, and I took the middle seats, and Gavin, Glenda, and Ainsley sat at the other end. Vera hadn't obviously arranged the seating as she had the other nights, and I wondered if she had given up on encouraging us to schmooze with her partners.

"I see what I want," said my husband as soon as he opened the menu. He pointed to something called beef Piccarumba, described as hand-diced Pennygown beef steak slowly simmered in a rich Tobermory ale gravy, with a puff pastry lid. "I know my wife will have me back on the fish-and-salad band wagon as soon as we get home. Until then, I will load up on Scottish calories and cholesterol."

Miss Gloria ordered a burger with beet root and onion relish and hand-cut chips and smoked back bacon, and I went for another helping of fried haddock fillets with chips and peas on the side.

"Do you mind if I order some hors d'oeuvres for the table?" I asked. "Since we're almost to the end of our excursions, I need to get a few more Scottish specialties under my belt."

"Go for it," said Vera.

I ordered a smoked salmon mousse and a cullen skink, described as natural smoked haddock embraced with cream, potatoes, and leeks, with hand-rolled homemade bread on the side. I would need to remember that lovely turn of phrase— *haddock embraced with cream*. At the last minute I added scallops, mushrooms on toast, and something called mac and cheese bonbons, because whatever they were, who could possibly resist such a description?

The waitress filled our wine glasses and soon brought out the starters. As Nathan and William discussed the adventures they'd endured on the golf course, I took notes on the food and the incredibly cozy ambience, with the dark wood and stone around the hearth lit up by the crackling fire, and tried to jot phrases about how I might describe Scottish food in general. Before coming to this country, I hadn't exactly known what to expect. This cuisine didn't strike me as similar to French or German food. Even people who hadn't visited those countries might be able to name their food specialties. Germany leaned toward meat and potatoes, while France was famous for its sophisticated fine dining. I was finding that the essence of Scottish food had crept up on me more slowly.

Our dinners arrived with more wine, and I began to feel a little fuzzy and warm, woozy with alcohol and tired from the events of the past few days. Caught between conversations at each end of the table, and full of food and wine, my mind began to drift.

Miss Gloria snapped my attention back to the table by tapping a fork on her water glass. "This has been an amazing trip, and I'm so grateful I was included." She cleared her throat and looked directly at Gavin. "I've been thinking about what happened in the Glencoe Valley and our conversation on the ferry. Although I am a pretty tough customer and I'll be fine, I think, for your sakes, limiting your liability and such, it would be a good idea if I talked directly with your publisher to tell him exactly what happened with me. That way he can make a judgment about any potential legal matters before moving forward."

All conversation at the table lurched to a halt, and now everyone was staring at her.

"That sounds like a reasonable plan," I said, just to break the awkward silence.

"It can't hurt to be cautious, and I'm imagining he would want to know, don't you think?" she added.

Vera looked stricken and pale. "I think you should do what you feel is best." She paused, as if there was a "but" coming. Instead, she stood up and left the table, her husband right on her heels. For tonight, the party was over.

Chapter
Twenty-Three

"Harmless as a setting dove," he agreed. "I'm too hungry to be a threat to anything but breakfast. Let a stray bannock come within reach, though, and I'll no answer for the consequences."

—Diana Gabaldon, *Outlander*

Nathan and I slept in a little bit and enjoyed some honeymoon snuggling. I spooned up against his muscular body, feeling perfectly content and still a little sleepy. "Did you ever wonder why I run into trouble everywhere I go?"

"You heard it here," he said, squeezing me. "You and Miss Gloria are magnets for trouble."

"You didn't have to agree so quickly," I said, poking him in the ribs. "People need help and we step up, that's all."

"Speaking of that, what's up with my sister?" he asked.

I told him in more detail about the conflict between Vera and her colleagues. "I suspect she wishes she'd never gotten into this project with them, but Gavin brings a level of recognition and money that would disappear without him." The alarm on my watch beeped, marking eight o'clock.

"Noooo," he said. "Turn that thing off. It's the first morning in ages I have my wife to myself."

I giggled. "We're leaving for Iona in a couple hours, but that leaves us time for breakfast and a walk out to the lighthouse if we get going now. You and I will see each other forever, but this is our only chance to see Tobermory." I threw the covers off to let him know I was serious.

We got dressed and went downstairs to the bar, my brain focused on coffee and my stomach on eggs and a double rasher of bacon and, if I was lucky, maple scones with loads of butter. Or cheese scones—those would be amazing too. Miss Gloria was not in the breakfast room. I glanced at my phone. It was minutes past the time we'd decided to meet.

"I better go wake her up," I said to Nathan. "She'll not forgive us if she misses anything. Will you order the full Scottish breakfast for both of us?" I'd have to cut back on the amount I was eating once I got home, but breakfast in this adorable hotel was not the place to start.

I trotted up the stairs and knocked on her door but got no answer. Maybe she'd gone outside to cuddle Tobermory the cat before breakfast? She had told me on the way upstairs to bed last night that she was missing Sparky and T-bone something terrible. As I went back down the hall, I checked my phone again and noticed that Miss Gloria had left a message that I hadn't seen on the way out because I'd been distracted by Nathan.

"Gone for a walk to the lighthouse with Glenda. I should be back in time for breakfast. Remember how I told you how kind she was yesterday? She feels terrible about upsetting me, and wanted to make it up to me by taking me on the walk to the lighthouse. It's another thin place that she says I need to experience. She's really much sweeter than we thought. She realized I was upset by my experience with those goggles and wanted to show me something she thought I'd really appreciate. She says it might be the most amazing treasure out of all the thin places in Scotland, and that most people don't get there."

This was bad. I could feel it in my bones. I didn't like the way she explained it to me, justifying her decision and then repeating it, which meant Glenda must have given her a real sales job. I hurtled down the stairs two steps at a time and bolted into the bar. Nathan was explaining to the waitress that yes, in fact, he did mean to order three full Scottish fries plus extra scones and butter for the table.

"Hold everything," I said, stopping Nathan mid-order. "We've got to get to the lighthouse. Miss Gloria might be in trouble."

We hurried out the door and trotted down Main Street until we reached the point where the path leading to the lighthouse began. On the way, I explained why I was so worried. "I suspect Gavin and Glenda fear that Miss Gloria's experience could scotch the publisher's interest in going ahead with the goggles. The way she talked last night at dinner, they would have to feel certain she's going to call their editor. There's no telling what they might do to keep this from happening. I don't like it one bit that Glenda has cut her out of the pack and is taking her somewhere remote."

"Have you noticed anything over the past week that would make you suspect Glenda of nefarious intent?" asked my husband as we trotted toward the lighthouse. "You have hardly mentioned her to me."

I thought this over as we jogged. "I'm free associating here . . . She accused Grace of trying to poison her, though Grace denies this. And Grace also says Gavin made a pass at her. Does Glenda know this? Imagine how humiliating that would be. Ainsley, Vera, and Glenda seemed to have had a falling out in college, but I don't have a clue why. And everyone knew Joseph Booth at least slightly, though no one wants to discuss it. And last but not least, Glenda doesn't eat much—that always gives me pause."

A couple walking two large black Labrador retrievers emerged from the opening in the vegetation.

"Have you seen two ladies going this direction, one of them older with white hair and a big smile?" Nathan patted his head to mimic our friend's wispy halo.

Because of her thick accent, I couldn't understand everything the woman answered, but they had definitely seen Miss Gloria enter the path with a second woman. Apparently, they both seemed fine, friendly even. And I heard the man mention Rubna Nan Gall, which Vera had told us was the name of the lighthouse.

"Is there a road?" Nathan asked. "Any way to get there in a car?"

The two locals looked at each other and shook their heads. "The only way to the lighthouse is this." The woman gestured at the narrow path.

"It's a coastal foot path," the man added. "Two kilometers to the lighthouse, twenty-five minutes if you walk at a brisk pace."

"Call the police," Nathan told them firmly. "Find out if they can send a rescue boat to the lighthouse. It's an emergency." He was terrified for our friend, I could see that. And his worry made me feel even more frightened.

Nathan took off without waiting for me. But that was fine, the sooner he got there, the better Miss Gloria's chances. The adrenaline coursing through my veins allowed me to run faster than my lungs and legs thought possible. I only stopped for a moment to pick up a fallen tree limb the size of a baseball bat, which might serve me as a weapon if I needed one. When I finally burst out of the greenery, panting like one of the black dogs, I could see the lighthouse keeper's cottage on the left and a long path leading to the lighthouse on the right. A weathered stone wall ran the length of the path until it met a wire fence guarding the lighthouse. Past the fence, two figures stood at the end of the rocky promontory.

Nathan hurtled in their direction. "Stop right now!" he hollered, but the wind was blowing hard off the water, and with it, his warning bounced back to me.

To my utter horror, the taller figure gave the smaller shape a good shove off the rocks and into the cold waters of the Mull Sound.

Chapter Twenty-Four

I wanted to cook for my mother in my own home, as though the act of feeding and nurturing her would unravel our rage like a kinked phone cord.
　　　　　　　　　　　　—Elissa Altman, *Motherland*

Nathan vaulted the fence that guarded the lighthouse, pushed Glenda away from the edge, and dove into the sound. There was splashing and yelling. Glenda scaled the fence and bolted back in my direction.

I stood at the bottom of the steps leading to the keeper's house, legs wide, blocking her retreat. "Do not even think about trying to get past me," I growled, brandishing the big stick I'd grabbed from the wooded path. "You've done enough damage, and the gig is up, as we say in my country." The fight seemed to drain out of her. Cowering and shaking, she sank down to the bottom step.

Nathan towed Miss Gloria back to the rocks in a lifeguard carry, his arm across her chest, and helped her clamber out of the water. He hoisted her over the fence, and then he hopped over, and they made their way toward us, both of them dripping and shivering. A bit of blood ran down my friend's shins where she must have scraped skin off on the rocks. She shook herself off like a wet dog, and I insisted that she take my sweatshirt. She pulled it over her head and tucked in her arms.

"I'll take over from here," Nathan said to me, grabbing Glenda's wrists and twisting them behind her back. He tugged her to her feet. "You take care of Gloria."

But Miss Gloria sprang to the top step, her hands perched at her waist. "Wait just a doggone minute. Before you take her anywhere, I want to know what the heck you were thinking?" she asked Glenda. "What did I ever do to you?"

At first I thought Glenda would remain mute. But then she lifted her chin defiantly and began to speak, her angry gaze pinned on my friend. "Did you not hear yourself last night at dinner? Why would you feel entitled to barge into our country and destroy this project? This book means everything to my Gavin's reputation. And our future together . . . Bad enough that awful slut Grace tried to ruin Gavin by casting false accusations about his loyalty to me."

Miss Gloria crossed her arms over her chest and wrinkled her nose. "I was doing you a favor by speaking up about the possible liability issues you risked with those goggles."

Glenda practically snarled in reply. "It was no favor, sister, and I was not about to let one dotty old lady ruin our triumph."

She was clearly off the deep end, and I thought it would be best to direct her away from Miss Gloria.

"Was Joseph Booth out to get your husband as well?" I asked, because I couldn't keep the question inside. "Is that why he had to die?"

"Joseph Booth?" Glenda's lips began to quiver. "He tried to ruin my Gavin years ago by casting aspersions on his work, claiming it was his. Gavin fired him, as well he should have. And Booth slunk away, tail between legs. But he returned to haunt us when he read in the news about how big our book was going to be. This time, he wasn't going to give up and leave town."

She broke into wrenching sobs, and Nathan met my gaze over her head.

"I'm going to take her in. Will you and Gloria be all right?"

"We could wait here for a boat or have the authorities bring in a stretcher," I said tentatively to my friend.

"Nonsense," she said. "I can make the trek back to the hotel on my own two feet. In fact, I could do it on one leg, hands tied behind my back." She and I chuckled, remembering a silly slapstick scene we loved from Monty Python. Then we watched Nathan bind Glenda's wrists with his belt.

"And by the way," Miss Gloria told Nathan as he finished securing Glenda, "I am a very good swimmer. I was more in danger of drowning from the rescue effort." She sounded a little bit huffy but softened her words with a smile. She started along the path leading to the keeper's quarters, and I followed. After about ten minutes, we stopped to rest, and

Nathan disappeared down the path with Glenda, with a firm grip on her bound wrists.

While we rested for a few minutes, I looked my friend over carefully. She seemed a little tired. Other than that, she wasn't bleeding much or bruised, and she appeared to have her wits about her—none the worse for the excitement.

She noticed me watching and jutted her chin out a bit. "She must have thought I was a frail old lady who could be easily dispatched. She was about to jump in and try to hold my head underwater, but I think she lost her nerve. It turns out maybe she's the one who can't swim."

"Why did you agree to come here with her? When did you start getting suspicious of her intentions? Wait," I said, realizing that I shouldn't badger her. She ought to be saving her strength for the walk. And Nathan would want to hear everything she had to say, and probably the cops would too. "Don't answer that. Let's concentrate on getting you back to the hotel, into dry clothing, and with a hot drink and some breakfast."

When we reached the end of the path, an ambulance, a police car, and a small crowd were waiting. Nathan emerged from the crowd. "The police already whisked Glenda away to the station. Now, how about we get you medically checked out?"

Miss Gloria waved away all the offers of help, insisting she was perfectly fine.

"I refuse your kind concern," she said. "All I need is time to take a shower, and then I'll see you in the bar for breakfast.

I'm famished. And I want to hear about everything that led up to this ridiculous event."

She stumped off in the direction of the hotel, obviously not wanting to miss the dénouement in which she had played a pivotal role.

*   *   *

When my friend appeared at breakfast, her hair tousled and damp, the waitress plied her with coffee and a heaped plate of steaming eggs and bacon, fresh scones on the side.

As Miss Gloria tucked into her eggs, Helen broached the subject of returning right home to Edinburgh and skipping Iona. "First of all," she said, I think you should be checked out by a real medical expert. I mentioned that yesterday, but today I have to insist. And second of all, you've got to be exhausted. It's time to call it a day and go on home to Edinburgh. Vera and Ainsley have to finish their work, and William and I will stay on with them. Nathan can drive you and Hayley home."

Miss Gloria narrowed her eyes and stared my mother-in-law down. "There is not a ghost of a chance that I am missing Iona. I have read just about every book on the subject. It is possibly the thinnest place in Scotland. And please don't tell me we'll visit another time, because what are the chances I will be back here?"

She looked around the table at each of us. And not one of us was willing to assure her she would have other chances. We were a long way from home, and she was not a young woman.

"Although I'm hoping to return because we didn't get to see Doune Castle or Falkland. And I'd love to get to the

Highlands. Remember how beautiful Inverness looked in *Outlander*?" she asked. "Those scenes were filmed in Falkland, not Inverness."

I could only shake my head at the depth of her spunk.

"Before we pack up and get ready to go, how about we all have a chat?" Nathan said, looking first at his sister and then at her friend, Ainsley. "I believe some explanations are owed. And I would like to hear the details of what happened this morning."

"I'll start and then we can work backward. I should have known better," said Miss Gloria. "I apologize for scaring you people to death. But I woke up early and was out taking a little stroll and chatting with Tobermory the cat. And then I ran into Glenda. And she told me how sorry she was about the experience with the goggles and that my distress was making them rethink the whole project." She picked up the last slice of crispy bacon on her plate and crunched it down. "I shouldn't have believed her because when has she sounded sorry about anything? But this time I believed she was completely sincere."

"She has a way of hiding her worst thoughts and feelings and looking innocent," Vera said. "She always has. But go ahead, tell us the rest."

Miss Gloria took a sip of coffee. "Anyway, she said that there was a battle in this inlet, which I already knew, right, Hayley?"

I nodded, reaching for a split scone and buttering it, then loading it with several strips of crisp bacon. Now that Miss Gloria was safe and my heart rate and pulse had receded to a normal level, my hunger had set in with a vengeance.

"Glenda mentioned that as they'd done their research for the book. People often talked about their experiences here in Mull because it was known as a thin place. Especially"—she paused—"at the point by the lighthouse." She let out a big sigh.

"You would think being eighty something years old that I would not be quite so susceptible. But honestly, it was irresistible to see what she meant, and I figured I could leave if it got too intense. And as I told Hayley yesterday, there wasn't a snowball's chance in hell that I'd wear any goggles. And to my knowledge, my ancestors weren't involved in the battle, so I figured how bad could it be? The light was so beautiful, and I knew you all wouldn't be up for a while. And my legs needed stretching, not to mention the fact that I've eaten like a linebacker all week. Hate to ruin my girlish figure."

She patted her stomach, paused again, and looked at each of the concerned faces around the table. "I feel like I'm a teenager explaining why I wrecked the family car or something, but I want you to understand that my decision to go with her wasn't something dumb and impulsive."

She waited until each of us nodded that we understood what she'd said. Even if not all of us believed it. In fact, I could imagine the gears churning in Nathan's head as he swore silently that he would never again leave either of us alone.

"Then we walked to the lighthouse and along the way had the nicest chat about living in Key West on a houseboat," Miss Gloria said. "Or so I thought. You'll cringe when you hear this, but I even invited her to come visit."

"Wow," I said, "she snowed you good."

"I feel like an idiot about that," my friend said. "I like to think I'm a pretty shrewd judge of character. Anyway, then we arrived at the point at the end of the path. By the way, I don't know if you noticed, but we could rent that sweet little house if we come for another vacation. The only problem is we'd have to get some muscle to carry our suitcases and our food in."

"I happen to know where we could find some muscle," I said, laughing and running a hand down Nathan's arm. "Keep talking: you got to the lighthouse . . ."

"And that's the point where I acted like a demented old fool. Glenda told me that I'd be able to see and feel things a whole lot better on the other side of the fence, right up next to the water. And she started to climb over and encouraged me to join her, and I did. In my defense, my antennae were thrumming, and I do believe I was getting vibes from the people who'd fought that battle. It's kind of hard to explain what happens, but it's like these people from history desperately want me to know the real story."

She rubbed a hand over her eyes, and I hoped that describing all this now wasn't too much for her. I was feeling a little queasy remembering how terrifying it had been to see her perched on the rocks and then shoved off.

"By that time, Nathan and I had arrived and saw you with her on the jetty. I totally panicked," I said.

"Yeah, well, with good reason." Her voice was glum. "I climbed over, and then she gave me a mean push. Let me assure you, that water is cold! And next thing you know, this big lug is splashing around in the drink with me, and I thought he might accidentally do me in." She grinned at Nathan, who was shaking his head at the wonder of this old lady's spunk.

William came into the lobby from the street, spotted us in the breakfast area, and joined us at the table. "What did you find out?" Vera asked. She looked so worried—actually, she'd looked worried from almost the first moment I met her, and that had only gotten worse.

He glanced around the table, his gaze lingering on his wife's face. "Gavin insists he had nothing to do with this incident and that it wasn't premeditated. He says Glenda acted on the spur of the moment. Everyone's upset about the project, especially the two of them. I gather that Miss Gloria announcing she was going to contact the publisher and ask to put the whole thing on pause is what finally tipped Glenda over the edge. At first they thought you were a batty old lady and you could blather on and it wouldn't make a difference." He shifted his gaze to my friend. "Maybe she thought she could talk you out of that plan, or maybe she thought it was time to dispense with you altogether. She hasn't confirmed that she meant to do you in."

"It seems obvious though, doesn't it?" I asked.

Miss Gloria grimaced and thunked her hand to her forehead. "I didn't even think twice about saying that because they were so solicitous and reasonable on the ferry. I believed that they really cared how I was doing and regretted the whole goggles incident. I've acted like an idiot all week, as though my brains leaked out on the plane coming to Scotland."

"It's not your fault," said William. "Many things got under Glenda's skin, and Gavin said she was wound really tight. She was afraid that the project would be canceled, and her husband would be shamed. And they stood to lose a lot of money, right?" He looked at Vera and then Ainsley for confirmation.

"It's true," Vera said. "When Gavin got involved, our advance quadrupled."

"Actually, it was ten times the first offer," Ainsley said, her voice flat.

William turned back to Miss Gloria. "She must have got it in her head that if she could make you go away, things would go on as normal. Or that's what Gavin was telling the cops. There's probably more to it. And I don't respect a man who's willing to throw his wife under the bus."

"Thank goodness for that," I said. "And there's definitely more. She as much as admitted she shoved Joseph Booth off the wheel. It sounds as if she was desperately afraid of losing Gavin and would go to any lengths to protect him and his work."

Chapter Twenty-Five

I like recipes to be written the same way you would give driving directions to your house to people whom you really want to arrive.
—Gabrielle Hamilton, "What I Learned from a Legend," *The New York Times Magazine,* November 4, 2020

We packed up the cars and, after a few minutes of jockeying, settled on Nathan driving one of the vehicles with Helen, Miss Gloria, and me as passengers. William, Vera, and Ainsley took the other, as the two women insisted they had a lot of thinking to do about whether and how they'd be able to salvage their project.

"If you see a car in the distance on this road and the pull-off before it, you'd best use it. The tourists on this island have no idea what they're doing," Vera warned my husband. "I'd say remember to drive on the left, but there's only one lane available. You can't possibly get lost—keep driving until you get to the tiny ferry landing. That's it."

We set off across the island, admiring the shades of green in the fields, dotted with white curly-haired sheep and furry brown Highland cows, with the blue ocean in the distance. Miss Gloria exclaimed about all of it, having missed the drive from the Oban ferry to Tobermory.

"I swear, this is the most beautiful country I've ever seen." She snickered. "My husband would have said that I say that about every place I visit, and that's probably true. But for a small place, don't they have everything? Mountains, oceans, animals, gorgeous stone ruins—amazing although violent history." She reached over and squeezed my shoulder. "Thank you again for bringing me on your honeymoon. I will never forget this."

"You're always welcome," I said, smiling back at her. "I won't forget it either. A week with only Nathan and me would pale in comparison."

Nathan snorted, glancing at her in his rearview mirror. "I'm only glad you survived it," he added.

"The curious thing about this whole expedition is that Gavin's confession only solves about a tenth of the questions raised in one short week. For example, if Glenda was an attempted murderess, why in the world was she the one who got poisoned? And did she really push Joseph Booth off the Falkirk Wheel. And why?" I asked.

Miss Gloria said, "Having been on the receiving end of a good shove from that woman, I wouldn't put it past her to have done him in as well."

"So possibly Glenda was upset enough with a man she supposedly didn't know, to the point she was willing to murder him?" I asked again. "I'm so curious to know what might have happened between them back in the days when these women were students."

"And I cannot understand for the life of me why my daughter and her friend Ainsley are keeping mum about all of this," said Helen. "How could they have worked with a woman this closely over this much time and have no idea what she was up to? I agree with you, Hayley," Helen added, "I don't think we have a tenth of the story."

After almost an hour of a hair-raising drive on the one-lane road, we reached the parking area. We pulled in between two empty buses and started to walk toward the ferry landing. A blond boy wearing a black tracksuit was playing traditional Scottish music on the bagpipes. I felt a shiver of excitement as the little boat approached the dock.

"I have a surprise for you," Helen said to Miss Gloria as we waited in a short line to board. "I've arranged for a private tour of the ruins of the abbey and the nunnery, and the cemetery if we have time. You don't have to come, of course—"

Miss Gloria hugged her hard. "Perfect—I'm thrilled. Did you know that this island holds one of the best-preserved medieval nunneries in Britain?" she asked Nathan and me. "The space between the physical and the spiritual here is said to be as thin as tissue paper." Looking tearful, she hugged Helen a second time.

Helen blushed, seeming pleased, even though she was not a hugging sort of person. "Do you want to come along?" she asked Nathan and me.

"I'm pretty sure Vera has a walk in mind for us," I said. "But I can't wait to hear about your tour."

Ainsley, Vera, and William arrived and got in line. "There's a cute little restaurant when we walk off the dock," Vera said. "If anyone is hungry after that big breakfast? Or we could meet up for a scone and tea after we explore the island?"

"Let's do that," Miss Gloria said. "I can't wait to get started."

The tiny ferry's engine began to grind, and we hurried aboard for the five-minute ride to the island. We docked at a large cement pier, flanked by big rocks and water in shades of blue from turquoise to navy. Miss Gloria and Helen disembarked first and strode off in the direction of the Iona Abbey.

"I'm going to sit in the coffee shop and make some calls and sketch out a new timeline," Ainsley said to Vera. "This project is beginning to feel like pinning jelly to a wall. Text me when you're on the way back, and I'll get us a table on the patio outside."

Chapter
Twenty-Six

Guilt isn't always in the form of an upset stomach or ele-vated pulse. Sometimes it's the smooth texture of a truffle or as light as a drained bottle of cereal milk.
—Saumya Dave, *Well-Behaved Indian Women*

Vera led us on a path running south along the water until we reached a fork. We took the right turn that would cross the island. On either side were fenced-in areas of grass populated by grazing sheep. I stopped short, watching one ewe move across the grass on her front knees. Almost as if she was praying. The wonders of Scotland just kept coming. I took a short video in case Miss Gloria didn't get to see this on the way to the abbey.

"This grassy plain topography is called a *machair*," William told us. "It's a low-lying area, as you can see, and so in danger of flooding and erosion by sea level rise. If you keep going along the water, you'd reach the bay where St. Columba arrived in his coracle from Ireland, to bring Christianity to the Scottish heathens." He laughed. "Isn't there always some-one attempting to convert the heathens?"

"Coracle?" Nathan asked.

"A round boat made of wicker and bound with leather," William told him. "He would have needed God on his side to make it across St. George's channel."

We trudged up a short hill and then down the path to a stunning beach made entirely of pebbles. Before the beach on a grassy area, someone had built a labyrinth made of pinkish rocks. I paused to take a deep breath and freeze the moment in my mind, so I'd remember this astonishing view and the feeling of sacred peace on the island. So far on this trip, I didn't seem to have the knack for tingling in thin places. But this island was special.

The four of us sat on the beach, sorting through the tumble of stones and looking out across the water. Hard to imagine that thousands of miles away, these same waves lapped ashore on the Smathers and Higgs and Fort Zachary Taylor beaches in Key West. The same water and environmental threats and human foibles connected us from island to island across all that distance. A gust of wind whipped across the bay, and I leaned into Nathan, as always appreciating his warm bulk. He helped me feel safe and grounded in so many ways.

Vera was making a small stack of smooth stones. "Sometimes you get lucky here and find pieces of green Iona marble," she said.

"We should never have let you go on this trip by yourselves," said William after a period of silence. "I don't know if I will ever forgive myself for putting you in danger. I knew something was wrong with this project, but I let you go without me anyway."

Vera cut him off, her voice sounding impatient. "You didn't put us in danger. And none of us understood how crazy Glenda had gotten. I think even Gavin was shocked at the lengths to which she was prepared to go."

"It boggles the mind to imagine that he wouldn't have noticed," I said. "The lesson, I suppose, is that we should pay closer attention to our spouses. To all the people we love, really."

Vera's face got even more serious. I looked with a laser focus into Vera's eyes, suggesting as strongly as I could nonverbally that this would be a good time for her to share what she'd been carrying alone. I couldn't say it out loud because she was Nathan's sister, and she had been so stressed. I didn't know her well now, but I hoped I was going to come to know her better and better over the long term.

She stacked the stones in front of her into a small cairn, the clacking of each on the next beating a soft and slow rhythm. "Each of us allows ourself to be blinded by someone or something from time to time, don't you think? I know that my kidnapping incident has caused me to shut off memories from the past. And shutting off part of your history means you don't have the benefit of that knowledge going forward. If there's a warning light blinking, you might not even see it."

I waited, letting her talk, hoping that neither of the guys would jump in to reassure her that she was fine and that she didn't have to tell her story if she wasn't ready. I thought she was ready. And I thought it would help her put the past horror to rest if we all could listen. I picked up Nathan's big hand and squeezed. He squeezed mine back, and we waited.

She met her husband's gaze and then dropped her focus to the stones again. "I was hanging out with some of my friends—the friends our mother disapproved of," she said, lifting her gaze to Nathan.

Nathan laughed. "That was just about everyone, right?"

"In this case, she was probably right. Anyway, we were hanging out behind the minute mart, bored to tears, and wishing something exciting would happen. And this guy showed up in a nice car and got out to chat. He was older than us, and handsome too."

I scrunched up my face, looked at Nathan with one squinted eye, wondering if this guy had really been as handsome and charming as Vera remembered. She had been basically a kid when this happened, so she couldn't have had the same perspective then as now. Vera was quiet, and I thought I should give her a nudge of affirmation. And maybe a joke to lighten the moment a tiny bit.

"We all see men through our own lens," I said. "What's handsome to one might be overdone or too slick to another. For me, I like them big and muscular and tough on the outside and soft like a mollusk under the surface."

Even Nathan laughed.

"I'm not sure I should take that as a compliment," he said.

"Oh, it is," I said. "I wouldn't have anyone else any other way. But back to the story." I turned to focus on Vera again. "How did he insinuate himself into your group?"

Her face looked pained. "Well, he bought us some beers. Which of course should've been another sign that he was bad company. But there wasn't a lot of excitement for teenagers in our town. And he was older than we were, and he wore what I thought were fancy clothes. And he was a smooth talker. And a few of us couldn't turn away. Some of the other kids started to drift home, and I realized that it was getting dark and my mother would be freaking out, and I said I had to go. He kind of cut me out of the herd and asked if I would like a ride. Said he was going my way."

She sighed and dropped her chin to her knees. "I should have questioned that also, because how did he even know what *my way* was? He didn't. He just wanted to get me in his car. And he did. I got in and we drove off, and I was feeling this mixture of amazing excitement laced with powerful fear."

She looked out over the water, and I could almost picture how she might have felt, getting noticed by a dashing older guy. She would have been beautiful, willowy with green eyes and wavy hair. And desperate to get some space between her and the rules and warnings of her parents and brother.

"When we reached his house, he forced me to go inside and down into the basement. By this time I was getting scared, beginning to wonder how I'd get away. And then he locked the door. There was a daybed and a television and a little refrigerator filled with beer and candy bars. In the bathroom, I saw some things that must have belonged to another girl. If I hadn't been terrified before, I was then, realizing that maybe someone had been there ahead of me. I honestly believed he had killed before and would kill me now. But I kept thinking about my family and how they would be looking for me, and how sad they would be if I didn't come home. I did what he told me and waited for the right moment."

Her voice was so full of emotion I thought she might weep.

I glanced at the expressions on the faces of the two men, seeing the unbearable pain they shared as they listened to her unthinkable story.

"I was there a couple of hours. He'd taken my phone and I didn't know what time it was and I started to feel like I would never get out. He turned on the TV. It was one of those big old clunkers with a fuzzy picture, but clear enough to see a newscaster was talking about an abduction." She glanced at Nathan. "They had an interview with my father. A few of my friends had described me getting into the car with a man and driving away. He'd immediately called the police and the local TV station and demanded action. He was so angry and threatening, saying he would track down whoever had taken me and make sure this person would regret threatening me for the rest of his life. He swore he would personally tear him from limb to limb if he had harmed me." Another glance at my husband. "Remember how terrified we used to get when he was mad?"

Nathan nodded.

"I think this guy got scared realizing that someone had seen me go missing, and the cops were going to figure out where he was and that I was with him. He marched me outside once it got dark enough and stuffed me into the trunk of his car, and we drove away. At first, I was only scared and sad and hopeless, and then I got angry."

She looked at Nathan again. "Remember how dad tried to teach us how to survive anything? We had drills about safety, every kind of safety from fire to kidnapping. We thought he was being ridiculous. But I had filed that stuff away, and now I remembered about the latch inside the trunk. When I felt his car slow down, I popped the trunk and flung myself out, and once I stopped rolling on the gravel and could scramble to my feet, I ran like hell."

"You were the bravest girl in the world," Nathan said, reaching around me to give her a little hug.

"It messed me up good," said Vera, shaking her head sadly. "Especially because they never caught him. Not until last year anyway, when Hayley and my mother tracked him down. Do you know what it's like to be looking around everywhere you go because you know someone out there wants to kill you?"

I murmured something reassuring. But honestly, I couldn't imagine what it would be like to be scared out of my gourd like that all the time.

"Nathan will remember . . . I was not coping well with any of this, and I asked my parents if I could finish high school in Scotland. We'd been studying that country in history class, and I loved everything I'd read. Plus, our great-grandfather came from Edinburgh. I planned out what I'd say to my parents, and I had the application ready, and I told them I'd never again feel safe in the US. And thank God they said yes because I met my William there and the rest is history, as they say. I needed to get away from them too, because I was certain that they blamed me for what happened."

"But they never would have blamed you—" Nathan started, but she cut him off.

"It didn't matter what was true and what wasn't. They were both so angry, and it felt like the anger was directed at me."

William said, "I'm so sorry, sweetheart. Thank you for telling us." He took her hand and kissed the palm. "I hate that you felt all alone with that fear." He hesitated and then asked, "Why didn't you tell us what was going on with your work partners? How Glenda was going off the rails. Maybe Nathan and I could have done something sooner and avoided a lot of scary problems for all of you. Avoided having Miss Gloria traumatized."

Vera flinched and I could tell that comment had hit her hard. She would hate the idea of harming Miss Gloria. "I knew she was nutty, but I didn't imagine she'd try to hurt someone. I didn't want to believe that."

"The thing is," I said, "she is so tough, my friend. She will now have bragging rights about how she was instrumental in capturing a killer and how Nathan almost drowned her in the process. Trust me, she will love this."

Vera still looked stricken. "I didn't tell you because I was desperately embarrassed. And all that got mixed up with what happened between us way back then in University. I hoped and hoped and hoped that I could lay that to rest. And it felt awful and ugly, exactly like what happened after the kidnapping. It was like those feelings came rushing back in and overwhelmed every bit of judgment left. Except that I wasn't seeing anything too clearly."

She stood up with an egg-sized pebble in each hand. "They say you should choose two stones, one to toss in the bay to symbolize something you need to let go of, something to leave behind." She wound up and threw one of her pebbles a good distance into the water, where it made a perfect splash. "The other comes with you, a new direction."

She showed us a beautiful, translucent green stone, and then slid it into her pocket and brushed off her hands. "I promise I will tell you everything once we get home. Mother will want to hear it too. Shall we go and meet the others for tea?"

I followed her lead: one stone in the water and one to take home. I heard the plunk, plunk of two more rocks hitting the bay behind me as I followed Vera down the path.

Chapter
Twenty-Seven

*She hadn't been blessed enough to have a conversation
about rhubarb varieties with anyone in years.*
—J. Ryan Stradal, *The Lager Queen of Minnesota*

We returned to St. Andrews that night, all of us tired
out after the events of the last few days and a gorgeous
and emotional day on Iona. After a bowl of soup, Miss Gloria
and I decided we were best off heading directly to bed. William
persuaded Nathan to stay up a while watching cricket
matches on TV. Miss Gloria and I started down the hall to
our rooms, bickering over who got the cats, Archie and Louise,
for the night.

Vera called to us. "Before you disappear under your covers,
I've just now had a phone call from Ainsley. Her chef,
Grace, has absolutely insisted on making dinner for all of us
tomorrow." She came down the hall and paused at Miss Gloria's
doorway. "I haven't said yes or no because I wasn't sure
whether you'd be up for that on your last night. You've seen
a lot of my friends, and it hasn't all been wonderful." She

grimaced. "I'm so sorry the trip has gone this way. All you'll be able to remember is someone trying to drown you and someone else nearly dying from the dinner party supposedly thrown in your honor."

"Are you kidding?" Miss Gloria said. "Her dinner was divine, and the only one who suffered any ill effects was Glenda, and she deserved a good stomachache."

"Agreed," I said. "As long as the husbands are in, we are too. I better stick with my new husband this last night. I haven't seen much of him on this so-called honeymoon."

Vera laughed. "I'll be sure to check."

* * *

After a long, restful sleep, we spent our last day in Scotland exploring the ruins of St. Andrews Cathedral and more of the town. We climbed St. Rules Tower for a stunning view over the countryside and the sea, and finished shopping for souvenirs and packing.

At six PM, we strolled across town to Ainsley and Dougal's condo, retracing the steps we'd taken at the beginning of the trip. After greeting us warmly, Ainsley escorted us to the roof for cocktails. For a moment, I imagined that Gavin and Glenda would be joining us as they had all week, and that thought made me feel jumpy. Miss Gloria looked a bit wary as well, and I suspected she must be sensing the same. The chatter was light—the weather, the music we'd heard, what Grace would serve tonight. Ainsley and Vera both appeared a bit pale and stilted, trying too hard to act normal on our final evening in Scotland.

Ainsley's phone chimed and she glanced at it and smiled. "That's Grace, calling us to dinner. Shall we go down?" We followed her down the sweep of stairs to the big dining room and took the seats that we were assigned. This time, the napkins and placemats featured a blue and green plaid with thick black lines interspersed with thinner red ones.

Miss Gloria's face lit up. "My clan's plaid. This is so lovely and thoughtful."

"There is some contention about whether this is the correct tartan for the MacDonalds of Glencoe, but Dougal's researched it, and this seems correct to us. We are desperately sorry about how upset you got in Glencoe, and this is by way of apology. I have a package of napkins for you to take home with you as well." She grinned. "I wasn't sure how much room was left in your suitcase." I thought Miss Gloria might cry at the kindness of our hostess.

"Now," Ainsley said, turning to me, "something that Hayley in particular will appreciate: Grace knocked herself out making special dishes. The menu tonight will be a first plate of Cullen skink risotto made with potatoes, corn, and garnished with smoked haddock, followed by Grace's most recent creation, cock-a-leekie kabob served with mashed potatoes."

I felt my stomach rumble in enthusiastic response. "This looks amazing," I said as Grace began to ferry in the appetizer plates.

"I swear to you no one put anything suspicious in any of these dishes," Grace said. "I watched like a hawk. No one crossed the threshold of my kitchen who I hadn't personally approved. And I am so grateful that you were willing to try me again."

Ainsley nodded at her and smiled. "It all looks delicious, and no one blames you for what Glenda did. And we're skipping the salad course, anyway, right?"

Grace grinned in return. "Right."

We ate a leisurely dinner and filled in Ainsley's husband about the many events of the trip, including Glenda's arrest in Tobermory.

"I can't wait to get a copy of this book," said Miss Gloria. "I absolutely adored every place you took us," she added, then glowered a bit. "Except for that cursed wheel."

"And you understand thin places better than anyone I've ever met," Vera said, nodding with appreciation. "I wanted to write this book because I've always felt a tremor of emotion in those places we visited, a connection to the people who came before us. But what I feel seems pale in comparison to what you describe."

"That's why she's such an amazing guide at the Key West Cemetery," I said. "She senses the lives of the people who are put to rest there. And she tells their stories in a way that brings them to life."

"And I believe that helps their spirits rest more easily," Miss Gloria said modestly.

"What will happen with the book?" I asked. "It seems a shame to lose all that you've worked on."

"We won't lose it all. But we have a few details to iron out," Vera said. "Gavin's agreed to pull out, so all the virtual reality nonsense will be gone. Once we explained what happened to

Miss Gloria, the publisher vetoed those goggles. He is not at all prepared to take the financial and emotional risks of possible future lawsuits. We'll have to rely on my words and our photos to communicate how special these places are. We'll lose some money, because Gavin was a huge draw."

All through this discussion, Ainsley had been silent, watching the others talk. "Can we talk about what happened earlier this week?"

She looked at Vera, who nodded her assent.

"Let's wait a minute for Grace, who has a few missing pieces."

Grace bustled into the room to clear our dishes, and then placed one plate of cheese and homemade crackers on the table, and another of shortbread cookies sprinkled with sugar that sparkled in the light of the chandelier. Then she stood behind Ainsley, her hand on the top rung of the ladderback chair.

"First," Ainsley said, looking around at each of us solemnly. "Grace would like to explain what she thinks happened that night at dinner." Then she smiled at Grace with reassurance. "Take your time."

Grace swallowed hard and clenched her hands together. She seemed nervous—either about what she had to say or to whom she was saying it. And by now, I was intensely curious, and I was certain Nathan was as well.

"Everything was kind of a blur that night," Grace began. "It was a big party, as you remember, and for better or worse, we'd planned a lot of dishes that needed tweaks right before I served them."

"We were showing off a bit, weren't we?" asked Ainsley with a smile.

Grace smiled back. "That's why I opted for the green salad with herbs as the last course before dessert. I could make it ahead and then toss it with the dressing at the last minute." She cleared her throat.

"I couldn't figure out how Glenda received the only plate that had poisonous leaves on it. And how did the police determine that plate came from Glenda? I finally remembered that Glenda wouldn't allow me to clear it. She's a slow eater." She glanced at Vera and Ainsley for confirmation. "She snapped at me a bit when I tried to take hers, saying that she didn't care if everyone else was finished, she hated to be rushed."

"When I finished clearing, her plate didn't fit on the counter with the others, so I had to stash it on the other side of the stove." She glanced at Ainsley. "Remember you'd told me to leave off the celery?"

Ainsley nodded. "She claims to be allergic. And I am slightly sympathetic as it doesn't agree with me either."

"Anyway, backing up a bit, before I served the salad," Grace continued, "Glenda went to the ladies' room. She was in the kitchen when I returned, where she made a big fuss about reminding me about her diet. Later I wondered whether she'd brought those poison leaves meaning to add them to Ainsley's dish, the one other plate without celery. She must not have realized that there were two special dishes. Only after she ate and began to feel unwell did she realize that she had put the leaves in the plate I served to her."

"You're saying she meant to poison Ainsley? Or did she accidentally overdose on poison herself and try to pin it on Ainsley or you?" I asked, unable to keep from wondering a little whether Grace had poisoned Glenda to protect Ainsley. But from what?

Grace nodded. "One of those, I can't be sure which. I suppose the police will have to sort that out."

"Very wise," my husband said. He had his arms crossed over his chest and was glowering a bit. "In fact, I spoke with the detective in charge of the case, and he confirmed that Glenda intended to make Ainsley sick, but Grace mixed up the plates."

"But why would she do such a thing?" I asked.

"She wanted us off the project," said Vera stiffly. "She was protecting her husband and her marriage and their version of the book. I believe she thought we were aiming to push Gavin out if we could manage it. Which we couldn't have done, because the publisher adored him and his ideas. It the end, it was her shenanigans that ruined him."

"And," Grace admitted, "she wanted to punish me."

"She was a talented gardener who knew herbs and would know about poisonous doses. It seemed unlikely that she'd put enough in her own plate to make herself seriously ill. Instead, she dosed my dish, and later was horrified to recognize the symptoms of foxglove poisoning in herself. If I had gotten sick, the finger would have pointed clearly at Grace," said Ainsley.

Every one of us at the table turned to look at Grace.

"Maybe it was the wrong thing to do, but I approached Glenda about the pass her husband made at me. But she rebuffed me, using some terrible words that I won't stoop to repeating," the chef said.

Ainsley said, "Even though one part of her knew what Gavin was like, she must have been psychologically unable to accept this version of his nature. She was feeling desperate enough to poison me, and that way take Grace down in the process. And maybe she even thought we'd drop out of the project and leave it all to them."

Nathan shrugged. "Hopefully between interviews with both Gavin and Glenda, we'll get a fuller picture."

"One more thing then, who was the mystery man who visited this house the morning of the dinner party?" I asked. "Was he related to all this in some way?" I suspected the man was Joseph Booth, but better to let them tell this, especially since I didn't have the why nailed down.

"It's excruciating to say, but I can answer that question," Ainsley said. "For that, we would have to go back to our time at University."

Vera reached across the table to squeeze her fingers.

"The man was Joseph Booth." She sighed. "I hadn't seen him for years. We were so young back then at University and so foolish," Ainsley added. "I was quite taken with Gavin, actually gaga over him. Apologies to you darling," she said to her husband, who had an appalled expression on his face. "He was vibrant and attractive and full of life in his lectures. History came vividly alive when he talked about it. And he was in great favor with the administration because of his popularity with the students and his writing."

She glanced at Dougal again. "I wanted to be a famous artist, and yet I doubted I could make that happen. Gavin gleamed with power and promise and certainty at a time when I felt so uncertain about everything—that's my only excuse. His power seemed sexy, I suppose. I thought I had fallen in love with him, and so I accepted his advances."

Vera groaned. "We were all a bit in love with him, I think. And he ran through every pretty young woman he took a fancy to, like a rushing stream over rocks. But he had the biggest thing for Ainsley." She looked around the table. "My friend is beautiful now, but she was a showstopper then—the kind of sparkling beauty that unfairly belongs to youth. And she was not a diva, like some other people we know."

Ainsley shrugged her thanks. "May we move on from that sordid moment?" She didn't wait for anyone to answer. "Joseph—Mr. Booth—was one of Gavin's research assistants. He occasionally ran the small group precepts for Gavin's large lectures, and he was responsible for holding individual meetings with us about our projects. He was equally as bright as Gavin." She dropped her head into her hands. "This is so hard. I feel that I'm to blame for Joseph's death because I sent him rushing away the morning of our dinner party. I thought he was reliving old feelings, old jealousies. That he couldn't stomach the thought of me working so closely with Gavin. But I think what he really wanted was for me to acknowledge that Gavin had stolen his materials and crafted a career based on his brilliant ideas."

I remembered the newspaper article that Joseph's aunt had called me about, with the outraged notes written in the margins. That had obviously infuriated Joseph, scraping scabs off old wounds. And therefore he risked approaching Ainsley the day before he fell from the wheel.

Ainsley continued. "After leaving University, he made a new life for himself as a software engineer. But he couldn't bear the idea of this big book based on his ideas, yet credited to Gavin. He resented Gavin's success in academia, as he'd always dreamed of becoming a teacher. And saddest of all, he never married."

"Joseph was desperately, tragically in love with Ainsley," Vera said softly. "I remember that so clearly."

Ainsley shuddered and took a deep breath. "Back in college, I refused his declarations of interest because I was involved with Gavin, and I believed he was serious about me. Joseph tried his best to persuade me that Gavin wasn't worthy of me. And when that didn't work, he insisted that Gavin was an intellectual hack who had stolen his proprietary software template. I thought he was merely trying to pry my affections away from Gavin because he was jealous. I told him to go away."

"It was hard," said Vera. "We had no idea what to do. Joseph Booth insisted he wanted to save Ainsley from Gavin's rot." She looked down at her plate, toyed with a section of shortbread. "None of us believed him."

"Joseph wanted to marry me," Ainsley said. "I refused." She wiped her hands on one of the plaid napkins. "I didn't realize that Gavin was also seeing Glenda and that he was serious about her."

"Or her about him, more likely," said Vera. "And what Glenda wanted Glenda got."

"I finally told Gavin what Joseph had said. He was firm with me," Ainsley continued. "He explained that Joseph, like other research assistants before him, was filled with envy and would take him down with pleasure in an instant, even if it meant manufacturing stories. And he ended by saying that I was a lovely girl, but I should go out and find a man my own age. A *boy*, I think he said. I was completely humiliated."

"It was awful," said Vera. "And I was recovering from my terrible kidnapping incident and felt so tainted, as though no one would ever want me either. We poured our hearts out to each other and swore we would never tell each other's terrible secrets."

Ainsley's voice dropped to a whisper. "After that, Gavin managed to turn the administration against Joseph and squeeze him out of his position at St. Andrews. There were rumors of his impropriety with students for years after."

"Which is rich, considering what Gavin did," Vera said, her voice full of disgust. "That pretty much ended our friendships with Glenda until the idea of this book project came up."

All of this made me feel so sad. Especially as I remembered visiting Joseph's family and witnessing their heartbreak. How it must have cost him to hide everything that had happened from his mother. And now the powerful reaction that both Vera and Ainsley had when they saw Joseph Booth splayed on the concrete decking made so much more sense. That unexpected tragedy must have brought a surge of guilt to each of them. I suspected they did not share that with anyone, including each other. Except Grace had heard Ainsley sobbing the night after we visited the wheel and decided that was important enough to drive to Glencoe in order to tell me.

"So Glenda pushed that poor man off the wheel when he tried to accost her about his intellectual property," Miss Gloria said.

"That's the working hypothesis at the police station," Nathan said. "The question is, what sense did it make that she would go after you, Gloria?"

"That's easy," she said with a big grin. "I was on to her—I smelled her rot, as Joseph might have said. It was only a matter of time before I'd have figured the whole thing out. Plus I'd threatened to take my story to the publisher right at dinner in Tobermory. And worst of all, I told her on that walk that if she was so afraid of losing Gavin to another woman, maybe it was time to cut him loose." She glanced at Ainsley and then Grace, and finally shrugged. "She couldn't endure that notion. So I had to go."

*　*　*

I dragged my suitcase to the family room, thinking it felt as though we'd only just arrived. And yet, with all that had happened, it also seemed like forever since we'd left home. Miss Gloria was perched on a chair at the kitchen table, cattycorner to William, and he was watching her face carefully. Neither of them even glanced at me, so I knew something serious was going on.

"We are so grateful for the hospitality that you and Vera have extended to us," said Miss Gloria. "I cannot tell you how much it has meant to me to visit this country and be welcomed into your family."

"You must know that it has been our complete pleasure and delight," said William.

Miss Gloria bit her lip. "Before we go, there's something really bothering me and I wondered if I could ask . . ." She paused, looking almost tearful. "About your family. And mine. And our history together."

William leaned toward her and took her hand in his. I watched for any sign that he might be mocking her. But on his face, I saw only thoughtful concern. "Of course, you can ask me anything."

She nodded her gratitude. "It's about the massacre at Glencoe. I realize this happened over three hundred years ago. But I felt the pain of those people when we visited, even before I wore those dumb goggles. I could literally feel the terror and the hurt right here in my chest when these people they'd been hosting turned on them. It lingers." She pressed her hand to her chest. Her lips trembled as she tried to form the last words. "How do you feel about that history? I guess that's what I'm trying to grasp."

He reached across the table and took her free hand, so he was holding both of her small hands in his big ones. "I am deeply ashamed of that bit of our history. If I could go back and change it so that a clan of innocent people was not destroyed by my ancestors, I would. I would. As it isn't possible, I hope you'll accept my sincerest apology. I am so sorry."

"Of course," she said. "Thank you for that kindness. I've learned some things about my own ancestors as well. They were not angels. Not that their faults and weaknesses excuse the massacre, but I realized that nothing is black and white in history. And I believe that some of your soldier ancestors actually warned my people and saved them. We can hope we're descended from that sort of bloodline."

*　*　*

While we waited in the Edinburgh airport for the trip home, I phoned Bettina and Violet Booth to tell them that Glenda had been arrested for the attempted murder of Miss Gloria and would soon be charged with Joseph's murder as well.

"It doesn't make your loss any less, but I thought you'd like to know."

"Thank you," they said in a sad chorus.

"We've found more documents stored away in his closet, and we've hired a lawyer to represent his estate's interests," Bettina added. "Maybe it will be enough to go forward with a lawsuit. It won't change the fact that our Joseph is gone, but that horrible man should not earn one red cent from our boy's mind. And his bylines based on Joseph's work should be expunged."

Violet tagged on, "We'd love to have you and your husband to stay with us any time you come to Scotland. "As you know, we have a spare room. We so appreciate your interest and kindness."

Chapter Twenty-Eight

But keeping people active at a wake was essential. Being busy, like working, allayed grief. By splitting cakes and heaping on berries and cream, the mourners could start to get their minds off death.
—Diane Mott Davidson, *Catering to Nobody*

By the time we finally arrived home to houseboat row, it was evening, and I had never been gladder to be anywhere. The sun had set but it was still light, the kind of rosy, warm light that settled over our island every June. Almost peachy in color, like a ripe mango, which I suddenly craved. As we walked down the finger toward our boats, I could see Miss Gloria's cats, T-bone and Sparky, splayed out on her deck. An excited yipping came from our boat: Ziggy, who could sense Nathan's presence from a mile away.

"I loved seeing Scotland, and I can't thank you enough for bringing me along," Miss Gloria said to me and Nathan. "But my gosh, is it good to be home. I will see you in the morning. This old lady is going straight to bed."

I squeezed her into a big hug. "If you go to bed too early, you'll wake up in the middle of the night," I said.

"I'll take my chances," she said with a big grin. "If I wake up, I'll have a snack and go back to sleep, exactly like a normal cat." She trotted over to her house, Nathan following behind with her suitcase. She hopped from the walk to her deck and scooped up a cat in each arm, black-coated Sparky on the right and orange tiger T-bone on the left.

"I met some lovely Scottish kitties, but they dinna hold a candle to you," she told them, kissing them each on the head and squeezing them until they squirmed to be put down.

"Archie," she explained as they followed her into her living room, "was a very handsome gray tiger, but especially shy. Don't you know I won him over by the end? I offered to send him that flopping fish toy that you guys love, but Vera said it would scare him to death. I should save it for a braver cat. Louise, on the other hand, had a lot to say and talked to me constantly. Oh, and there was Tobermory, a big orange tiger who was named after the town he lived in. Can you imagine if I'd named one of you Key West? So silly! Wait till you see what I brought you from Scotland."

Nathan came back empty-handed but chuckling.

"Thanks for including her," I said, circling my arms around his waist. "Even though we almost did her in, I know she'll never forget it. Nor will I."

He hugged me hard and kissed me on the lips. "I'm going to take Ziggy for a spin and grab the mail," he said.

"I'll see if there's anything to eat in this place," I said. I opened the door, and both Evinrude and Ziggy rushed out. "I missed you guys so much!" I patted Ziggy's head on his way to Nathan, and gathered up the cat to bury my face in his fur. "You most of all."

Inside the houseboat, I smelled a sweet fruity odor and noticed that my mother had left a bowl of pink mangos on the table with a note: *Welcome home! We missed you so. Call when you can. Salad in the fridge.*

I opened the refrigerator and dished out two plates of chicken salad with toasted almonds and mango chunks, and warmed up the last two cheese scones from the freezer. I poured us each a half glass of wine, because why not? Arriving safely home to this cozy beautiful space was well worth a celebration.

Nathan and Ziggy came clattering in, and the dog headed toward me with a slobbery doggy grin on his face. I kissed him on the head and gave him a treat.

"I think it's mostly junk mail," Nathan said.

Just then, my phone dinged with an incoming message. The subject line looked almost as though it had been written in spidery hand lettering. *Hayley Snow Bransford.* I was still getting used to that name and not one hundred percent sure I wouldn't stick with my maiden name, maybe use Nathan's for fancy social occasions or if we had a family sometime way off in the future. Nathan insisted he was fine with either. At the top of the e-mail, the sender had written the date, and "Peebles, Scotland."

Dear Hayley, we can't thank you enough for caring about Joseph and helping us solve the mystery of his tragic fall. As a token of our deep gratitude, we agree that you should be the rightful heir to our prize-winning scone recipe. We will leave it to your judgment as to whether you publish. In some ways, it would be a shame to have those secret scones expire with a couple of old women. And besides, we are already deep at work on next year's entry.

You and your family are always welcome in our home. As you know and has been said once, we have a spare room and would welcome your cheerful company anytime.

With much affection, Violet and Bettina Booth

Underneath the note was the recipe, titled "Cinnamon Scones from the Kitchen of Violet and Bettina Booth." My heart lurched at the thought of them choosing me to share something this special. I felt tears prick my eyes at the depth of their loss and the reach of their kindness. They were thanking me and giving me credit even before they'd heard the case was wrapped up. They were so sure I had helped them and would continue to do so. I showed the e-mail to Nathan.

"Very sweet," he said, a small smile on his lips. "You make friends wherever you go, which is one of the reasons I'm madly in love with you." Now he looked a little sheepish. "Do you mind if I pop over to the station? Could you save my plate? The chief's in his office, and he'd like to fill me in on what I've missed."

"Go ahead," I said, waving him out. "I'll unpack and call my mother."

She would be more impressed with the ladies sharing their scone recipe than Nathan ever could. I sat on the flowered couch with my supper, the cat draped purring across my lap, and dialed my mom.

"Hayley! You're home! We missed you in the worst way. Was it the most amazing trip? Did you see everything you wanted to? And how did you like Nathan's sister? And did Helen behave herself?"

I started to laugh. "Are you going to let me get a word in edgewise?" And then I told her the whole story about Joseph Booth falling from the wheel and Miss Gloria's horrible experience with the virtual reality goggles, followed by her near drowning at the lighthouse.

"She won't describe it that way at all. She thinks she would have been fine even if we hadn't come along to rescue her. And we didn't want to tell you while we were still in Scotland because I was afraid it would freak you out," I said.

"It would have freaked me out—I'm freaked out now," said my mother. I heard her summarizing what happened to her husband, Sam. "I'm going to put Sam on speakerphone, if that's okay—he wants to hear this too."

"And I forgot to even mention the attempted poisoning," I added, after assuring both of them that we were all alive and none the worse for wear.

"Good gravy," said my mother, "next time we are not letting you go without us."

"We did have muscle," I said. "We had Nathan and Vera's husband, William, although they got distracted by the golf."

"Can you put Gloria on the line? I'd like to hear her voice for myself," my mother asked.

I glanced over at her houseboat. The windows were dark except for the lighthouse nightlight she kept in the kitchen. "Her lights are already out, so I suspect she's sawing logs with the cats. And Nathan's gone over to the station to find out whether the police department has survived without him."

"Is Gloria okay?" asked Sam. "That sounds like a lot of excitement for an old lady."

"She seems fine. We all agreed we wouldn't have traded any of it for something more boring and safe, even if we had the chance. We saw the most amazing places." I filled them in a bit more about the beauty of Glencoe and how Miss Gloria had experienced her ancestors in both a quiet way and in a bloody battle.

"I think the thing she's most upset about still is that all this happened after the Campbells had taken advantage of ten days of hospitality from the McDonalds. That's what she can't get over, how those soldiers got friendly with the family and then turned on them. Anyway, I'll let her tell it. Is there anything new with Ray?"

"He's still not talking," my mother said. "Connie will need your support. I think it's been hard for her having you away."

"I may pop down and see how she is tonight. I'm tired, but if I don't stay up a while, I'll regret it later. See you tomorrow for lunch?"

"Absolutely," said mom. "What are you craving from our island?"

"I was thinking about mangoes all week long, but you scratched that itch. And the chicken salad is divine. I would love to have a Caprese sandwich from that southernmost place on the beach."

"Done!" she said. "See you there a little before noon."

I scraped the last of the chicken salad onto a bite of scone and finished it while sorting through the mail, tossing the junk, and dividing the rest into items for Nathan to look at and things for me. Then I put my dishes into the tiny dishwasher and went outside. It was still a little hot and muggy—this was June, after all. But a tiny breeze had started up so that I could hear the Renharts' wind chimes on the other side of Miss Gloria's boat, and the low murmur of conversation and music from up the finger. I headed toward Connie and Ray's.

Connie was waiting on her deck and threw her arms around me and squeezed. "That felt like the longest week ever! Did you have an amazing trip? We sure missed you here."

"It's good to be missed, that's for sure. And really good to be home. But Scotland is the most beautiful, beautiful country, and believe it or not we had so much excitement."

"This being you, I do believe it." She poured us each a glass of prosecco, and I gave her the short version of the events of the trip. "Vera looks exactly like her mother must have looked thirty years ago. Her book is going to be amazing, even though nothing like what her compadres had planned." I summarized what had happened with Glenda and Miss Gloria's near-death experience. "I won't tell you all of the details because she will want to, I'm sure. Tell me about Ray?"

She looked immediately bereft. "Our lawyer says that unless he can come up with some new information, the prosecution has a pretty good case against him."

"But what does Ray think?"

Connie shrugged. "He's known everyone in the gallery for ages. He actually went to art school with Jag, and they were the two stars of their graduating class. And the woman who owns the gallery attended the same school two years earlier. So they have history together and a lot of loyalty."

"Do you know them both?" I asked.

She nodded slowly. "Carly is very talented. She does collage and modern abstract stuff. But I think she figured out that business is really her strongest suit."

"Hence, the gallery," I said, suddenly feeling a wave of exhaustion from the jet lag and the trip as a whole. "I'll run by tomorrow and chat with him, but right now if I don't go to bed, I might end up sleeping on your deck."

Chapter
Twenty-Nine

Life, it turns out, is hard. Restaurants shouldn't be.
—Frank Bruni, "The Best Restaurant if you're
Over 50?" *The New York Times*, March 31, 2019

I woke up from a deep sleep feeling sluggish and disoriented. It took a few minutes of absorbing the sounds of Houseboat Row—Miss Gloria describing her trip to someone on the dock, Ziggy woofing at a seagull, and a motorboat starting up nearby—for me to figure out where I was and where I'd been. I remembered waking up from a dream about Miss Gloria's ancestors around three in the morning—bloody envy was the theme. After being startled awake, I tossed and turned, wondering if the people of Glencoe had felt any inklings of danger from the soldiers staying with them. Was it a complete surprise? Or perhaps they'd had twinges of worry that they'd suppressed until it was too late. Wide awake and a little spooked, I'd gotten out of bed and worked on my pieces for the next edition of *Key Zest* for an hour and a half before falling back into a hard sleep.

I rolled out of bed and poured myself a cup of the coffee that Nathan must have made several hours earlier, which reminded me of the stale coffee I'd served to the policeman in Vera's kitchen. I took the coffee and a plate of Cole's Peace mango toast and sliced fresh mango out on the small back deck and read over the paragraphs I'd written in the night and during the plane trip home. The hardest part to get right was always the opening salvo—how to sum up Scottish food in a way that might be interesting for both local Key Westers and tourists.

My mind kept returning to the mystery of Glenda's motive for pushing Joseph Booth off the Falkirk Wheel and attempting a similar stunt with Miss Gloria. How had she gone from friend to dangerous enemy? I thought of her husband's history of relationships with Ainsley and other students, and her learning that he'd made a pass at Grace the cook and who knew how many others. She might have felt that hanging onto his affections and his success was like sand running through her fingers. Or even rushing water.

The truth was, Glenda's envy made her sick from the inside out.

My mind shifted over to the problem with Ray—a trio of old friends in a wickedly competitive business. One woman, two men—three artists, all operating in a tiny gallery in a pricey tourist district.

On a hunch, I googled Ray. A page about his occasional showings in Key West loaded, followed by some older mentions from art school. Ray had come in second and third in several events, and first for the Tallahassee International

Juried Competition organized by the Florida State University Museum of Fine Arts and juried by faculty from the College of Fine Arts. I also found a notice of his engagement to Carly, the owner of his gallery on Duval Street. Good gravy, did Connie know this? Then I went back to the notices of each of the competitions Ray had placed in and combed through them more carefully. Jag had placed in several, but always behind Ray.

I dialed his cell. After a bit of chitchat about my trip and his baby, I cut to the chase. "How's the weapons charge case going?"

He was silent for a few moments. "Not well."

"Did you ever tell Connie you were engaged to Carly?"

"I didn't see the point." His voice was pleading. "It was a mistake and we were both young and foolish and fortunately figured it out before we'd actually gotten married and ruined our friendship in the process. And it would have made things totally awkward at the gallery if Connie knew."

"Tell me about Jag," I said.

Long pause. "He's a wonderful artist. And an old friend."

"Maybe not quite at your level? And maybe hasn't been all along? And one more question, does he tend to hold a grudge?"

At this point, the walls of Ray's silence broke down. "You'd think friends only want the best for each other, right? But in the creative arts, we scrap so hard to make a living and get acknowledgment from the outside world. When someone close to you is getting that feedback and you aren't, it's a bitter pill."

"And maybe Jag wasn't satisfied with your rivalry all along?" I asked. "I don't think he's quite as talented as you."

"I'm not sure about that," Ray said. "Maybe I've had more luck. But I could sense that he'd grown sour lately, even though he didn't show it on the surface." He was quiet for a moment. "When I won the Anne McKee grant and he didn't, and then the big commission for the artwork at City Hall, he kind of lost it. He's always had an edge, but over the past few months, he's done some things that scared me. I've been afraid to confront him for fear he would hurt my family. And that would kill me," he ended.

"You can't go on like this. I'm going to ask Nathan and a couple of the guys to stop over and ask some questions at the gallery," I said. "Okay?"

"Okay."

* * *

Halfway through my grilled caprese sandwich from the food truck overlooking the water at the Southernmost House, three police SUVs parked at the curb, with blue lights flashing. Nathan strode down to the small beach with Officer Steve Torrence and Chief Sean Brandenburg in tow, all three of them in polyester blue.

I nearly choked on my sandwich, set it on the plate in front of me, and held up my hands. "Wow, you brought out the big guns."

My mother let out a peal of laughter. "I'd tell them anything if they showed up looking like that."

"We just wanted to say welcome home," said Steve, leaning in for a hug.

The chief hugged me too and kissed my mother on the cheek. "Stay out of trouble, you two." They walked back to their squad cars as Nathan explained that Jag had confessed after ten minutes of grilling. "He set Ray up so the gallery owner thought he was stealing things. And then one of Jag's paintings was destroyed, and it looked like Ray had done that. Ray grew more and more on edge. He finally pulled his gun when Jag hired a few kids to set off cap guns outside the gallery. I suspect he'll still be charged, but hopefully something lessor now that we know he was being provoked."

"How in the world did you figure this out?" my mother asked me.

"I talked to Ray this morning. His situation felt so similar to what happened in Scotland. Take envy, ambition, competition, and throw in a couple of powerful relationships from the past. All hell breaks loose."

Sam said to Nathan, "Sounds like your wife was in the thick of this as usual."

Nathan rolled his eyes. "Try as I might, I can't seem to talk her into staying out of police business. One might be tempted to say that I've lost control of the situation. If I had any to begin with."

"It's got to be a strong love for a detective to be married to a slightly unconventional person who has a knack for getting into dangerous situations," my mother said.

Nathan threw his head back and laughed. "You hit the nail on that head."

"Can you stay for lunch?" I asked.

He shook his head. "I'm way behind on everything."

"I'll walk you out then," I said. "Be right back," I told Mom and Sam.

At his car, Nathan folded me into his arms, and for a moment I felt tucked away in the warmth and safety of his bulk, my personal human shield. It was unreasonable to count on him for every whisper of protection in every dangerous situation. I had to rely on myself too. But still, being in his arms felt so good.

"I'll never doubt your instincts again," he said, resting his chin on the top of my head. "And I was wrong to hide my family from you. I've already heard from my sister and my mother. They adore you. You won them all over. They love Miss Gloria too."

I pulled away so I could look at him in the eye. "Haven't met your father yet."

He grimaced. "I'll put that on the list. With one more item."

"That is?"

"A honeymoon from that honeymoon."

Recipes

Susan Hamrick's Cock-a-Leekie Soup

Grace the chef serves this soup at Ainsley and Dougal's dinner. One of our Scotland trip mates, Susan, gave me permission to share her recipe, which I imagine to be similar to Grace's soup. Although the addition of prunes may sound odd, Susan tells me that traditional cock-a-leekie soup does contain diced prunes.

Ingredients

4 lb chicken thighs, bone in and skin removed
10 c. water
1 onion, chopped
⅓ c. barley (or substitute 1 lb peeled, cubed potatoes)
1 10-oz can condensed chicken broth
7 leeks, cleaned and sliced
2 stalks celery, thinly sliced
1 sprig fresh thyme, chopped

1 tbsp fresh parsley, chopped
1 tsp salt
½ T. ground black pepper
6 pitted prunes, chopped (optional)

To prepare the leeks, trim off roots and coarse dark green tops. Cut in half lengthwise, and wash under running water thoroughly, to remove any grit or soil. Then slice. Slice the celery. Chop the thyme, parsley, and prunes.

In a large stock pot, combine chicken, water, leeks, onion, and barley or potatoes. Bring to a boil, and reduce heat to simmer for an hour.

Remove chicken, discard bones. Chop meat into bite-size pieces and return to the pot. (You could refrigerate the stock overnight at this point, and skim the congealed fat off the top the next day before reheating.)

Add rest of ingredients, including the chicken broth, celery, thyme, parsley, prunes, salt, and ground black pepper. Simmer for another 30 minutes or until vegetables are tender.

Leftovers can be frozen.

Shepherd's Pie

Hayley's stepdad, Sam, makes this dish to send them off on the journey. This is a little bit fancy—fancy enough for company, but not a lot of trouble. Especially if you're not fussy about the size of the dice and use your food processor to slice everything up, as I did.

Ingredients

1 T. olive oil
1 lb ground beef
1½ medium white or red onion, peeled and diced
2 medium carrots, diced
2 stalks celery, diced
2 cloves garlic, peeled and minced
¼ cup all-purpose flour
¼ cup dry red wine
2 c. beef stock
2 T. tomato paste
2 T. Worcestershire sauce
1 bay leaf
2 T. chopped fresh parsley
1 c. green beans cut into 1-inch lengths
Optional:
2 sprigs fresh rosemary
½ c. frozen peas or corn

For the Topping

Potatoes, about 5, peeled and chopped
2 turnips, peeled and chopped
Butter
Milk or cream
Salt and pepper

Brown the beef. Set this aside on paper towels to drain. Sauté the onions, carrots, celery, and garlic in a little olive oil until soft. Add the flour and let this cook for a few minutes with the vegetables. Mix the tomato paste into a little of the beef stock so it doesn't get lumpy. Add that along, with the Worcestershire sauce, the remaining stock, and a bay leaf. Simmer this until bubbly and beginning to thicken.

In a 9" × 13" pan, layer the browned beef, followed by the vegetables and sauce, followed by the green beans and parsley. Set this aside while you finish the crust.

In a separate pan, simmer the turnips and potatoes in water until soft. (My turnips always need a little more time than potatoes, so I start them simmering 5 or 10 minutes ahead.) Drain and mash with a tablespoon or two of both butter and milk. And salt and pepper to taste. Spread the mashed potatoes over the top of the beef and vegetables.

Bake in a 350° oven for 30 minutes or until browning and bubbly.

Cheese Scones from Grace's Kitchen

It's easy to eat your weight in scones while in Scotland, as Hayley and I both found out. We've both been trying out recipes ever since returning from our trips. None of them have turned out badly, but this may be our favorite. It's adapted from the King Arthur Flour recipe and definitely earned a spot here.

Ingredients

2 c. unbleached all-purpose flour
1 T. baking powder (I use low sodium if possible)
1 c. shredded sharp cheddar cheese, plus ¼ c. more for the
    tops
heaping ¼ teaspoon salt
2–3 chopped scallions (or leeks or chives if you prefer)
6 T. cold butter, cut in pieces (I used Irish Kerrygold)
2 large eggs (1 separated, white reserved for glaze)
½ c. buttermilk or plain yogurt
1–3 tsp. of sharp mustard, if that appeals

Mix the dry ingredients together. Cut the butter into the dry mixture, using a pastry cutter. You want the butter to be in pea-sized pieces—try not to overwork the dough. Shred the cheese and chop the scallions, and stir these into the butter-flour mixture. Whip together the egg plus yolk, the buttermilk or yogurt, and mustard if using, and mix until the dough is moist.

Pat the dough onto a floured surface or parchment—I like a circle—and then cut into six or eight wedges, depending on the size you prefer. Transfer to a parchment-covered baking sheet. Paint the saved egg white on the tops of the scones, and sprinkle with shredded cheddar.

Bake at 375° for about 20 minutes or until the tops are browning.

Serve piping hot with more butter if you like!

Sam's Sort of Scottish Creamed Vegetable Soup

I make a lot of creamed vegetable soups in the colder seasons, but this one from Sam was so yummy, with a deep but light celery flavor.

Ingredients

1 large leek, white and light green parts
1 onion
1 clove garlic
2 T. butter
2 stalks of celery
1 large turnip
2 medium potatoes
1 celeriac root
1 box good-quality chicken stock
1 tsp. white pepper
¼ c. milk or to taste

Clean the leek well so you don't get grit in your dinner. Chop the leek, onion, celery, and garlic, and sauté these in melted butter on low heat until soft. Add the chicken broth.

Add the remainder of the vegetables and simmer until soft. I simmered the celeriac for 10 minutes before adding potatoes and turnip, because it felt firmer than the other vegetables when I cut it.

When the vegetables are soft, stir in the pepper. Using an immersion blender, blend the vegetable mixture until smooth. Add milk to your preferred thickness.

Taste for seasoning, and serve with cheese scones and a salad.

Cranachan

Scottish Cranachan was one of the signature desserts Hayley and company ate in Scotland at the Loch Long Hotel, along with sticky toffee pudding. It's so easy and yet so fancy looking—it would be quite at home at a dinner party.

Ingredients

3 T. rolled oats
1 pint of fresh raspberries
1 c. heavy cream or whipping cream
1 to 3 T. Scotch whiskey
2 T. honey

Toast the oats in a pan (no oil needed) until beginning to brown. (Watch carefully so they don't burn.)

Whip the cream until almost thick, then add the honey and whiskey—to taste. I used one T. of whiskey, and we agreed it could have used more. Fold the toasted oats into the cream.

Alternate layers of cream and fruit in a tall glass, ending with a dollop of cream. Refrigerate until ready to serve. This amount makes 4 smaller servings or 3 large. Can be doubled or tripled as needed!

Banana Date Scones

On one of our first days during our trip to Scotland, John and I got separated for a bit in the little town of Melrose. And he came back with an incredible banana date scone that he'd found in a small bakery. Actually, it was only part of a small scone because he had eaten the other half. I've been craving another ever since. I've tried to re-create them for you here. Hayley made these for Miss Gloria before they left on their trip.

Ingredients

1⅝ c. flour
⅙ c. brown sugar
2¼ tsp. baking powder
¾ tsp. cinnamon
¼ tsp. baking soda
¼ tsp. salt
⅜ cup cold unsalted butter
⅓ c. sour cream (could also be whole milk plain yogurt)
1 tsp. vanilla
1 ripe banana
½ c. chopped dates

Mix all the dry ingredients (up through the salt) together well. Cut in the cold butter until it's the size of small peas.

Mash the banana well, and stir in the sour cream and vanilla. Mix well. Add the dates and stir those in. Mix the wet ingredients into the dry.

Knead the dough briefly, and shape it into a circle on a floured surface. Flatten the circle and cut it into six pieces. Bake this at 425° for 10 to 12 minutes. I left it in for 10, and it could have used one or two more.

Serve with more butter and jam if you like it.

Sticky Toffee Pudding

We had this cake several times in Scotland, and it's delicious. Don't even think about skipping the caramel sauce!

Ingredients

¾ c. pitted, quartered dates
¾ c. water
2 tsp. vanilla extract
½ tsp. baking soda
¼ c. unsalted butter, at room temperature
½ c. firmly packed brown sugar
2 T. white sugar
2 eggs
1 c. flour
¾ tsp. baking powder
¾ tsp. salt

For Sticky Toffee Sauce

¼ c. firmly packed brown sugar
½ c. cream
2 T. unsalted butter
¼ tsp. vanilla extract

Place the dates, water, and vanilla in a small saucepan, and bring to a boil. Simmer until soft, which might take about

5 minutes. Remove from the heat, add the baking soda, mix well. Let the mixture cool. Meanwhile . . .

Cream butter with sugars. Beat in the eggs. Add the dry ingredients and finally the cooled date mixture. (Do not worry about leaving little chunks of dates—they will provide some nice texture.) Pour the batter into a well-buttered cake pan. (I also added a layer of parchment paper and buttered that for good measure.) Bake at 350° about 40–50 minutes, until a toothpick comes out clean. Turn the cake out onto a platter.

For the sauce, mix brown sugar, cream, and butter in a saucepan. Bring to a boil and simmer until thick, about 5 to 7 minutes. Remove from heat and add a splash of vanilla.

Poke holes in the cake and pour the sauce overall.

Serve warm if possible, with ice cream or whipped cream.

Coronation Chicken

This was one of the first lunches we had on our Scottish vacation. I saw "coronation chicken" listed on the menu and had to know what it was. It turns out to be curried chicken, but not just any curried chicken. The recipe was developed for the coronation of Queen Elizabeth II in 1953. Jacket potatoes are baked potatoes served with the crispy skin left on.

There is no slapping of curry powder into mayonnaise and proclaiming it done (which I have been guilty of myself.) The dish can be served as a sandwich (the real English versions insist this should be soft white bread), as a salad, or as the topping on a baked potato. One recipe called for Major Grey's chutney, another for chopped dried apricots, and others for chopped fresh mango. I chose good apricot jam and mango for this version. You could substitute whole yogurt or sour cream for the whipped cream if this seems too rich.

Ingredients

2–3 c. fresh roasted chicken*
1 T. butter
1–2 tsp. curry powder
1 small red onion, diced
1 T. tomato paste

¼ c. water or chicken broth
⅓ c. white wine
2 T. apricot jam
½ c. mayonnaise
½ c. whipped cream
1 tsp. lemon juice
Cayenne to taste
Fresh diced mango
Slivered almonds or scallions or both
2 baked potatoes

I roasted a large chicken the night before I made this salad, but you could use a roast chicken from the deli counter or bake chicken breasts and shred them. While you're preparing the sauce, put the potatoes in the oven at 350° for an hour to an hour and a half, until soft inside and crispy outside.

Melt the butter, stir in the curry and chopped onion, and cook over medium heat for a couple minutes, being careful not to burn. Add the tomato paste, water, and lemon juice. Simmer the mixture until reduced by about half, and quite thick. Mix in the apricot jam and a sprinkle of cayenne, and set this aside to cool.

In another bowl, combine the mayonnaise with the whipped cream. Stir in the curry mixture when it has cooled off. Fold in the chicken and then the mango, along with almonds or scallions as you prefer.

Refrigerate the chicken mixture until you're ready to serve. Cut the potatoes open, and squeeze them to allow space for the chicken to be piled on top. Serve with a salad and green vegetable. I don't know if Queen Elizabeth would have been happy with this version, but we found it rich and delicious!

* This amount of sauce could easily have covered 3 cups of shredded chicken.

Scottish Cheese Shortbread

While on the trip to Scotland that became the backdrop for the next Key West mystery, you can bet that I paid close attention to the food. They make wonderful cheese in the British Isles, but they don't generally serve it at cocktail hour as we do in the United States. On our Scottish menus, a cheese plate was frequently offered as a dessert option. Although I did try the sticky toffee pudding and Scottish Cranachan that are specialties in the country, I often chose the cheese. I think these delicate but spicy cheese crackers would make a wonderful addition to a cheese plate, whether served as an appetizer or dessert.

Ingredients

½ c. (1 stick) unsalted butter, at room temperature
¼ tsp. freshly ground black pepper
¼ tsp. cayenne pepper
8 oz. extra-sharp white Cheddar cheese, finely shredded
1 c. unbleached all-purpose flour

Beat the butter together with flour and the two kinds of pepper until mixed. Beat in the grated cheese until the dough begins to pull together.

Place the dough on a piece of parchment paper and shape it into a roll. Cover the dough and chill in the fridge for half an hour or more.

Preheat the oven to 350°. Slice the log into rounds, about ¼-inch thick, and arrange these on baking sheets covered with parchment.

Bake for 13–15 minutes, until the edges begin to brown.

Cool 10 minutes on the cookie sheets, and then move to a rack or plate to finish cooling. You will need to remind your guests that these aren't sweet cookies, but then they will vanish . . .

Cinnamon Scones from the Kitchen of Violet and Bettina Booth

I crave that prize-winning recipe that the Booth sisters shared with Hayley—as you may crave it by now as well! This recipe is my closest approximation. I cannot vouch for how close it comes to the prize winner, but it's awfully good. There seem to be several secrets to making light scones. Freeze and grate the butter. Work the dough as little as possible. And keep it cold in between steps.

Ingredients

2 c. all-purpose flour
2½ tsp. baking powder
1 tsp. ground cinnamon (don't skimp on quality here—I used Penzeys)
¼ tsp. salt
½ c. (1 stick) unsalted butter, frozen (I like Irish Kerrygold)
½ c. heavy cream (plus 2 T. for brushing)
½ c. packed light or dark brown sugar
1 large egg
1 tsp. pure vanilla extract

For the icing

1 c. confectioner's sugar
3 T. freshly-brewed coffee
¼ tsp. vanilla extract

Mix together the flour, baking powder, salt, and cinnamon. Grate the frozen butter onto a plate. Rub the butter into the dry ingredients using your fingers or a pastry cutter, until the butter is the size of peas.

In another bowl, whisk together the heavy cream, vanilla, egg, and brown sugar. Mix this lightly into the flour and butter mixture. On a piece of parchment paper, shape the dough into a disk, and with a floured knife cut the disk into eight triangles. Put the scone dough back into the refrigerator while the oven heats to 400°. Move the parchment with the scones onto a baking sheet. Paint the scone tops with the remaining cream and sprinkle them with sugar.

Bake the scones for 20–22 minutes until they begin to brown. You could serve them as is, but why leave off the killer icing?

For the icing, whisk the confectioner's sugar with coffee and vanilla until smooth. If you don't like the idea of coffee, you could substitute milk. But honestly, that hint of coffee is amazing! When the scones have cooled, drizzle them with icing. (You will probably have leftovers, which can be used on your next batch. Or eaten with a spoon— just sayin' . . .)

We froze the extras that weren't eaten on the spot, and they were delicious when defrosted.

Acknowledgments

I n June 2019, I was fortunate to take a trip through parts of Scotland and Ireland. The adventure was made more amazing by the presence of family and friends, to whom the book is dedicated. Warm thanks go to the organizer and musical tour guide, Jack Beck; to our unflappable driver, David; and to the musicians we met along the way, including Alan Reid. It was an astonishing experience! As I wrote, I found these books helpful for detail and inspiration: *Powerful Places in Scotland* by Gary White and Elyn Aviva, *Around a Thin Place: An Iona Pilgrimage Guide* by Jane Bentley, and *Outlander Kitchen: The Official Outlander Companion Cookbook* by Theresa Carle-Sanders with a foreword by Diana Gabaldon.

I apologize to the people of Scotland for the way I used the Falkirk Wheel. The wheel is real, but the unpleasantness happened strictly in my imagination. I am grateful to Susan Cerulean, Jeff Chanton, Robin Elizabeth, and Susan Hamrick, who helped me remember trip details for several scenes. I borrowed Robin's words to describe her experience of noticing the people who had lived in the past in Glencoe. Miss Gloria's experience while wearing the goggles came from my imagination. Susan Cerulean and Jeff Chanton helped

Acknowledgments

fill in the details of the solstice parade. Thank you to Susan Hamrick for her recipe for cock-a-leekie soup. And thanks go to Bunnie Smith who, in exchange for a generous donation to the FKSPCA, allowed me to use her cats, Archie and Louise, in the book. Tobermory the cat is also real, though he did not pay a cent to be mentioned.

My sincerest gratitude must go to Angelo Pompano and Christine Falcone, my long-time friends and writers' group, who saved me over and over from sloppy plot turns and a lack of imagination. I was under a strict deadline for this book, and they kept right up as I churned the pages out. Hayley and the gang thank them too! Chris is brilliant with titles, and I thank her for *Bloody Blades: Crossing the Thresholds of History*. Thank you also to my Facebook friends, who are always willing to brainstorm a murderous plot twist. A particular thank you goes to Pat Ruta McGhan for her lovely description of Nathan's love for Hayley, which I borrowed for Janet. And a big hurrah to Margo Sue Bittner for the splendid title suggestion.

A warm thank-you to my agent, Paige Wheeler, who has stuck with me from the beginning and found a fine second home for the Key West mysteries with Crooked Lane books. Thanks to Matt Martz, Melissa Rechter, Madeline Rathle, Jenny Chen, and all the staff at Crooked Lane for producing and publishing a beautiful book. I'm very grateful for amazing editorial guidance from Sandy Harding, and the gorgeous cover design from Greisbach and Martucci.

Thanks to every reader, bookseller, and librarian who helps me keep the series going. You make all the hard work

Acknowledgments

worthwhile! Thanks to my beloved pals at Jungle Red Writers, Hallie Ephron, Hank Phillippi Ryan, Rhys Bowen, Deborah Crombie, Julia Spencer-Fleming, and Jenn McKinlay, for support, brilliant ideas, and a lot of laughter. And last but never least, my thanks go to John, fabulous life partner and supporter—the Jamie to my Claire. *Tha goal agam ort!*

Lucy Burdette, Key West, Florida
December 2020